Deadly Tides at Mont-Saint-Michel

Sandrine Perrot - Brittany Mystery Series
Book 3

Christophe Villain

Copyright © 2023 by Christophe Villain

All rights reserved.

No part of this book may be reproduced in any form or by any electronic or mechanical means, including information storage and retrieval systems, without written permission from the author, except for the use of brief quotations in a book review.

Christophe Villain
Pettenkoferstr. 2
45470 Muelheim
Germany
author@christophe-villain.com

Coverdesign by Giusy Amé
Translation by Terry Laster
Copy editing and proofreading by Elizabeth Ward

Auberge Saint Michel

A cloudless sky stretched over the Emerald Coast and the bay of Le Mont-Saint-Michel – a picture-perfect day for a trip to the sea. Sandrine was off-duty this Sunday, and when Léon unexpectedly rang her up in the morning to invite her for an outing, she didn't think twice. The roof of the dark green Karmann Ghia convertible was down, and the wind was streaming through her brown, shoulder-length hair. She threw her arms up and closed her eyes for a moment, determined to savour every moment of the day.

A few miles past Cancale, they turned off the main road and onto the narrow Route de la Baie, which hugged the curve of the bay. They drove leisurely through the sleepy coastal villages. For Sandrine, it was a treat to be chauffeured around without the urgency of needing to be somewhere at a specific time. As they moved along, she marvelled at the vibrant sails puffing out in the wind propelling fragile-looking, three-wheeled carts across the tidal flats, almost like a flock of oversized butterflies.

"So, where are we actually headed?" she asked Léon, who had a knack for surprises.

"That way."

He pointed towards Le Mont-Saint-Michel. The tidal

island, crowned by its famous Gothic abbey, jutted dramatically out of the expansive bay, which stretched all the way to the distant horizon where it met the English Channel. Sandrine thought she could see the gilded figure of Saint Michael, the patron saint of France, glittering atop the church in the clear midday sun.

"You've lived here for several months and haven't visited Le Mont-Saint-Michel yet. Truly a travesty."

"Won't it be crowded with this lovely weather? It's early June, and the weekend too."

"Sure, we're not the only ones who set out this morning. But it will be much quieter now during the off-season than in July or August when crowds of people jostle their way up the narrow lane to tour the abbey," he replied. "We need to seize the opportunity and explore the place before the school holidays begin."

It was true Sandrine hadn't actually managed to visit the site yet, despite being able to see the island from her garden in Cancale on clear days, and having intended to do so multiple times. Something always came up, usually related to her job as a Police Capitaine at the Saint-Malo precinct. She was delighted that Léon had been aware of this and invited her on this outing. She leaned over and gently kissed him on the cheek.

"Thank you for the invitation. Visiting the island has been high on my wish list. With a little luck we'll find a nice restaurant, I'm already getting a bit peckish."

She glanced at her watch. It was nearly lunchtime, and her kitchen had offered no more than a cup of coffee and a slice of cold pizza from the previous day. *I really need to get into the habit of shopping more regularly. But then, I'd also have to cook more often.* Not a prospect that filled her with enthusiasm.

"I can imagine," he replied, grinning in a way that suggested he had another surprise planned for her. She vaguely remembered him mentioning that he had worked in a restaurant on Le

Mont years ago. He must know the area well and had probably made a reservation.

"We can't go much farther with the car."

Léon turned and drove along the parking lots that had been built in recent years on the landside of the bay. A new bridge had replaced the causeway, allowing the sea to flow around Le Mont once more and gradually wash away the sediment that had been accumulating for decades.

He stopped at a closed gate.

"Why didn't you use one of the other parking lots we passed? There were plenty of open spots."

He entered some numbers into the keypad of the parking machine, and the gate lifted.

"This one is more convenient. Reserved for hotel guests who are staying overnight. I happen to have the access code," he said, grinning. He drove to the end of the nearly empty lot and parked the car in the shade of a tree.

"How do we get across? It seems to be quite a distance away," Sandrine asked.

"From here, we'll have to take one of the shuttle buses. The hotel parking lot is right next to the departure point. With this weather, that's a clear advantage." The car's temperature display was hovering just below 90 degrees Fahrenheit, and not a cloud was in sight. The forecast for the coming days was more of the same.

A narrow pathway through the dense hedge surrounding the parking lot led directly to Place des Navettes, where the tourist centre was located, along with the shuttle buses known as the *Passeurs*, ready for departure.

"We're in luck; the line is short. Most tourists already arrived in the morning, so it's a bit quieter now," Léon said, quickening his pace. He didn't want to miss the Passeur and be forced to wait for the next one under the scorching midday sun. The doors of the boxy bus were open and a man in an orange safety vest waved them on. Sandrine passed up the open seats, choosing to stand in front of one of the large windows. She didn't want anyone blocking her view of the bay.

Moments later, the doors closed and the bus began to move. Along the way, they stopped twice to pick up more tourists, then the bus passed through a gate and drove onto the bridge that curved gently towards Le Mont-Saint-Michel. Sandrine looked out over the salt marshes, where sheep were grazing and the tidal flats that stretched to the horizon. The view was only interrupted by the channels of three rivers – the Couesnon, Sée, and Sélune – that emptied into the bay here.

"It's a shame it's low tide. I would have liked to have seen the Mount at high tide."

"We won't see much of the sea today; the water is still receding. High tide is between seven and eight in the evening. Unfortunately, I have to work around that time."

"That's fine. By then, we'll have likely explored the village several times over, and our feet will be aching. Let's just enjoy the trip."

Léon owned the Club Équinoxe in Saint-Malo, and weekends were his busiest work times. But she couldn't complain – her hours were anything but regular. Criminals rarely took weekends off, after all.

"It must be awe-inspiring to see the water turn the Mount into an island," said Sandrine.

"That doesn't happen too often, actually only during spring tides. If I've read the forecast correctly, the next one is predicted for this Tuesday. Then, the sea rises past the rear section of the bridge, and anyone who wants to keep their feet dry can't get in or out of the place."

That morning, she had opted for a straight-cut black dress that reached down to her calves and a pair of delicate leather sandals. She was glad she didn't have to cross a flooded bridge. A pleasant meal, preferably with a view of the bay, was more to her liking.

"You look beautiful." He leaned toward her. "I must say, I like you better without your weapon."

"I thought you had a soft spot for dangerous women," she said with a wink.

"You're dangerous enough without a gun," he replied seriously.

Sandrine studied him closely. They often trained together in Mixed Martial Arts, but she doubted his comment was pointing in that direction. She liked Léon, a lot, but he deserved someone with a less complicated life than hers. And she had always been upfront about that.

"The gun and the job are a package deal."

"I could get used to that."

She maintained eye contact with him for a few breaths until the shuttle bus suddenly braked, and Sandrine grabbed onto his arm to keep her balance. With a gentle jolt, the vehicle came to a stop.

"We're here," she said, and it suited her just fine. The direction their conversation had taken felt a bit too serious for the moment.

Sandrine stepped off the bus and leaned against the bridge railing. Before her, the rock and the steep walls of the Gothic abbey rose, from this angle, all the way into the bright blue sky. She tilted her head back, shielding her eyes with a hand, and looked up at the monastery that occupied the entire upper part of the island.

"Impressive," she murmured.

"Even more so when you consider that the church has burned down multiple times since its construction. Ten times, if

I recall correctly. The Benedictine monks have always rebuilt the monastery, each time taller and more beautiful."

"Are there still monks here?"

"In the Middle Ages, there were always between 50 and 60. During the Revolution, the abbey was closed and the last ones were driven out, but now some have returned to Le Mont – about a dozen monks and nuns. You can sometimes see them praying in the church."

He lifted his smartphone, and she glanced at the display.

"I took the liberty of purchasing two tickets online. I figured you'd want to explore."

"Of course. We must take a look inside the monastery."

"But first, let's eat. My stomach is already growling."

Léon offered his arm, and Sandrine linked hers with his. Leisurely, they strolled past the patrol car and armed police officers, entering the small town through the outermost of the three city gates, the Porte de l'Avancée. The town was wedged between the medieval city walls and the rugged cliffs. The Grande Rue, the town's only street, wound its way uphill, lined with dozens of hotels and shops, leading up to the abbey's entrance.

As they had anticipated, the restaurants and souvenir shops were bustling, but things were still reasonably relaxed – especially compared to weekends during the high season when tourists are crammed shoulder to shoulder into restaurants and snack bars. At that thought, Sandrine glanced at her watch.

"Finding a table at a decent restaurant might be a bit challenging around this time," she said.

"No worries, we're expected," Léon assured her.

He led her to an imposing four-storey stone building in the lower part of Grande Rue, its dark blue awnings offering some shade from the midday sun. 'Auberge St. Michel' was written in gold lettering on the windows, revealing a fully occupied dining room. She looked at him sceptically, but he just smiled and opened the door to the Auberge.

A woman, perhaps in her early thirties, dressed in a hue that matched her tightly combed-back blonde hair, waved and approached them as soon as they entered the restaurant.

"Bonjour, Léon." She kissed him on both cheeks and extended a hand to Sandrine.

"You must be the mysterious woman he often talks about. My name's Blanche." Her smile was open and disarming. "We can skip the formalities, especially since you're a friend of Léon's, who is practically family."

"I'm not mysterious at all," Sandrine replied.

So he talks about me. She shot Léon a curious glance, thinking she saw a hint of a blush. Clearly, what the woman had said was true.

"I'm sure Léon brings many of his friends here. The restaurant looks utterly charming, and I bet the food is superb."

"Do you have a table for us? We're starving." Léon interrupted her stream of words. Was he afraid Blanche would spill even more beans about him? Sandrine smirked; she should have a longer chat with this woman. She seemed to know him well.

"Of course, the family table in the bar is reserved."

Blanche led them past the open kitchen and up the staircase, which was carpeted in dark blue, to the upper floor. 'Bar du Mont' was inscribed above the entrance to a room roughly half the size of the restaurant below. Light poured in through the open windows, illuminating several round tables, the largest of which was set for lunch. On the opposite side, a row of tall bar stools stood in front of a dark imposing wooden bar. Bottles and glasses filled a softly illuminated mirrored shelf. A solid billiard table occupied a corner, its balls scattered as if someone had abruptly abandoned their game.

Blanche guided them to the table. Sandrine counted eight place settings. Clearly, they were expecting more guests.

"Finally! I was starting to worry I'd have to eat all of this alone," called out a man about Léon's age who was standing behind the bar, polishing wine glasses. He tossed the cloth onto the counter and approached them, embracing Léon and giving him a hearty slap on the back. "Good to see you."

"This is Jean, an old friend." Léon introduced him to Sandrine. "The boss's son."

"The younger son of the boss," Jean corrected Léon. Even to an untrained observer, it wouldn't have gone unnoticed how his expression darkened for a fleeting moment. Yet he seemed to quickly shake off the shadowy thoughts and smiled at them warmly.

"Come, we've prepared something delicious. I hope you've brought your appetites."

"Absolutely."

Léon pulled out a chair for her, and she took her seat at the table. Blanche returned, carrying a tray with several glasses of champagne.

"A little something before the meal," she said, handing Sandrine one of the tall glasses.

"Thank you, Blanche."

The woman laughed. "Charlotte. Blanche is my sister."

"Twins," Léon explained. "Not even their mother can tell them apart."

"That's not true at all. I can certainly distinguish between them." A casually yet elegantly dressed woman, with the self-assurance of someone accustomed to the spotlight, approached the table.

"A mother knows her children. Camille Barnais," she introduced herself, extending a hand to Sandrine. "I'm pleased to meet you."

"It looks like we've almost got the whole family here," said Jean. "Only Father is missing."

"And Michel," his mother corrected him.

"He's living here again?" Léon sounded surprised.

"The prodigal son returned unexpectedly a few weeks ago, and he's being celebrated," Jean responded, his voice tinged with a bitterness that was hard to miss.

"No fighting at the table," Camille instructed. "Take your seats."

Blanche returned with baguettes and small bowls of salted butter, which she placed beside the plates. Condensation formed on the porcelain; they must have come straight from the refrigerator.

"I've prepared a traditional menu I hope you'll enjoy," Jean explained.

He went back to the bar and opened a cabinet door, behind which hid a dumbwaiter. On a tray, an array of small plates and bowls awaited, which he brought to the table. The twins, whom Sandrine could hardly tell apart, took their seats. Two place settings remained unoccupied.

"Here comes Father," Blanche said, glancing at a narrow door that presumably led to a back room.

A man who looked like an older version of Jean entered. He carried two bottles of wine in one hand and supported himself with a cane topped by a silver handle in the other. Charlotte sprang up and offered to take the wine from him, but he declined.

"Auguste Barnais," he introduced himself to Sandrine. "The fortunate husband of the most wonderful of all women." He threw Camille a smile in which his love for her was unmistakable to anyone who saw it.

"Old charmer," she dismissed him, amused. "Join us before you miss the first course."

"I may not be very hungry, but I'll certainly enjoy a glass," he said, placing the two bottles on the table and taking his seat. "A superb light rosé from Burgundy. Judging by the aroma, Jean is preparing rack of salt marsh lamb. A marvellous pairing."

He handed one of the bottles to Blanche, who opened it with the skill one might expect from the daughter of a restaurateur, and poured a glass for everyone. Auguste raised his glass to Sandrine. His hand trembled, and wine splashed onto the sleeve of his jacket.

"Damn," she heard him mutter softly. He dabbed at the fabric with a napkin.

"I'm going to take care of this; go ahead and start, I'll be back shortly." Ignoring the twins' objections, he stood up and left the bar.

Jean returned with a tray, placing a long casserole dish containing a meat terrine in the centre of the table.

"A Breton terrine with porcini mushrooms, for our guests from Brittany. Then we have oven-baked mussels with a blend of herbs, oysters, and a few salmon pastries."

He distributed the small bowls with the tiny portions intended to whet their appetites. A wonderful aroma wafted up, making Sandrine's stomach softly rumble in anticipation.

She speared one of the mussels just as Auguste returned. *That was quick. I can't even spot the stain anymore.*

Camille must have caught her gaze.

"My husband is a fashion dinosaur," she said, rolling her eyes. "He buys multiples of his favourite things, so he doesn't have to think too long about what to wear in the morning."

"It's a very nice shirt. What's wrong with it?" he responded.

"Nothing at all," she replied. "But a little variety wouldn't hurt."

"You provide all the variety I need in my life," he said, blowing a kiss to his wife, who smiled back in return.

Jean was an exceptionally talented chef who clearly took joy in pampering his guests.

"May I?" he asked, offering Sandrine a plate of gratinated oysters. "You're sure to enjoy these. I got them from Cancale this morning. You live there, don't you?"

"Yes, you're right. I moved to Brittany this spring."

"Then it'll only take you another twenty years to call yourself a true Cancalaise," he teased.

"Who knows if I'll be here that long. My profession isn't exactly conducive to settling down," she replied.

"You're with the police, aren't you?" Camille looked at her curiously.

"With the Police Nationale in Saint-Malo," Sandrine confirmed.

"Then Léon better behave himself or he'll end up in handcuffs," the twins chuckled. Their playful banter suggested they were quite familiar with him.

"I have nothing to worry about; aside from a few parking tickets, I'm a law-abiding citizen," Léon said.

"In stark contrast to some," Jean muttered. His father shot him an annoyed glance, which he ignored.

"You have to try the rack of lamb." Auguste handed her a plate with a portion of lamb. She suspected he wanted to change the subject. Sandrine didn't want to be rude and tried it.

"It is superb – spicy, yet mild."

"It's from a salt meadow lamb," Auguste explained.

"What's so special about these lambs?"

"It's a local specialty. During spring tides, the meadows around Le Mont-Saint-Michel get completely flooded, leaving sea salt deposits and fostering unique plants like glasswort, sea mustard, and other salt-tolerant herbs. These give the lambs that graze there their distinctive flavour," Auguste explained. He took a sip of the tea he had poured for himself before leaning back in his chair and momentarily closing his eyes. Sandrine could see that the family meal was beginning to tire him out, and he was struggling to stay engaged. Judging by the smile that lingered on his lips though, his thoughts seemed to be drifting to pleasant memories. At one point, Sandrine thought she heard him chuckle softly.

A tall, blond man who looked like a younger version of Auguste entered the room, and Jean abruptly broke off his conversation with Sandrine. Out of the corner of her eye, she noticed Léon also straighten up slightly, shifting his attention to the newcomer. A subtle air of hostility swept over the gathering, which had only moments before been engaged in cheerful conversation.

"Hello, Léon," the man greeted him, ignoring Sandrine and the rest of the family.

"Hello, Michel. Back home?"

"Sooner or later, everyone settles down," he responded vaguely.

Auguste emerged from his reverie, his face glowing with an inner radiance. He was clearly pleased to see his son.

"Michel, it's wonderful that you've joined us. Come, have a seat. Your brother has outdone himself in the kitchen once again."

Jean moved his chair back slightly and crossed his arms over his chest. No smile appeared on his face to encourage Michel to stay. There wasn't much love lost between the brothers, it seemed. The twins, who had just been chattering happily, fell silent. Blanche stood up, feigning a need to fetch more bread.

"I'd love to, but I'm short on time right now. I'm planning to take the boat out tomorrow, and I need to make a lot of preparations."

The light in Auguste's eyes dimmed, and his shoulders slumped. He tried in vain to hide his disappointment.

"That's too bad. Maybe next time."

"There will surely be an opportunity to catch up on old times soon," Michel said, directing his words to Léon, but his voice lacked any of the warmth that characterised the rest of the family.

"Of course." Léon's words were polite but amounted to nothing more than an empty platitude. *That's not like him at all. He doesn't seem to like Michel.*

"What time are you going to head out on the boat?" Camille asked.

"Very early tomorrow. The weather is supposed to be excellent, and I've been working a lot this past week."

Jean's sceptical look made it abundantly clear how little he thought of his brother's work.

Camille glanced at the clock. "I was planning on stopping by the marina. My cousin Céleste invited me for a coastal trip next weekend, and my sailing shoes and rain jacket are on the boat. I need them."

"I can bring your things back when I return," Michel said.

"I'd rather do it myself," she decided. "A water pipe has burst at the house on Rue de Dinan, so I need to head to Saint-Malo anyway to check on things. I'll stop by the boat and quickly grab my stuff. It's no trouble at all."

"It's unnecessary," Michel countered. "Organising the repairs is enough work as it is. You know how hard it is to get a craftsman on short notice, especially on a Sunday."

"It's hardly a detour. And no more arguing."

She stood and picked up a chocolate truffle from a dainty bowl next to Jean's plate.

"May I?"

"Of course."

"Jean has such a sweet tooth. He never finishes a meal without some chocolate." She playfully tousled her younger son's hair, who ducked and pulled his head away.

"He doesn't usually share." Camille popped the chocolate truffle into her mouth and nodded with delight.

"Can I take your car?" she asked Jean. "Mine's in the shop."

"I can drive you," he offered. "The printers called; the new menus are ready and I was planning to pick them up on the way. Then on the way back, I wanted to speak with the harbourmaster – something I'd like to settle before Michel sets sail, even if my brother thinks it's unnecessary."

"Nonsense, you've got enough on your plate here and I might stay overnight in Saint-Malo. I can swing by the printers on my way back tomorrow."

"As you wish," he conceded, seeming to recognise that she was going to do what she wanted regardless.

"I'll be on my way as well," Michel said, taking his leave and exiting the bar through the back door, the same one his father had used.

"Drive carefully." Jean pulled the keys out of his pocket and handed them to his mother. "No dents this time, please."

"Oh, come on, a car without a few dents lacks character, just like a good man," she replied. She kissed Auguste, waved goodbye to the others, and left the room.

Léon leaned towards Sandrine and whispered, "Camille is a fantastic woman who can do everything except drive."

Charlotte, sitting next to her, nodded in agreement. "Léon is right about that. I don't like driving the bulky SUV either, but sometimes I have to when I'm fetching materials for the renovation."

"Is the Auberge being renovated?" asked Sandrine.

"No, fortunately not. I work upstairs," she said, pointing to the ceiling.

"Upstairs means in Le Mont-Saint-Michel the abbey," Léon explained after noticing Sandrine's puzzled look. "Charlotte is a civil engineer and specialises in rescuing old walls."

"Blanche is a historian," added Charlotte. "You see, the entire family is closely linked to the monastery."

After dessert, which Sandrine ended up not skipping after all, they said their goodbyes to the Barnais family. Auguste seemed distant, almost as if he barely noticed their departure. Jean started clearing the table, while Charlotte walked them to the door and bid them goodbye.

"Isn't that Michel?" Sandrine pointed to a man carrying a small backpack slung over his left shoulder, talking on the phone as he walked.

"Looks like it," Léon replied. "He's probably heading to the boat. I assume he's planning to spend the night onboard so he can set sail early."

Michel strode down the street, soon lost to their sight amid the tourists.

"Then I hope his day improves. From his expression, it didn't look like he was having a pleasant conversation."

"Is that the suspicious cop coming out in you? Hotel owners deal with unreliable suppliers, disgruntled guests, or the tax office all the time. Maybe he just needs to fix something on the boat. Auguste used it frequently in the past, but these last few years, it's just been docked. I wonder why he hasn't sold it. The upkeep isn't cheap."

"What time are our tickets for, anyway?"

They had a thirty-minute window during which they could enter the abbey, and Sandrine didn't want to miss it. She was looking forward to the view from the apex of the Mount. The air was clear; perhaps she could spot her house or at least see Cancale from there.

"We have plenty of time to take a look around the place."

At a leisurely pace, they strolled up the lane towards the abbey's entrance.

Saint-Malo

They'd spent some time in the souvenir shops along Grande Rue and climbed up a staircase onto the fortress wall that completely encircled the town when Sandrine's phone rang.

"Not again. It's Sunday," she muttered under her breath.

"What's up?"

She showed him the phone. Adel's name was on the display. Her first impulse was to decline the call, but then she reluctantly answered.

"I'm off-duty and have no intention of letting anyone ruin my Sunday," she greeted her colleague. She listened to him in silence for a moment. "Fine. I'll need a little over an hour. We'll meet at the quay."

She ended the call and slipped her phone into her tiny purse.

"Work calling?"

"I'm afraid so."

"Crime never sleeps." He didn't do a good job of hiding his disappointment.

"At least we had a splendid morning and an excellent lunch with pleasant company. Next time we'll go somewhere with no cell reception," she jokingly suggested. She rose onto her tiptoes and gave him a kiss on the cheek. "But I have to go back now."

"Murder and mayhem plaguing Brittany?"

"I don't know yet. Adel was unusually vague. For some reason, he thinks my presence is needed. He wouldn't interrupt my weekend without cause. Something must have struck him as odd."

"Then I'll take you there."

"That's so sweet of you. I'll make it up to you, I promise."

Léon pulled up at Quai Saint-Vincent in Saint-Malo, before the walls of the old Corsair city. On the broad sidewalk between the multi-lane road and the marina, a handful of police, fire, and rescue vehicles were parked. A yellow crane truck maneuvered clumsily until it finally positioned parallel to the harbour basin. The heads of two divers peeked out from the murky, dirty water. Sandrine didn't envy them their job.

"Your colleague looks pretty grumpy over there. Should I have stopped further away?"

"Nonsense. Even policewomen have a private life." She kissed him goodbye. "Thank you for the lovely day. It's a shame it had to end like this."

"Agreed. We'll make up for it soon."

"I'd like that."

Sandrine got out of the car and approached Brigadier Luc Poutin, who eyed her with blatant curiosity.

"Where's Adel?" she asked, referring to her colleague whom she trusted far more than him.

"He's by the crane. Where the diver's vehicle is parked." He cleared his throat noisily and spat into the water. In her presence, the older policeman acted even more boorish than usual, but she had no desire to call him out or reprimand him.

She found Brigadier Chief de Police Adel Azarou near the

cabin of the crane truck, where he was talking to a diver who was swimming in the harbour basin. Upon her arrival, he signalled the driver to lower the steel cables.

"Hello, Adel."

"Hello, Sandrine. Sorry about the weekend. Really."

"My dad always said to keep your eyes wide open when choosing a career. Guess I didn't listen well enough. What happened here?"

"A car went off the road, broke through the barrier chain between the bollards and plunged into the harbour."

"The driver?"

He shook his head. "The diver said they found a body in the car. A woman, but that's all he could tell. Now they're attaching the tow cables to the frame. We should find out who was in the wreck soon."

Sandrine stepped to the edge of the harbour basin and looked down at the dark, oily water where empty plastic bottles floated and bubbles from the divers popped at the surface. In front of her stretched a forest of sailboat masts, and to her right ran the medieval city wall, behind which townhouses stood in parallel to the yacht harbour. There, onlookers had gathered, eager not to miss the recovery operation as they stuffed themselves with chocolate crêpes and lemonade.

"A fatal traffic accident. The standby team should be able to handle this on their own. Why did you call me?"

"We have several witnesses who reported that the car was being pursued and got rammed in the roundabout. After that, the driver lost control, floored it, and sped into the harbour."

"Is there evidence to back that up?"

"The forensics team found glass shards from a taillight. The location seems to match." He pointed toward the exit of the roundabout. "Jean-Claude and his team are done here and taking a coffee break. Once the car is secured, they'll be busy with gathering evidence from it for the rest of the day."

Sandrine knew the little crêpe stand next to the children's carousel by the city gate. She looked over and recognised the head of forensics and some of his crew. She wasn't the only one whose weekend had been spoiled.

A patrol car pulled up to the kerb, and a man in a grey suit stepped out. Adel whistled in surprise.

"What brings our boss here on a Sunday?"

Sandrine looked curiously at Commissaire Jean Matisse, the head of the police station. She had no idea what he wanted, but it was unlikely he would have interrupted his weekend for a mere traffic accident, even a fatal one. Or did he already know more about the incident than she did?

"You'd better handle this one," said Adel, walking over to the fire chief who signalled the crane operator to slowly tighten the rope.

"Bonjour, Capitaine Perrot," Matisse greeted her.

"Bonjour, Monsieur le Commissaire. Shouldn't you be spending your Sunday with your family? We can handle a car accident just fine on our own."

"You shouldn't be the only one forced to work overtime on the weekend." He scrutinised her discreetly. "You look like you had more pleasant plans for today than dealing with a traffic accident?"

"Actually, I was already on my way back when Adel called," she replied, bending the truth slightly.

"I'd like to speak with you. Privately." His voice took on a serious tone that instilled a sense of unease in her. They took a few steps aside until Sandrine was confident that no one could eavesdrop on their conversation. The prying eyes of journalists, who had gathered behind the police tape, followed them, and more than one camera was pointed in their direction.

"There's news, and not all of it is good," he began.

"As always."

"Prosecutor Lagarde has left us and taken a position in Rennes."

"I heard about that already. Good for him."

In reality, she had toasted this news with Rosalie last week, glad to be rid of the incompetent man. His successor could hardly be any worse.

"We've been assigned a new prosecuting judge." The usually self-assured man avoided eye contact with her at that moment, only heightening her sense of apprehension.

"Do I know him?"

"You could say that," Commissaire Matisse replied, glancing at a taxi that pulled up to the kerb. "I would have liked to break it to you more gently, but here he comes."

A man stepped out of the taxi, and for a moment, Sandrine's breath caught.

"This can't be happening," she muttered. *Merde.*

"I'm afraid it is."

"Antoine de Chezac. What a pleasure," she muttered sarcastically. *What did I do to deserve this?* She had been forced to collaborate with him multiple times in Paris; later, he had overseen the disciplinary process that had almost cost her career. In her first case in Saint-Malo, they had clashed on several unfortunate occasions when he had withheld vital information.

"He will vividly remember how you publicly outmanoeuvred him during the investigations of the death on the coastal path," Commissaire Matisse said.

"He asked for it and more than deserved it."

"He's not the kind to forgive or forget when you make him look bad. Especially since you're a woman."

She knew that all too well from her own experience. The man had relished the prospect of destroying her career.

"What did he do to get banished to the sticks? He'd never leave Paris voluntarily."

"Apparently, working outside Paris for a while is now seen as a career booster. I suppose it's some kind of populist trend."

She kept her eyes on the man. With practiced ease, Antoine de Chezac strolled past the throng of journalists. Deborah Binet, the reporter from *Ouest-France*, recognised him instantly and pelted him with questions. With a feigned smile, as if the attention was unwelcome, he turned to the reporters and launched into a speech about his challenging new role in Saint-Malo – no doubt a spiel he had been rehearsing for days. All hot air, no substance. Sandrine knew him well enough to predict the platitudes he'd use. She sighed. With him as a supervisor, her job would become significantly more difficult. The man was cunning and career-driven. He would subordinate everything to advance his career, including investigative work. A case he couldn't win would be swiftly buried.

"Any chance we could get Lagarde back?" she asked Matisse.

"That's a rhetorical question, isn't it?"

She shrugged in resignation. *Unfortunately.*

The engine of the crane truck roared to life, and the pull ropes tightened. The divers must have run the belts through the car's interior and secured them. Sandrine stood beside Adel and watched intently for the spot where the car would surface. She took a deep breath in and out. In a few minutes, she would be facing a corpse, and she'd have to act professionally. How the police treated the incident would hinge on her expertise. She couldn't afford mistakes. Especially not with Antoine de Chezac breathing down her neck, lying in wait to catch her in a misstep.

A black car top broke the surface, and inch by inch, an SUV emerged. Water poured from its interior and splashed into the basin. The driver's body was tilted to the side, making the face unrecognisable from the quay. Sandrine knew only that a life had been unnecessarily lost here today, and her stomach tightened slightly.

"Lieutenant Perrot," Antoine de Chezac addressed her. She instantly recognised his nasal voice dripping with condescension.

"Capitaine," she corrected him, without taking her eyes off the vehicle. The man knew precisely her rank; the incorrect title was a calculated move to intimidate her. He had been responsible for her demotion to lieutenant and clearly wanted to remind her that he had the power to do it again, should she give him even the slightest reason.

"Yes, I forgot." He skipped the pretence of an apology. "In Paris, you always arrived at crime scenes on your motorcycle. This is the first time I've seen you in a dress. It suits you exceedingly well; perhaps you should consider wearing one to work more often. It makes you appear considerably more feminine." His eyes scanned over her body like the antennae of a repulsive insect. She forced herself not to recoil from his intrusive demeanour or slap him for the inappropriate remark.

"Capitaine Perrot is off-duty today. She is here at my request," Commissaire Matisse explained.

I don't need your help, she thought. *I can handle this guy on my own.*

"Is that necessary? A simple traffic accident surely doesn't require such a high-profile investigator," de Chezac said, his voice tinged with palpable mockery. "And your forensics guys would much rather be having coffee than recording this accident."

"They already did that before you got here." The commissaire's voice took on a sharper tone, which effortlessly glided off the judge's armour of snobbery.

"Watch out!" called the fire brigade chief. The crane arm swung over the quay, slowly lowering the heavy vehicle to the ground.

Jean-Claude Mazet, who couldn't have missed de Chezac's

criticisms of him and his team, walked over to the car with one of his men and peered through the window.

"A body, female," he called out to them.

They followed him to the car. Mazet stepped aside, and Sandrine looked in. The driver was hanging in her seatbelt, her eyes still widened in terror. Her hair and clothes clung to her soaking wet body. Sandrine gasped. The sight of the woman was like a hard punch to the gut, and she took a step back.

"You're quite sensitive today," Judge de Chezac sneered. "That's not like you at all."

Wordlessly, she turned and walked over to Adel's car, parked a few feet away. He opened the door for her, and she perched sideways on the passenger seat. Her chest had tightened so much that breathing became painful.

"What's wrong?" her assistant asked.

"Our investigator seems a bit frail today. I'd assumed she was accustomed to the sight of corpses," Monsieur le Juge de Chezac said, looking around for approval. But people averted their eyes in awkward silence. Only Poutin grinned broadly.

"Shut your mouth," Sandrine said, her voice icy.

"Excuse me?" De Chezac straightened up, as if ready to chastise her, but she paid no more attention to him. The man wasn't worth it.

"The victim's name is Camille Barnais, and she runs a hotel in Le Mont-Saint-Michel. We had lunch together just two hours ago."

"*Merde.*" Adel leaned against the car. "That's really tough."

"How do I break it to her family?" The question was more for herself than for him.

"I can do it," he offered.

"Thank you, but that's my job, as is figuring out what happened here," she said. "I have to call Léon."

She watched the paramedics open the door, lift Camille Barnais out, and place her on a stretcher. As the ambulance drove off, she grasped the frame of the Peugeot with both hands and pulled herself up.

"Come on," she said to Adel, walking toward the SUV with steps she wished felt steadier.

"Are you okay?" Matisse whispered.

"I'm fine. It was just the surprise. I wasn't prepared to see Camille."

"It's always a shock to encounter a victim you personally know. Do you want Azarou to take the case?"

"I didn't know her well, but I owe it to her to find out what led to this accident. Adel and I will handle it together. Can you please keep de Chezac off my back, at least for a while?"

"I'll do my best."

Matisse stepped aside, and Sandrine circled the vehicle. Swiftly, she pulled on a pair of disposable gloves. She crouched down at various spots to examine the body of the car without touching anything. Even if the harbour water had washed away most of the evidence, she followed protocol to the letter.

"The taillight is shattered. When can you tell me if the fragments you found on the road match this?" she asked Jean-Claude Mazet, who stood beside her.

"First thing tomorrow morning. We're pulling an all-nighter," he replied.

"That dent on the rear right looks fresh."

"Absolutely. We'll take a sample of the paint. It must have been a red vehicle. According to witnesses, a van. In a day or two, we should know the exact make. Marie is already reviewing the traffic cam footage; we might spot the two vehicles. With any luck, the license plate will be visible."

"Let's hope so."

"Looks like a hit-and-run," Adel said quietly, joining her. De Chezac had already begun speaking to the journalists, giving his account of the incident. She could accuse him of many things, and shirking his duties to get into the papers was one of them. He'd be a household name in Saint-Malo before long.

"Camille Barnais was on her way to inspect water damage at one of her properties on Rue de Dinan. As far as I know, the family owns multiple houses in the city. They also have a yacht docked here. She mentioned she wanted to grab a few things from the boat."

Sandrine recalled how Camille's family had teased her about her poor driving skills. Maybe this really was just a tragic accident, and the collision had caused Camille to hit the gas pedal instead of the brake in a panic.

"Everything seems to point to an accident," Adel said.

"It looks that way, but let's not jump to conclusions. Can you drive me to Le Mont-Saint-Michel? I want to speak with the family before the journalists descend upon them."

"Of course," he replied. "Dubois and Poutin will wrap things up here. The SUV will be taken to the station for examination." He glanced at the new prosecuting judge. "And he's doing a splendid job with the press. Maybe he'll keep them busy for a while before they decide to pester the family."

"He's good at that, but I'm afraid not everyone will be distracted." She scanned the crowd for Deborah Binet but couldn't spot her.

They climbed into Adel's white Peugeot 306 and left the crime scene. She was relieved to escape de Chezac's presence but was increasingly apprehensive about the conversation with the family. How would she break the news of Camille's death to Auguste? She couldn't forget the loving expression that had lit up his eyes whenever he'd looked at his wife. It was clear how deeply he loved her, even after many years of marriage when other couples had long since drifted apart. The impact her death would have on him was almost unimaginable.

. . .

An employee of the hotel led Sandrine and Adel into the bar where she had eaten with Camille and the family just a few hours before.

"How dreadful," the woman muttered repeatedly.

"The family already knows about the accident?" *Someone beat me to the punch.*

"Certainly. A female reporter was here just before you and was asking intrusive questions. A disagreeable person. Jean promptly showed her the door."

Deborah Binet immediately came to mind. That's why Sandrine hadn't spotted the journalist among her colleagues. Someone must have tipped her off about the identity of the deceased. Instead of getting distracted by the chatter of the new magistrate, she had driven straight to Le Mont-Saint-Michel. No wonder Jean had thrown her out. The woman had an excellent nose for a story but the emotional intelligence and tact of a Rottweiler.

The family members were waiting for them. Auguste and the twins sat together at a table near the windows. Blanche wiped her reddened eyes with a handkerchief and then crumpled it between her fingers. Next to their father sat a priest in a black cassock. She estimated the man to be well over seventy, perhaps even eighty. His snow-white hair and beard were neatly trimmed. Grey eyes scrutinised Sandrine intensely, veering on hostility, before shifting to Adel and darkening further.

Jean stood behind the bar, his forearms on the counter, and Michel leaned his hip against the windowsill. The palpable tension between the brothers filled the air. She felt as if she had walked into an argument that had momentarily paused due to her arrival, but would surely resume as soon as she left and the family was alone again.

"I'm sorry," she said. "I wish I could have been the one to give you this sad news first."

Auguste Barnais' gaze remained fixed on the table. There

was no indication that he was even aware of her presence. The priest laid a hand on his arm, and the man looked up and gave her a feeble nod. She was uncertain whether he recognised her in that moment. Words failed her when it came to offering him any appropriate comfort – if such a thing was even possible.

"How did it happen?" Charlotte asked. Sandrine was thankful for the question; when it came to facts, she felt less helpless.

"Don't be rude, offer our guests a seat first." Auguste's voice sounded lifeless, and his words came out as if carefully rehearsed. A faint smile appeared on his face, which seemed strangely disconcerting to Sandrine at that moment.

She took a seat, while Adel remained standing by the door.

"We can't say for certain yet, but all signs point to a collision with another car at the Quai Saint-Vincent roundabout. Camille's car veered off the road, broke through the barrier, and plunged into the harbour. Unfortunately, she couldn't free herself from the vehicle in time."

"A collision?" Michel straightened up and took a step forward. "With whom?"

"We don't know yet. The unidentified driver fled the scene, without alerting the police."

"A hit-and-run?" Charlotte looked at her in disbelief.

"Do you have any idea who could have done this?" Michel added.

"That's utterly irrelevant. Mother is dead; that's all that matters. Catching the guy won't bring her back," Jean snarled.

"Don't get upset. I just want whoever is responsible to be held accountable," Michel replied defensively.

Auguste looked at his son. "We need to stick together now. At least your mother lived to see you return to the family fold and keep the tradition alive."

"Indeed," the priest agreed.

"Père Martin is an old family friend," Charlotte explained.

"And our spiritual guide," her father added. "We'll go to church later to pray for Camille."

The priest nodded in agreement. "She's in a better place now."

"Where we'll soon be reunited."

Sandrine had to strain to hear Auguste's hoarse whisper.

Jean shot an angry glance at the old priest, but Blanche motioned for him to keep his cool. Sandrine suspected that the comforting presence of Père Martin was helping Auguste cope with the devastating news without completely falling apart, and his children tolerated the priest mostly for their father's sake.

"I need some fresh air." Michel abruptly left the room, as if fleeing the scene. Auguste looked as if he wanted to stop him but decided against it.

"She must've been on her way to the boat to get her things." Jean poured himself a Cognac and downed it in one go. "Michel could've brought everything back tomorrow evening when he returned from his tour. This was a senseless accident. I'd offered to drive her, but she turned me down. If only I had insisted ..." He let the sentence hang in the air.

"When Mum set her mind to something, there was no talking her out of it." Blanche stood up, wrapped an arm around her brother's shoulders, and pulled him close.

Auguste, too, rose to his feet, albeit laboriously.

"Marie," he addressed the waitress who was still standing by the door, "you're going to have to manage without us at the restaurant today. We're going to the church to pray for Camille."

"Of course, Monsieur Barnais. We'll manage. There won't be any complaints."

"Jean, go get Michel; I want him to come with us."

His son reluctantly placed the bottle back in the cabinet and left the room. Judging by his expression, he'd have preferred his brother's absence.

"I don't think there's anything more you can do for us,"

Auguste Barnais said, turning to Sandrine. "I don't mean to be rude, but we'd like some privacy now."

"I understand." She stood up, said her goodbyes, and left the room.

As she walked out, she noticed Michel pacing back and forth along the fortress wall across the street, gesticulating wildly as he spoke on the phone. It was the second obviously distressing phone call she had witnessed him making that day. Sandrine couldn't help but wonder what was so urgent that he couldn't postpone it.

* * *

They sat on two camping chairs behind Club Équinoxe. Léon looked thoughtfully across the half-full parking lot, where Sandrine's old Citroën 2CV was parked.

"How did Auguste and the kids take the news?"

"Not well. A female journalist got there before me and ambushed them with questions before we could even inform the family about the accident."

"What a piece of work."

Sandrine now knew for sure that it was Deborah Binet who had left the accident scene before her. Unsurprisingly, several missed calls from the journalist were on her phone. Despite knowing that Sandrine wouldn't disclose anything about ongoing cases, she kept trying her luck. Persistence was one of the woman's strong suits.

"As for Auguste, he's hard to read; he almost seemed to be in a trance."

"Probably the meds," Léon replied tersely.

"What do you mean?"

"Advanced-stage cancer. He missed the window for any chance of recovery a long time ago. Auguste avoids doctors like the plague."

"Painkillers?"

"That's my guess."

Now it became clear to her why the man had gradually seemed to drift off during dinner. The medication must have started to take effect.

"Blanche was crying. Michel and Jean were at each other's throats. I got the feeling they'd had a big argument before I arrived."

"Blanche and Charlotte worshipped their mother. No idea how they'll cope with the loss. I'll visit them in the coming days. Want to come along?"

"I'd normally say yes, but I'm afraid my presence won't exactly soothe their pain. After all, I'm the one handling the case."

"Did you get transferred to the traffic police and forget to tell me?"

"Hit-and-run with fatal consequences. Here in Saint-Malo, that's a serious offense. We're not in Paris. It will probably make the front page of the newspapers here tomorrow."

"I hope you catch the driver, even if it won't bring Camille back." He stretched out his legs and looked up at the sky, which was slowly darkening. "The family is quite religious, at least the parents. If there's any truth to it all, Camille should have made it 'up there' by now. The thought must be helping Auguste cope with his pain."

"That's what the priest who was present claimed, at least."

"Père Martin? He's still visiting the Barnais family?"

"That's how he was introduced to me."

"He's been leading Mass at the local pilgrimage church, Église Saint-Pierre, since I was a kid. He also regularly hears the family's confessions."

"After I left, they planned to go to the church together to pay their respects to the deceased."

"That will give them some comfort. The current parish

priest will likely have no objections to Père Martin conducting a Mass for Camille in the church."

"He's not part of the parish?" Sandrine queried.

"Not for years. The man must be over eighty. As far as I know, he lives with his nephew, who is a chaplain in Pontorson. Père Martin used to bike to Le Mont-Saint-Michel every day. That's at least a forty-minute ride. Keeps you in shape. There was always a place set for him at the Barnais family table."

"If he no longer holds an official position in the community, why does he go to such lengths daily?"

"Old habits, perhaps. As far as I know, he used to frequent the Saint-Aubert Chapel on the north side of the island to pray or meditate there."

"I can see that. The way he carries himself, he's clearly big on traditions and customs."

"The man is pretty conservative. No idea what century he's stuck in, but women carrying weapons and catching criminals are definitely not to his taste. He's probably praying for your soul right now. Was Adel with you?"

"Père Martin gave him a look that could leave bruises."

He chuckled softly. "I can easily imagine that. Tourists are already a thorn in his side, but a Muslim in his pilgrimage site would surely get his blood boiling."

"What happened between Michel and Jean?" Sandrine changed the subject.

He sat up, and his chair scraped across the asphalt.

"That's a story as complicated as it is messy. Michel is something of the black sheep of the Barnais family. He got kicked out of school for drug-dealing, left the family, and moved to Saint-Malo. His police record should be quite colourful. He's not exactly welcome here," he said, thumbing towards the club behind him.

"Is he still dealing drugs?" *That might explain his phone calls.*

31

"Drugs, fake IDs, stolen car parts – anything that brings in money."

"And now he's back on Le Mont with his family?"

"It seems that way. Surprised me too, but word is he's run up debts with the wrong kind of people and things got too hot for him here."

"Do you think his father is settling his debts? Auguste didn't strike me as someone who throws money around carelessly," Sandrine asked.

"Like I said, it's a complicated family. They are quite well-off, but the Auberge has always been the centrepiece. Everything revolves around it. By family tradition, it's handed down to the eldest son, for generations. And that would be Michel."

"So that explains Jean's comment about the prodigal son returning."

"Jean has been slaving away for the hotel these past years, and he's had a big part in its success. Why would he be thrilled about his brother showing up out of the blue and being favoured by Auguste? Especially now, with Camille ..." Léon trailed off.

"So he's on the verge of losing the Auberge to Michel."

"It seems that way. I can't imagine that after losing Camille, he'd have the strength or will to fight the cancer for much longer."

"And the daughters?"

"They pitch in at the Auberge now and then, but they're both independent women. Charlotte is a civil engineer and owns a successful planning firm specialising in the preservation of historic buildings. You know she's currently overseeing the renovation of the abbey. Blanche studied medieval history and is considered an authority on the history of Brittany. Some of her books are bestsellers, especially the popular science ones. You'll find some copies in the monastery's bookstore. When Auguste passes away, they won't be left empty-handed. Knowing them, they won't be pleased if the Auberge falls into Michel's hands."

"And they suspect their brother sees his inheritance more as a mere investment?"

"I'd be very surprised if they have any serious doubt that he'll sell the Auberge the moment it's in his possession. He probably already has some willing buyers lined up, ready to shell out a pretty penny."

The metal door to the club squeaked open, and a woman with buzz-cut hair and colourful tattoos on her arms poked her head out. "Jacques is here and he wants his money."

Sandrine looked at Léon curiously.

Léon grinned at her. "Don't worry, it's not the mob at my door, here to extort protection money. Jacques is the head of the cleaning company. The guy doesn't trust banks and only takes cash. Probably stashes it all under his mattress. He thinks it's safer that way."

"No one would ever think to look there," noted the woman at the door sarcastically.

"Duty calls," he said, standing up. "Thanks for delivering the news in person, but I've got to run now."

"Of course." She took him in her arms and hugged him tightly for a moment before stepping back and saying goodbye.

An Accident?

Inès Boni, the office manager, intercepted Sandrine before she could settle at her desk.

"Marie wants you to come by. She said it's urgent."

"I'd better head there right away, then."

Sandrine knew Marie Abondio, the 'Mistress of Bits and Bytes' as her boss Jean-Claude Mazet called her, wasn't one for drama or exaggeration. If Marie claimed to have stumbled upon something significant, Sandrine trusted it to be true.

"Is Adel here yet?"

"He's already in forensics."

"Then they'll both be waiting for me." She set her bag on the desk and hung her coat over her chair.

"Le Commissaire also wants you to stop by. The press release is ready, and he'd like your approval."

"No problem, but forensics comes first."

A traffic accident that resulted in death was big news in Saint-Malo. If Marie had uncovered something, Sandrine wanted to know before the press did.

. . .

Marie and Adel sat together in front of a screen and waved her over as soon as she entered the room.

"What's going on?"

"I was able to splice together footage from various surveillance cameras around the area so that we can see the accident and the preceding moments with sufficient clarity. I think we can reconstruct what happened." Marie pulled up another chair, and Sandrine joined them.

It was a video she'd rather not watch. Seeing a woman she had just dined and laughed with yesterday plunge to her death was not something she looked forward to. The thought of being trapped in a sinking car, facing a slow yet inevitable death, was an image she'd rather banish from her mind.

"Here she comes into frame," Marie commented on the video. A black SUV appeared and soon vanished from the camera's view. "And here's her pursuer." She paused the video and pointed at a red van – a Peugeot Boxer, an older model, as far as Sandrine could tell from the blurry image.

"Why 'pursuer'?" she asked.

"The van has been following her since I first identified her within city limits, several miles before the accident. As I move further from the city centre, I have fewer recordings, but there's still plenty to sift through. Maybe I can find earlier footage to determine when and where the van first appeared. As you can see, there were two men in the car. They tailgated her for quite a distance."

"Could be a coincidence," Sandrine said. "Maybe they were headed in the same direction."

"I doubt it," the technician replied, and pressed play. The SUV reappeared. The images jarringly switched from camera to camera.

"Something's off with that woman. Just look at how she's driving. Like an absolute rookie. Speeding up, then slowing down, and she can't even stay in her lane." Marie pointed at the markings that Camille's car crossed frequently, as if she were intoxicated.

"Her family used to tease her about being a terrible driver." Sandrine recalled how Jean had asked his mother to return his car without any new dents. His offer to give her a ride had been politely but firmly declined. That had clearly been a mistake.

"They have ample reason to," said Adel. "The traffic police have issued quite a stack of tickets to Madame Barnais. Mostly for illegal parking. Occasionally, she was a bit heavy-footed." He looked at the screen. "If she always drove as poorly as she does in this footage, it's a wonder she hasn't racked up a lot more."

"Let it run again," Sandrine requested.

Marie restarted the footage from the beginning and shifted her chair a bit to the side. She absent-mindedly played with the colourful wooden beads braided into her hair as Sandrine focused intently on the monitor. The transporter maintained a constant distance from Camille Barnais' car, regardless of how fast or slow she drove. Her pursuers could have easily overtaken her multiple times on the two-lane road without breaking the speed limit. But they didn't. Why?

"A plumber," she said, pointing at the vehicle now visible from the side. "The advertising is clearly visible."

"I already checked that. It's a one-man operation from Saint-Servan. Should I send a patrol car over?" Adel looked at her inquisitively.

"Wait, the best is yet to come," Marie interrupted. "Here, they're on the Chaussee du Sillon, just before the harbour area." Her finger traced the car on the monitor. "Now she reaches the first roundabout at Quai Saint-Vincent. Watch this!"

Camille turned on her blinker to enter the roundabout when the transporter suddenly sped up and rammed her from behind. Sandrine whistled in astonishment. *So that's where the dent came from.*

"This is no accident; they intentionally rammed her," Adel exclaimed.

"Wait."

Both cars sped through the first of the roundabouts. The Peugeot Boxer was still tailing the woman. As they exited the next roundabout, they sideswiped the rear of the SUV. Glass shards from the blinker scattered on the ground. Camille Barnais jerked the wheel. Startled or panicked, she must've floored the gas pedal. The heavy vehicle lurched forward and veered across the road toward the wide sidewalk. The iron chain between the bollards ripped apart and whipped through the air. The car skidded across the Quai and plunged into the harbour basin. The red Peugeot paused momentarily, then sped off, leaving Camille Barnais trapped in the half-submerged car.

"What bastards," said Adel. "They deliberately forced her off the road."

"Exactly." Marie leaned back, satisfied with the work for which she'd undoubtedly spent the whole night at the precinct.

"Excellent work," Sandrine praised the young forensic technician. "The question is whether they intended to kill Camille Barnais or if the chase just got out of hand," she mused.

"It looks pretty clear-cut to me," Adel said decisively. "Why would they tail her through half the city if they didn't have this spot at the harbour in mind?"

"I agree. We can safely rule out a random accident. But what significance does the Quai Saint-Vincent have? That's where an observer turned into an aggressive assailant. If we figure out the reason, we're a step closer to solving this." She patted Adel on the shoulder. "You take care of the car, and I'll talk to Dr. Hervé and our boss in the meantime. That should help us see the bigger picture."

***

She knocked on the frame of the open door, and her boss waved her in.

"Capitaine Perrot, have a seat."

He handed her a sheet of paper: the press release, which she read attentively.

"Please write it up as an unsolved hit-and-run; that way we're playing it safe."

He leaned back and gave her a sceptical look. "I initially thought this was just a traffic accident – dramatic, sure, but not something the criminal investigation department needed to get involved with."

Sandrine pulled a chair up to the desk. "I've come to believe there's more to this accident than we initially thought yesterday."

"And this isn't just because you knew the victim and want to clear any doubts?" He rested his forearms on the table and leaned in. "De Chezac has you in his crosshairs. If you blow a simple traffic accident out of proportion, he'll use it to hang you."

"I highly doubt that. You don't know the man nearly as well as I do. He relishes nothing more than cases that can be inflated. If we're right in our suspicions, he'll revel in this investigation like a pig in mud. A high-profile victim and a mysterious accident are just the sort of spice he needs to keep his face in the papers."

"Spill it then, what caught your eye?"

"It wasn't me. Marie Abondio pulled an all-nighter reviewing the surveillance footage." She relayed how a Peugeot had followed Camille Barnais before ultimately forcing her off the road on Quai Saint-Vincent.

Commissaire Matisse nodded approvingly. "We knew there was a collision with a red van at the roundabout. If it's true that the car had been tailgating her halfway through the city, then you do have a case on your hands."

"We can already prove that much, thanks to forensic evidence."

"And what's your next move?"

"We're paying the owner of the van a visit."

"Good, let's see what comes of it before I inform our new prosecuting judge."

"That's probably wise. He'll want something concrete." She stood up and took her leave.

"The van's registered to a Gerard Dupuit," Adel informed her as they drove. "His wife said we could find him on Rue de Dinan." He noticed her quizzical look. "It's in the Old Town."

"Let's hope she's right. By now, the radio should be broadcasting that we're looking for a man on hit-and-run charges. He might have already skipped town."

Rue de Dinan was also the street where Camille Barnais had intended to go to deal with a burst water pipe. Same area, and the car involved in the accident belonged to a plumber. A strange coincidence?

Ten minutes later, they pulled up on the narrow, cobblestone street. Parked in front of a four-storey house was the red Peugeot Boxer they had seen in the video.

'Le Plombier de Saint-Malo' was boldly lettered on the side. The front left fender was dented. She kicked the bumper which wobbled alarmingly, but a wire wrapped around it kept it attached to the body of the car. Sandrine crouched down in front of it.

"These look like black paint streaks. This is undoubtedly the car involved in the accident."

Adel took his phone and called for a traffic unit to secure the vehicle until forensic technicians could tow it away.

"Let's go have a word with this guy," he said, crossing the street. From a window, the sound of a hammer striking metal echoed throughout. The man was clearly going about his work as if nothing had happened.

"Hold on a second."

Sandrine stopped her colleague and glanced at the nameplates next to the buzzers. On the second floor was the office of Suzanne Leriche, the psychotherapist of Aimée Vilette who had been murdered in Saint-Malo just two months ago. Another strange coincidence. She pressed the buzzer, and shortly afterward the door's electronic lock buzzed open. A musty smell of damp plaster hit them, and dark stains marred the white walls.

On the second floor, Suzanne Leriche opened the door. "Sandrine?" She looked at her in astonishment.

"And this is Brigadier Chief de Police Adel Azarou, my colleague."

"Pleased to meet you. But what brings the police to my office? I hope no one I know has been murdered again."

"That's quite possible, you might know the victim."

Camille Barnais had mentioned a burst water pipe in one of her properties. Suzanne Leriche was thus one of her tenants. This didn't necessarily mean the two women knew each other, but Sandrine assumed as much.

"We need to speak with your plumber."

"Are you going to arrest him?" The psychologist sounded concerned.

"That remains to be seen."

The woman pressed both hands against the door frame, blocking their way.

"Suzanne?"

"Do you have a search warrant?"

"Do we need one?" Sandrine asked, surprised. She hadn't expected this reaction.

"A water pipe burst. Of course, it happened on a Sunday, and Gerard is the only plumber who works at weekends. I'll let you in, but only if you promise not to arrest him until he's finished here."

Sandrine caught the serious look on the psychologist's face. This was no joke.

"Monsieur Dupuit, there's someone here who wants to speak with you," she called over her shoulder into the office.

"I'm sorry, but this is a matter of survival," she said as she turned back to Sandrine. "I can't subject my clients, let alone the other tenants in the building, to another day of dripping water from the ceiling. Some of the files are already soaked, and the computer has given up the ghost."

A gaunt man with a bald head, rolled-up sleeves and wet knees appeared behind her. "You're looking for me?"

"Capitaine Perrot and Brigadier Chief Azarou from the Police Nationale. Do you own the red Peugeot Boxer parked outside?"

"Since when do the police send their top brass for a car theft?" He grinned and pulled a pack of cigarettes from the breast pocket of his shirt.

"No smoking on the job," Suzanne Leriche chided him.

"Alright, boss." Reluctantly, he put them away.

"If someone's been killed, the top brass does get involved," Adel said.

"Someone's been killed? How did that happen?" asked the plumber.

"We were hoping you could enlighten us," replied Sandrine.

"Yesterday Madame Leriche called me out of my weekend. I even had tickets for a soccer game."

"And Madame Leriche is also paying your Sunday surcharge, correct?" Suzanne shot him a stern look.

"Of course. Anyway, I parked the van downstairs and got to work up here. It wasn't easy shutting off the water – everything's pretty rusted in this building. So, I needed some penetrating oil to remove the rust and get the valve working. I went back to the car, and it was gone. Stolen. Believe me, I cursed up a storm. The whole street must've heard it."

"I did actually hear his cursing from up here," Suzanne Leriche confirmed.

"Did you report the theft straight away?" Adel inquired.

"No, how could I? My phone was in the car."

"So why is it parked on the street now?"

"First, I had to deal with the water issue in the building. It was already flooding down the stairs. By the time I had that under control, the van was back – on the opposite side of the street, with a big dent on the front left side and torn ignition cables. I was just relieved to get it back, tools and all. These days, you hear about kids stealing cars for kicks and joyriding them into scrap metal."

"I can vouch for that," said the psychologist. "Gerard had been working here all afternoon."

"Exactly. And Madame Leriche had been breathing down my neck the whole time," he grumbled, making it clear he wasn't thrilled about being monitored. "After finishing up, I called the police. I need a report for insurance purposes. Am I in hot water?"

"Something like that. We have to take the van for the investigation," replied Adel.

"Damn it. How am I supposed to work?" He pulled a cigarette from his pack and stuck it in his mouth. "I don't give a damn, I need this now," he said, pushing past Suzanne Leriche and heading down the stairs.

"Can I at least take out the tools I need for the repair?"

"Sure, that's on me," Sandrine decided.

Adel followed the plumber to make sure Gerard took only

his tools. He was convinced that Gerard Dupuit had nothing to do with what happened on the Quai – it seemed more like a targeted attack than an accident.

"Thank you. The man might not have the best manners, but he's a lifesaver for people like me in need," said Suzanne.

"I heard that about my manners!" Gerard yelled from below. "That's defamation and will be added as an extra charge on the invoice."

The psychologist let out a deep breath. "Thank you for not taking him."

"There's no reason to. Your plumber has a watertight alibi."

"Clever pun, although I'm not in the mood for humour," Suzanne said, nudging a half-filled bucket of water that stood in the hallway.

"Couldn't help myself." A hint of a grin tugged at Sandrine's lips.

"Is this about the accident at the port? I heard about it last night."

"Yes, it seems the person who stole your handyman's van was involved."

"Poor Camille. I feel so terrible about what happened to her," Suzanne said. "How is Auguste taking it?"

"You know the family?"

"Of course. They're my landlords. Plus they're friends with my parents and used to visit us quite often. They own several properties in the city, including this one, and lots of land in the surrounding area."

"Saint-Malo is indeed a small world."

"If they've sent you, this can't be an ordinary accident, can it?"

"Just like you, I have to maintain confidentiality," Sandrine replied. "But you're right, there are some discrepancies that need to be sorted out before I can close the case."

"I hope you catch the bastard who did this."

"Depends on what we find in your handyman's van. Fingers crossed the thief was dumb enough to leave some fingerprints behind."

"Of course." Suzanne hesitated for a moment before continuing. "Why don't you come over for dinner sometime? I'd love to have the company."

"Thank you. That would be nice."

"See you soon, then."

"Depends on how the investigation goes. I'll call."

On the stairs, the plumber approached her. "You have to give your statement on the record today," Sandrine informed him.

"I won't be much longer here, unless Madame the psychologist notices there's another dripping faucet somewhere in the house. I'll stop by the police station on my way home."

"Just don't forget."

She stepped onto the street. Adel was talking with a uniformed police officer whose patrol car was parked behind the Peugeot Boxer.

"The tow truck is on its way. Jean-Claude is sending one of his guys to take an initial look inside the van and oversee the loading."

"Then let's head back. I'm eager to see if Inès got hold of Dr. Hervé on the phone."

"Do you have any specific suspicions?"

"Just a gut feeling, but I have no idea whether it will lead us anywhere."

"Usually, your gut feelings are pretty reliable."

"I hope so."

They got in the car and drove back to the precinct.

On the way to her boss's office, she stopped by Inès Boni's desk.

"Did you manage to get Dr. Hervé on the phone?"

"Of course, I happen to have his personal cell number."

"Why am I not surprised?"

"Because I'm efficient," the office manager replied. "He sent a sample to the lab in Rennes. If you initiate an official investigation, he could expedite your autopsy and flag it as urgent. Otherwise, it could take three to four weeks before the results are on the table. The lab is swamped, and traffic accidents are usually at the bottom of the queue."

"I'll talk to Commissaire Matisse, he'll agree," Sandrine said.

"Then I'll get the paperwork ready," Inès responded. "You're already expected. The new prosecuting judge is with him. And here's a printout that Marie dropped off for you."

"I'm in no hurry; they can finish their meeting in peace. There's still a report I need to write," she said, trying to wriggle out of it.

"No dice, you're expected. I've been instructed to send you straight to them as soon as you walk into the office."

"We'll see what that guy's cooked up this time," she mumbled.

Matisse waved her in. The two men sat at the round conference table, which her boss only used for official occasions. "Please have a seat."

"Thank you."

Sandrine took a chair, being careful to maintain as much distance from de Chezac as possible without being conspicuously rude.

"Commissaire Matisse just told me that you want to turn this traffic accident into a criminal case," the prosecuting judge began as soon as she sat down. "What has changed your opinion since yesterday?"

"The facts," she replied curtly.

"Not relying on female intuition again, I hope?" De Chezac's smug smile seemed to indicate that he was throwing down the gauntlet, knowing his advantage as her superior.

She ignored his comment and continued.

"The van was stolen on Sunday on Rue de Dinan, about an hour before the accident and shortly after Madame Barnais left Le Mont-Saint-Michel. The drivers targeted the woman and followed her through the city to Quai Saint-Vincent, where they intentionally caused this tragic event that led to her death. After the collision, the thieves returned the van to the same place they had stolen it from. The sole purpose of the theft was to track Camille Barnais and involve her in this incident."

"Does the owner have an alibi?" Matisse asked.

"He was repairing a broken water pipe on Sunday. The customer was present and confirmed he was there the entire time, and that the van was stolen. Gerard Dupuit reported the theft to the police that evening."

"Is the witness reliable?"

"Without a doubt."

"Possibly reckless youths on a joyride that went awry," suggested de Chezac.

"That's not the impression we have."

Sandrine slid the printout she had received from Marie Abondio to the commissaire. "A surveillance camera got a good shot of the guys in the stolen van."

The picture showed two men, between thirty and forty, wearing baseball caps and sunglasses.

"It will be tough to identify them, but we might get lucky and find fingerprints. People who can hot-wire a car are often in the system."

De Chezac snatched the printout and examined it for a moment before dropping the sheet back onto the table.

"Alright, so we've got two guys who steal a plumber's van and cause a crash. That might ruffle some feathers in this little town, but I wouldn't make too big a deal out of it. That seems like something Dubois and Poutin can handle. No need to bring out the big guns." His smile widened.

Is he trying to sideline me? Is this his form of revenge? He can't be stupid enough to overlook what the facts indicate.

"There's more to it," she said, directing her comment to Commissaire Matisse. "These guys trailed Madame Barnais halfway through the city." She turned to de Chezac, who was about to reply. "This is made abundantly clear from the security camera footage, Monsieur le Juge."

She emphasised his title, 'Juge', a role whose authority Antoine de Chezac took great pride in.

"Were they targeting her?" Commissaire Matisse asked.

"They were certainly surveilling her; that much is clear. Her destination was an apartment on Rue de Dinan, but she didn't go straight there. When she turned into the harbour, that's when the two men acted. We're not sure if their intent was to merely frighten her, intimidate her, or actually drive her into the harbour. Maybe Camille Barnais, a notoriously terrible driver, panicked and the situation escalated unintentionally. We don't know yet, but we will find out."

"What could she have wanted at the harbour?" de Chezac inquired.

"That's where the family's yacht is moored. Camille Barnais intended to pick up some personal belongings before her son set off on a sailing trip."

"Should we take a look inside the boat?" Commissaire Matisse asked.

"The scant evidence hardly justifies a search warrant," the prosecuting judge stated, abruptly putting an end to the idea.

"It's no longer relevant. Michel Barnais was set to depart this morning. Brigadier Azarou spoke with the harbour master; he's already left the port. Whatever was on that boat is now beyond our reach."

"His mother dies and he opts for a sailing trip? Odd,"

observed Commissaire Matisse, while de Chezac seemed more disappointed that he hadn't been able to show Sandrine who was in charge of the investigation from now on.

"Everyone deals with grief in their own way. We shouldn't read too much into it. Maybe Michel Barnais needs some distance from his family," she said, finding it a plausible explanation given the strained relationship between the siblings.

"What's the next step?" the commissaire asked.

"Capitaine Perrot and I will go to Le Mont-Saint-Michel to question the family. Your brigadier can apprehend Michel Barnais as soon as the boat returns to the harbour," de Chezac decided. He was formally leading the investigation, and Sandrine had no choice but to comply with his instructions, whether she liked them or not. She found herself longing for his predecessor, who only showed up for press conferences.

"Which car will we be using?" she asked.

"My new service vehicle hasn't been delivered yet, so I'll be riding with you."

"When should we set off?"

"Best to go right away, so we can get it over with. A mountain of important work awaits me back at the office. Lagarde has left behind quite a mess."

Sandrine pulled up in front of the police station's main entrance in her Citroën 2CV. Antoine de Chezac was standing on the pavement waiting, but somehow missed her. The thin, tinny honk of her "ugly duckling" made him jump. He turned towards her and paused for a breath, frozen. She waved at him. Slowly he overcame his astonishment and approached the car. Sandrine leaned over the passenger seat and pushed the door open from the inside.

"Hop in, Monsieur le Juge," she called out to him.

"Are you serious?" He held the door and looked at her, shaking his head.

"It was your idea to use my car. This is all I have, unless you like motorcycles. I could arrange that."

"I doubt," he hesitated, "that this clunker will make it to Le Mont-Saint-Michel. Maybe we should get a patrol car to take us instead."

"Don't worry, this little gem can handle it; it's only thirty years old. Besides, we'll be less conspicuous this way."

"Less conspicuous? In this thing? We might as well hitch up a horse-drawn carriage."

"We're in the same boat," she replied.

"And which would that be?" he snapped back.

"My jurisdiction is the city, and yours is the Arrondissement of Saint-Malo. Le Mont-Saint-Michel falls under neither. The place is in the Arrondissement of Avranches, which is not even in Brittany but in Normandy. Because this is a rural area, the Gendarmerie Nationale calls the shots there. I have no idea if they like us; rumour has it they have something against people from the Police Nationale, especially those from Saint-Malo."

The prosecuting judge pondered for a moment, then leaned over to wipe imaginary dirt off the passenger seat before reluctantly settling into the 2CV.

"Next time, get yourself a reasonable car. We look utterly ridiculous in this thing."

"No one's going to see us, at least I hope not," she reassured him, against her better judgment. On the opposite side of the street was Deborah Binet's sports car, the journalist from *Ouest-France*. *She's probably already snapped a few pictures of us.* That woman would be hot on their trail. With the underpowered 2CV, there was little chance of shaking her off in her speedster. *Let's see what headlines we'll be reading tomorrow.*

She pulled the gear shift lever towards her and put the car into first gear. The ugly duckling started off with a little wobble.

. . .

De Chezac's phone rang as they made the turn towards Le Mont-Saint-Michel in Pontorson.

"Prosecuting Judge de Chezac," he said when he answered. "Ah, Madame la Juge. What a pleasant surprise." The furrows that dug into his forehead belied his chipper tone.

"Yes, we're on our way there ... No, it's purely about an accident in Saint-Malo ... No, we're not expanding our investigation, we simply aim to lay out the facts to the family and express our condolences."

He fell silent for a moment. A woman's voice could be heard from the phone, but the rumble of the 2CV's engine made it impossible to understand her words.

"That's very kind of you, but entirely unnecessary. We don't wish to waste your time ... Very well, if you insist. I'm pleased to make your acquaintance, after all, we're colleagues. Let's meet in the parking lot. *Bonne journée.*" He pocketed the phone.

"Damn it. We've been found out."

"Who discovered our little excursion?"

"A prosecuting judge named Amélie Bonnard from Avranches. Someone couldn't keep their mouth shut, and now she wants to be filled in. What's the need for their own prosecuting judge in such an insignificant place?"

"I'd say it's her prerogative. We are, after all, investigating in her district."

"Nonsense, this is our case. Camille Barnais owned an apartment in Saint-Malo, where she also met her unfortunate end. There's no reason for this Bonnard to meddle in our investigation."

Sandrine glanced in the rear-view mirror. Deborah Binet was still tailing her. By now, she knew her well enough to imagine her cursing, having to trundle along behind the sluggish 2CV. A smile slid across Sandrine's face; she didn't want to make it too easy for the journalist.

The duck shook noticeably in the airstream of a tourist bus

that whizzed by them, and Sandrine had to steer hard to keep on the road.

"It's life-threatening to drive with you," he said and pointed to the parking lot. "The woman is expecting us there."

Sandrine signalled and made the turn.

At the entrance to the parking lot, a patrol car was parked. A blonde woman with an old-fashioned up-do in a nondescript grey suit, and a man in uniform waited in the meagre shade of a small tree, smoking.

"Wasn't hard to spot them," de Chezac said, a hint of disdain colouring his tone. "Seems like they don't want to miss us."

Sandrine kept quiet in response to his comment. She had not yet met prosecuting Judge Bonnard personally and would let herself be surprised by what awaited her. People from Normandy could be quite unique, or so the Bretons said.

"Stay here and leave Madame le Juge to me; then everything should go smoothly," de Chezac instructed her.

"As you wish." Staying in the background wouldn't be difficult for her.

They parked next to the patrol car and got out. Normandy's prosecuting judge, a woman in her mid-fifties, looked up at them with a friendly expression. She stubbed out her cigarette in a tiny ashtray, which she then stored in her bulky grey faux-leather handbag that hung from a broad strap over her left shoulder.

"You must be Antoine de Chezac, Lagarde's successor. Welcome to Normandy," the woman greeted him. "I'm sure you're already missing Paris. I know I would be."

"I look forward to the work that awaits me here." He deftly sidestepped the topic.

"What a wonderful city, with all its culture and unique architecture. I wish I could spend more time there," she sighed.

For Sandrine's taste, the sigh was a bit theatrical, especially considering they were standing in front of one of France's most significant Gothic landmarks – a UNESCO World Heritage Site unparalleled in its grandeur. She struggled to think of buildings in Paris that could compete with this abbey by the sea. She recalled a quote from Victor Hugo: *"Le Mont-Saint-Michel is to France what the great pyramid is to Egypt."* It seemed quite apt to her.

"And then to be immediately thrown into such a complicated case," Amélie Bonnard continued. "I'm truly sorry. I would've wished for a more pleasant start for you in our region."

"Well, the investigation doesn't seem all that complicated to me," de Chezac responded. "A fatal car accident. As tragic as it is, nothing about it falls outside the scope of routine police work. I assure you, we'll have the hit-and-run driver in custody soon."

"That's immensely reassuring," she said, throwing him an admiring smile that de Chezac patronisingly returned.

"The Barnais family is quite prominent in this area," said the uniformed police officer who had been silently listening until now. "The case is already making waves."

Sandrine guessed that the man was rapidly approaching retirement. He must be one of Madame Bonnard's best, or she wouldn't have chosen him.

"I haven't introduced Commandant Charles Renouf yet. He's the head of the Gendarmerie in Avranches."

"Pleasure," said Sandrine, unable to muster a smile. Judging by the razor-sharp creases in his starched trousers and his upright posture, he was ex-military. She doubted he was comfortable in civilian clothing – if he owned any at all.

"Prominent?" De Chezac asked, voicing his doubt.

"Oh yes. The Auberge has existed for many generations in Le Mont-Saint-Michel. The family is respected and influential. At least in our humble region," Madame Bonnard explained.

"Why else would the press be tailing you?" Commandant

Renouf remarked, nodding in the direction of the sports car parked on the roadside some distance away.

"The press?" De Chezac turned around and followed the police officer's gaze.

Sandrine maintained eye contact with Normandy's prosecuting judge Amélie Bonnard, who wore a soft smile on her lips. She had evidently noticed Deborah Binet, who was observing their small group through the lens of a camera. *This woman is not the naive provincial she pretends to be. De Chezac had better watch out.*

"Deborah Binet from *Ouest-France*. She's been following us since we left the station," said Sandrine. Another person who didn't believe this was just a simple traffic accident, otherwise she wouldn't waste her time tailing them.

"I did my best to shake her off, but ..." She patted the fender of the red-and-black 2CV which, with 29 horsepower, was not exactly what one would call overpowered.

"You live up to your reputation," said Madame le Juge Bonnard. "You seem to miss very little."

She's heard of me? At least talked to someone who knows me, then.

"I have a reputation? Hopefully not a bad one. Don't believe everything you hear."

"We'd like to speak to the Barnais family," De Chezac said, evidently growing tired of a conversation that wasn't revolving around him and wanting to cut it short.

"Of course, understandable," Amélie Bonnard agreed. "Just a few formalities and you're good to go."

"What formalities?" Impatience crept audibly into his tone.

"Look over there." The woman extended her arm and pointed across the flat land. "Around there, you didn't just leave the Saint-Malo district, but also Brittany. I'm sorry to have to bring this up, but here in Normandy, specifically in the Manche department, your jurisdiction is quite limited. But you already know that."

"The case falls solely under the jurisdiction of the Saint-Malo police precinct," he replied.

"I'd personally agree with you, but the Prefect in Saint-Lô has a different view and has already communicated this to the Prefect in Rennes." She took a step closer to Sandrine. "Camille Barnais is his second cousin," she said in a conspiratorial tone. "But that has no bearing on our work. We're treating this case with the same level of attention as any other."

"I'm confident that's the case." De Chezac became more cautious. If Amélie Bonnard truly had the backing of her Prefect, and Sandrine had no doubt that she did, bypassing her was simply not an option.

"Here's how we will proceed." The prosecuting judge's tone remained gentle, but left no room for doubt about her authority, and that she would make life difficult for de Chezac if he tried to overstep it. Sandrine managed to suppress a smile at the last moment.

"From now on, the investigation will be a coordinated effort between our respective departments. Commandant Renouf will be fully involved and will work on the case with ..." she glanced at Sandrine, " ... with Capitaine Perrot."

"I can't agree to that," de Chezac retorted. Being cornered by a woman in a nondescript, old-fashioned outfit did not sit well with him and instantly ignited his resistance.

"I'm not sure you have much choice." Her previously friendly tone faded with each word. "The protocol may be different in Paris, but out here in the provinces, the authority lies with the designated prosecuting judge and for Le Mont-Saint-Michel, that's me."

Memories of her favourite high school teacher surfaced in her mind. She too had not put up with any nonsense Sandrine tried to dish out when she had skipped doing her homework, or played hooky from class.

"I ..." De Chezac straightened, his shoulders rising as if preparing for an offensive. The two locked eyes. After several breaths, his shoulders lowered and he nodded, reluctantly. The woman was right; here in the Avranches district, she was the one who called the shots.

"Commandant Renouf will serve as the liaison officer between Saint-Malo and Avranches," he finally conceded. "Who we ultimately assign from the Saint-Malo station to this case is my call." He managed to save face on that last point, even though it was Commissaire Matisse who had the final say on staffing, not him. "The case should be wrapped up soon; until then, Capitaine Perrot will lead the investigation."

"And Commandant Renouf will be fully involved in the investigation," the woman added. Sandrine felt a grin clawing its way up her throat and almost reaching her lips, but she held it back with all the discipline she could muster. Her relationship with de Chezac was already rocky enough without his thinking she was gloating over his perceived defeat.

"We're pleased to have Commandant Renouf join our team." Sandrine almost admired how quickly he swallowed his pride and brushed off his setback. He acted as though he had proposed this arrangement himself.

"Very well. Let's get rid of the pesky young woman from the press and pay a visit to the Barnais family. Follow us."

Commandant Renouf and Antoine de Chezac climbed into their cars. The magistrate walked over to Sandrine and looked at her red-and-black painted vintage car with the sunroof.

"I love your car. A French classic. The Charleston Special Edition, isn't it?"

"Correct. An inheritance from my aunt."

Amélie Bonnard turned her head slightly toward her. "I bet you could take the engine apart and put it back together again."

"Not as skilled as a trained mechanic, but yes, I can manage that."

"I'm starting to see what our mutual friend Matisse sees in you. We're going to get along just fine." She winked at her, then turned and walked back to the patrol car.

So Matisse had filled her in on our outing. He was looking out for me. As friendly and benign as Amélie Bonnard seems at first glance, she has backbone and isn't easily intimidated by de Chezac. I'd better not get on her bad side.

She climbed into her vintage duck and followed the patrol car heading toward Le Mont-Saint-Michel. At the gate before the bridge leading to the tidal island, they stopped. A uniformed officer from the local police approached her window. She watched as Amélie Bonnard spoke to her. The woman briefly glanced at the sports car. Deborah Binet's press pass and assertive manner wouldn't be of much use today. The journalist would be forced to park here and take the bus, like ordinary tourists. That would buy them at least twenty minutes before she reached the inn.

"That woman is clever," she said appreciatively.

"Hmm," grumbled de Chezac.

Armed police officers stood in the square before the town. Commandant Renouf waved at them, then turned left and drove through a smaller gate in the city wall. The adjacent Centre des Monuments Nationaux arched above the narrow road they passed under. Leaving the medieval building behind, they followed the patrol car up the winding hill. Sandrine recalled that the residential parking was situated here. They stopped beneath the towering walls of the abbey, in the shadow of a tree.

"Follow me," Judge Amélie Bonnard called out, marching up the wide staircase toward the abbey. De Chezac exhaled deeply before following her. Being led by a woman didn't sit well with him. At the top of the stairs, Judge Bonnard turned right, crossed a gravel plaza, and took another staircase – this one much narrower – that led downhill to the Grande Rue. De Chezac almost had to run to catch up with her.

"Your boss is quite the character," Renouf said suddenly, but quietly enough so that only Sandrine could hear him.

"I've had the pleasure of collaborating with him several times in Paris."

"And now he turns up here. Seems almost as if you're jinxed."

"At least your prosecuting judge isn't easily intimidated by him."

"Madame Bonnard might look like a friendly, easy-going country girl, but she's no-nonsense when it comes to her job. Not someone I'd want to cross."

"I don't plan to. I want to find out why Camille Barnais had to die and who's behind it. I'll leave the politics and the photo ops to them."

"Healthy attitude." The man nodded, seeming to agree with her approach.

The family gathered again in the upstairs bar, closed off to hotel guests. It didn't surprise Sandrine to see Père Martin sitting a distance away on an uncomfortable-looking chair. She wondered if he'd spent the night here or had cycled back from Pontorson that morning. Auguste seemed more alert and present than he was at their last meeting, likely having skipped any medication. The grieving man sat in a wing-back chair by the window, looking at them expectantly. Yet it was Jean whose appearance caught Sandrine's attention. His left eye was swollen and starting to turn bluish. Who had he fought with? Her first thought was Michel – the tension between the two men must have finally boiled over.

"I had an unfortunate fall. Down the cellar stairs." He preempted her question. At least he didn't claim to have run into a door – a common lie to cover up the consequences of a fight or domestic abuse.

"Accidents happen. Get well soon." It was left unsaid, but obvious to both that she didn't believe a word. The twins avoided her gaze. Sandrine suspected they knew what had occurred and wanted no part of it.

"We wish to express our deepest condolences," de Chezac began, his rehearsed speech likely delivered many times before.

Auguste waved him off. "Thank you for your sympathy, but right now facts about Camille's death are more important to us. There are rumours and innuendos in the papers suggesting her death might be more than just an accidental mishap. It's agonising not to hear anything concrete from the police."

"We're in the process of—"

He interrupted Judge de Chezac with a swift motion of his cane.

"Madame Perrot, you are a friend of Léon's, you sat at the table and dined with us. Camille liked you. We trust you. What happened? Why did my wife have to die?" His voice cracked at the word "die," and he took a deep breath, as if it had taken all his strength to utter it.

"I'm sorry, but I can't give a conclusive answer as of yet. According to our findings, your wife was driving along the Chaussée du Sillon towards the harbour to collect her belongings from the boat. At the roundabout on Quai Saint-Vincent, her car was hit by a van that had been stolen in town shortly before. The damage wasn't substantial, but the impact must have startled her. She sped up, either wanting to escape or perhaps mistaking the gas for the brake pedal in the moment. In any case, she lost control of the car, broke through the barrier, and plunged into the harbour. The airbag deployed, and the heavy vehicle sank quickly. She had no chance of getting out in time."

Auguste's fingers grasped his cane, and the muscles in his jaw tightened as he clenched his teeth. Blanche stood up, crouched beside the armchair, and took his hand. As harsh as the pain of loss was, the family seemed to stick together – at least those who were present.

"Have you identified the driver?" The priest's question surprised her. Since when was he concerned with earthly justice? He seemed like a man more interested in heavenly retribution.

"As I mentioned, the van was stolen just before the incident in Saint-Malo. Forensic experts are currently examining it. There's usually some evidence left behind. We have traffic camera footage that shows the driver. It won't be long before we can make a positive identification."

The priest's hands lay firmly on the armrests, his fingers gripping the wood like a clamp. "Vengeance is mine, says the Lord," he murmured, looking down.

"And it's my job to bring the perpetrators to earthly justice," she retorted, making it clear she wasn't relying on, or even waiting for, divine retribution.

Instead of quoting the Bible as expected, he pulled his lower lip up between his teeth and bit down. Was the man mourning, or was he forcing himself to hide something?

"Père Martin heard our confessions yesterday and prayed with the family for her soul's salvation at Église Saint-Pierre," she heard Auguste say. "Tomorrow, he will hold a Mass in Camille's memory."

"That's the least I can do for her. May the Lord take her into His grace." He sounded distracted, not like the staunch, combative priest she had met the day before. Something was weighing on the man, but what? Perhaps the conflict between the brothers troubled his soul.

"This is standard procedure, and I have to ask the questions, even if they seem inappropriate," she began, looking at each family member until they nodded. "Do you know of anyone who would have wanted to harm Camille?"

"No." Auguste struck the end of his cane onto the wooden floor, and the sound made Charlotte jump. "She was a wonderful person, and everyone loved her."

Not everyone, otherwise she'd still be alive. She didn't voice the thought, it would have been more than inappropriate. But from the wrinkles forming on Jean's forehead, she recognised he also harboured this thought and possibly had someone specific in mind. She would need to talk to him, but in private.

"Especially now that Michel has found his way back into the family, she was happier than ever," said Auguste. "After all, he's our son."

"The firstborn," Jean interjected.

"Exactly," Auguste replied in a curt tone that silenced him.

Sandrine looked over at Jean. "And what does that mean?"

Léon had already told her, but asking gave her the opportunity to observe the reactions of the family members when one of them articulated it.

"The Auberge dates back to the Middle Ages as an inn for pilgrims who came here on their journey. During the Hundred Years' War, we were besieged by the English. Although they couldn't capture the place, their cannons reduced the buildings to rubble. But the Auberge Saint-Michel was rebuilt and flourished. In our family, it has been passed down to the firstborn son for generations. It's tradition, and it's served us well," Auguste answered for him. Jean's fingers, which had been drumming on the wooden bar, went still. His expression froze and his gaze remained fixed on his father, who avoided his eyes. The twins' attention flitted between Auguste and their brother.

"Where is Michel now?" asked the magistrate, breaking the mounting tension between the two men before it could erupt into an argument.

"He took the boat out. We expect him back either this

evening or tomorrow morning. He'll be back in time for the memorial service," said Charlotte, who looked relieved to have avoided a family squabble in front of strangers. "He wants to grieve alone," she added, her sceptical expression suggesting she didn't quite believe her brother.

Sandrine had seen all kinds of reactions from grieving relatives; everyone dealt with the loss of a loved one in their own way. Perhaps solitude on a boat was Michel Barnais' method of coming to terms with his loss.

"To answer your question, I'm not aware of any disputes my mother was involved in. No threats, nothing like that," Jean said. "She was a peaceful person who got along well with everyone. I offered to drive her; I should have insisted. Instead, I gave her my car keys." He leaned on the table with his forearms, as though the strength had gone out of his legs.

"What car did she usually drive?" Maybe she had overlooked something obvious.

"She owns a small Peugeot. She only took the SUV because her car was in the shop." Suddenly, Jean sat upright. "You're suggesting it wasn't a random accident? Someone was targeting her or the car?"

"We're following up on all leads," she said evasively. She wouldn't disclose that the van had followed Camille halfway across town. Not yet.

"Then it's possible they thought it was me in the car, not her." He cast a meaningful glance at his father. He didn't need to elaborate on whom he suspected. The black eye spoke for itself.

"Don't jump to baseless conclusions," Auguste admonished him. "We were all here at the Auberge when Camille left. No one left Le Mont until we got word of her accident."

"Obviously, it wasn't necessary for anyone to leave Le Mont

for this to happen. It could easily have been commissioned by one of us," Jean muttered, just loud enough for Sandrine to hear.

"Don't dishonour your family." Red surged into Auguste's face, and anger flashed in his eyes.

The priest once again passed up the opportunity to cite appropriate Bible verses about obedience to one's father, which irked Sandrine. Even she, who had avoided church services for years, could have rattled off one or two on the spot.

Jean shot his father an angry look and stormed out.

"Come back!" Auguste called after him. But he was already gone.

"Let him go," pleaded Blanche. "He needs some time to cool down. Mother's death has hit him hard."

"It's hit all of us. He needs to accept his brother returning to the family and not let himself be consumed by jealousy." His voice sounded conciliatory, but the hardness in his eyes did not abate. "We're done here. Come back when you've caught the perpetrators," Auguste said decisively. Blanche helped her father out of the armchair. Leaning heavily on his cane and with an arm from his daughter for support, he left the room with unsteady steps.

"He needs you." Charlotte turned to the priest.

"As soon as he's recovered, we'll go to the chapel. A prayer will help."

"Thank you, Père. My father appreciates your support."

"Your family has done more for me and the church than I could ever repay."

"We'll also take our leave. Should we come across new information, we'll keep you posted," said Antoine de Chezac as he stood up. He had seized the opportunity to assume leadership of the group.

"I'll walk you to the door," offered Charlotte, escorting him out onto the Grande Rue. The sky had turned overcast and a chilly wind swept through the street. The flags and pennants on the wall fluttered wildly, and the metal sign above the entrance to the Auberge creaked. Sandrine paused beside the woman while the others headed for the parking lot.

"You must forgive my father," Charlotte pleaded.

"He's in pain, isn't he?"

"You know ... Léon must've told you."

"I hope that was alright."

"Of course. It's no secret. Everyone on Le Mont knows. Father refuses to take pain medication until he can barely stand it. Léon has been quite ... resourceful in that regard. Though perhaps I shouldn't mention that to a police officer." She gave Sandrine a sheepish smile.

"I understand. A little cannabis for the pain doesn't put me in an ethical bind, nor does it put him in any trouble."

"Jean is fundamentally a peaceful man, but right now, he's frustrated and angry. He pours his heart into the Auberge and keeps it running. Then Michel shows up, and Father celebrates his return."

"He'll inherit the hotel?"

"It's tradition."

"That black eye came from Michel, didn't it?"

"I won't comment on that."

"He clearly suspects his brother of being involved in the accident."

"I can't imagine that. Michel may be no saint, but he would never do anything to put our mother in danger."

"It was Jean's car. Maybe someone assumed he'd be the one driving it."

"Then it couldn't have been Michel; he knew Camille was using it." She shook her head vehemently. "No, that's impossible. In this regard, Father is right. It's jealousy speaking through him, understandable as it may be."

She glanced up at the windows as if to ensure that nobody could overhear them.

"Father won't be around much longer. Things are going to change a lot around here."

"Michel won't keep the Auberge going?"

"Jean would never work under him, and Michel himself has no love for the hotel. He'll sell it as soon as it lands in his hands."

Her statement confirmed the suspicion Sandrine had, one already voiced by Léon. The prospect of the Auberge Saint-Michel being sold would only fuel Jean's anger, especially coupled with his father's preferential treatment of Michel.

"For generations, the Auberge has been in the hands of the Barnais family. How does your father feel about the potential sale?"

"He's doing his best to ignore it and clings to this ridiculous tradition. A stubborn old man." She smiled gently. "But we love him. Jean, too."

"Thank you for your candid words."

"Find the culprit; maybe it'll bring some peace of mind to my father and brother."

"And you?"

"I believe in karma, divine justice, whatever you want to call it. No one who commits such an act will go unpunished."

"I wish I had your faith in that."

"Isn't a life without hatred worth striving for?" They held eye contact for a moment until Sandrine nodded. A beautiful idea, but she had seen too much evil go unpunished in her life. She preferred earthly justice.

"I have to go or they'll leave without me," she said, bidding Charlotte goodbye and crossing the street.

***

"We had bets going on whether you'd strangle de Chezac and dump him in the sea on the way," Adel greeted her. "But it looks like he's been spared." He set a pen on top of a half-read report on the table in front of him and looked at her expectantly, as if awaiting details.

"I had unexpected allies; otherwise, it could easily have come to that."

Inès Boni, standing behind the brigadier, allowed herself a knowing smile.

"Did you know that Amélie Bonnard was waiting for us?" Sandrine asked.

"Just after you left, she called to inquire about the Camille Barnais case. After all, she's a notable figure in her district. I assumed it's routine for her to want to speak with Commissaire Matisse. However, she has a reputation for not tolerating interference in her jurisdiction."

"She made that abundantly clear. She met de Chezac and me outside the town. Now we are collaborating with her on the case. Commandant Renouf has been designated by her to handle the investigation. We have to keep him informed and bring him along whenever any of us operates in Normandy."

Adel leaned back and interlaced his fingers behind his neck. The chair creaked ominously, and Sandrine wondered if it was about to tip over.

"We're moving up in the world. Our first international case. Team Perrot and Azarou investigating beyond borders."

"Normandy is still part of France, just like Brittany," Sandrine said, putting a damper on his enthusiasm.

"We are neither French, nor Breton. We are Malouin," Inès Boni stated, quoting the motto of the Malouins, residents of Saint-Malo who consider themselves distinct from the rest of Brittany.

"Now we have two investigating judges breathing down our necks instead of one." Sandrine sighed at the thought of coordinating between them and the increased paperwork that would fall on her and Adel.

"I don't know the woman, but it can't be much harder than

working with just de Chezac," he said, always trying to see the positive side.

"Madame Bonnard has a good grasp of human nature," Inès chimed in. "And Commandant Renouf is a distant relative of Brigadier Dubois. He can't be that bad."

"So far, he seems amiable, maybe a touch too formal, but certainly competent," Sandrine replied. "With some luck, we won't have to venture into the Avranches district for work anymore. The accident happened in Saint-Malo, and I bet the two guys who stole the van are from around here, too."

Adel turned the monitor toward her. He had uploaded the database.

"The car was thoroughly cleaned, but not well enough. Jean-Claude's people found a fingerprint. It belongs to our friend here." He tapped his index finger on a picture of a man.

"Jori Le Bihan. A known petty criminal. His file is pretty thick, but it's all minor stuff," Adel said.

"Not the type to orchestrate an assassination attempt." Sandrine leaned in to examine the photo. A gaunt, pale guy with greasy dark hair, glaring defiantly into the police camera.

"Absolutely not. That would be way out of his league."

"Then our initial assumption – that someone wanted to intimidate Camille Barnais and things spiralled out of control – may be spot-on."

"The guy's not exactly a criminal mastermind. Even he would wear gloves in a planned assassination attempt to avoid leaving fingerprints."

"Then the two guys must be panicking by now. We need to find Jori as soon as possible before he leaves the area."

"The alert's out, and a patrol has already been to his apartment. Our man has flown the coop. According to his girlfriend, he stuffed some clothes and money into a duffel bag, jumped into his car, and made a break for it. She hasn't heard from him since – or so she claims."

"I'll speak with Matisse. We need to extend the search beyond the department's borders."

"It's already in motion," Adel replied. "We haven't been as idle as you might think."

"What about his accomplice?"

"Jacques Chopard is in on it. Dubois and Poutin know the local petty criminals best. They're making the rounds in that scene." He uploaded a new file. "But what's interesting is, Le Bihan works for this guy: Albert Chauvin."

"Never heard of him."

"This guy has his fingers in most of the shady deals around here. He's been in custody more times than my mum makes couscous, but so far, no convictions. Officially, he runs several junk yards in Brittany and is a big player in online sales of used auto parts. Our colleagues suspect large-scale fencing and dealing in counterfeit parts, but they can't pin anything on him. The man is cautious and extraordinarily shrewd."

"What's his connection to Jori Le Bihan?" Sandrine asked.

"Jori works as a security guard for him."

"Then we should have a chat with this Chauvin."

Adel pulled his pistol from the drawer and holstered it. "I'd do the same if I were you," he advised her.

"Fencers rarely resort to overt violence."

"But junk yard owners are known for keeping large, vicious guard-dogs."

"That's a fair point." She donned her shoulder holster, grabbed her pistol and spare magazine, and tucked them away. "This should suffice."

As she left the police station, she asked Inès to tell the harbourmaster to notify them when the Barnais' boat docked. She wanted to know when Michel was back, and also to take a look inside.

* * *

They parked at the entrance of the junk yard. A sign reading 'Office' hung on a container, which had windows cut into it and was mounted on a wooden base. Someone honked, and the brigadier jumped aside. A tow truck carrying wrecked cars sped past them. Mud splashed up from the tyres, hitting Adel, who cursed the driver. Sandrine handed him a tissue.

"Thanks." He wiped the fabric of his Calvin Klein jeans, but all he achieved was smearing the dirt even farther. "If I catch that jerk ..."

She watched the truck vanish between gutted cars, stacked three high. A crane with a grabbing arm lifted one of the junk cars and dropped it into a massive press. Behind it stood a wall made of metal cubes. This was the final resting place for these cars that once were prized possessions. Judging by the activity on the grounds, business seemed good for Monsieur Chauvin.

"What brings you here? Surely you're not looking to scrap a car," greeted a woman sitting at a desk overflowing with paperwork. A scented candle burned on the windowsill, but it fought a losing battle against the stale cigarette smoke hanging in the air. "You look like the police. What are you trying to pin on Albert now?"

"Nothing. We're not interested in your boss. At least not at the moment."

"Then why are you standing here?" she snapped back.

"We'd like some information on one of your employees."

"Most of them don't take kindly to the police. They also don't like it when I talk to you." The woman pushed her glasses up the bridge of her narrow nose and glanced at the mud splatters on Adel's jeans. "It's a bit muddy here, and the drivers are in a hurry. They get paid by how much they deliver, after all. And fancy customers like you rarely find your way to us." Her facetious tone indicated she was more amused than apologetic.

"Fortunately, we're normally paid to keep our seats at the station nice and warm," Sandrine retorted. "If we were paid by the number of people we send to prison, we'd probably be visiting here more often."

"Well, aren't we all lucky as hell then?" the woman replied, eyeing Sandrine. For a moment, Sandrine thought she saw the faintest glimmer of a smile touch the woman's pale lips. The secretary pulled out a pack of Gauloises from her desk drawer and lit one up. She inhaled deeply then exhaled a cloud of smoke towards the running ceiling fan.

"Here comes Albert," she said, pointing at one of the windows.

Shortly after, someone kicked at the jammed door from the outside. A stocky man with a receding hairline and thinning hair stood in the doorway, eyeing them coldly. "Police?"

"Yep," said his secretary.

"We're looking for one of your employees," Sandrine added.

"That happens more often than you'd think," he said, pushing past them. Sandrine stepped aside; she had no desire to come into physical contact with him. She estimated the man to be in his late fifties. His scarred face and nose which had obviously been broken several times was evidence of a wild life, as were the burst capillaries on his cheeks. Clearly, he wasn't a stranger to alcohol.

Albert Chauvin removed his olive-green waxed jacket. His T-shirt was too short, and his belly hung over his belt. He tossed his cap toward the coat rack like a Frisbee; it missed and fell to the ground.

"One of these days, I'll get it," was all he said. He didn't bother to pick up the fallen hat. Taking off his rubber boots, he placed them behind his office chair on a folded newspaper. Only then did he turn back to Sandrine and Adel.

"Who are we looking for this time?"

"We're looking for Jori Le Bihan."

He turned to his secretary. "Have you seen Jori today, Fleur?"

She stubbed her cigarette into an overflowing ashtray.

"He didn't show up for work. Happens from time to time. Probably out partying with his friends."

Adel laid down the surveillance camera photo in front of her. "This is him, isn't it?"

"What did he do, speed?" she asked, pushing the picture aside.

"The police wouldn't send such a well-dressed officer for a mere ticket. You need to look closer, Fleur," Albert Chauvin interjected.

Sandrine didn't consider him a talkative man. Had he interrupted the woman to keep her from identifying Jori Le Bihan?

Albert reached across the table, pulling the photo towards himself. He looked at it for a while before shaking his head.

"Nah, he doesn't look like this. And Jori would never wear such a stupid cap." He tossed the photo carelessly back onto the table, but out of his secretary's reach.

"The man in the photo, whom we are certain is Jori Le Bihan, caused an accident."

"So what? We've all had fender benders before. If he was involved, send me the bill; I'll pay it and deduct it from his salary."

"I, for one, have never stolen a car to intentionally run someone off the road into a harbour. Instead of helping the victim in the wreck, your man let her drown and cowardly sped away." Sandrine directed her words more at the secretary than at Albert Chauvin.

Fleur's thin eyebrows lifted slightly. "The woman at the harbour?"

"Exactly," Adel confirmed.

"Nasty business," said Albert. "I can't imagine Jori doing that. But we can certainly give you his home address; you're likely to find him there."

"He's flown the coop, and his girlfriend has no idea where he went or if he plans to come back anytime soon."

Albert Chauvin raised both hands dramatically in the air.

"How could I further assist you? How would I know where he is? I'm not his babysitter."

"Did you know the victim?" Sandrine asked.

The man opened his mouth, but then hesitated. He had sensed a trap.

"You haven't told me who the victim is yet, and I don't read the newspapers."

"Madame Camille Barnais."

"Never heard of her. Sorry."

"It's rumoured you do business with her son." Sandrine didn't take her eyes off the man. "Michel Barnais."

"They're related?" he replied, acting surprised. "I didn't know that. I know Michel, but business? No. We play pool occasionally. He usually loses. Then we have a beer, chat about soccer, and go our separate ways. That's all."

"He's also said to be in the auto parts business."

Chauvin shook his head. "Not that I'm aware of. I have no idea how he makes his money. His folks are said to be well-off."

"Was Le Bihan travelling on your behalf?" she said, changing the subject.

"No, he's employed as a security guard, not a driver. Besides, we only use our own vans. My name is boldly written on them to avoid any confusion."

"If we find out he was acting on your behalf, we'll have another conversation – this time at the station." Adel leaned in, placing both hands menacingly on the man's desk.

"Tell my lawyer when to come. I know the way quite well."

He wasn't easily intimidated; he'd had too many dealings

with the police and had always managed to walk away unscathed. *But he'd also never been implicated in causing someone's death.* She was convinced that a small fry like Le Bihan wouldn't act without instructions from his boss. And now that she had met Chauvin, she believed he could very well have dispatched the man to prevent Camille Barnais from boarding the boat. The question was: why?

"We'll do that," she said. "But inform your lawyer that this is a murder investigation."

She wanted to rattle him, increase the pressure, even if she knew that at most Le Bihan would face a manslaughter charge. Judging by the brief twitch of his mouth, she had succeeded.

"We shall meet again," she said, then wished them goodbye.

"What do you think?" Azarou glanced at the office container. Fleur was watching them from one of the windows. She was probably making sure the police weren't sniffing around any further.

"The secretary knows something; otherwise, Chauvin wouldn't have cut her off," Sandrine said.

"I didn't get the impression she wanted to help the police. She's loyal to her boss." He started the engine, shifted into reverse, and made a U-turn. The woman behind the window disappeared in the smoke of another cigarette.

"I agree," she said, looking away from the dumpster. "That guy's knee-deep in this. I'm convinced he knew that Le Bihan had gone underground; otherwise, he wouldn't have offered the address so easily."

"Le Bihan is a foot soldier, not someone who acts independently. He completely botched the job. His boss probably told him to lie low."

"I don't know Chauvin well enough. What do you think, has he hidden his man somewhere or made him disappear entirely?"

"Chauvin? He's a con man, loan shark, and fence. Would he beat his debtors up? A resounding yes from me. But kill? That's not his style."

"Then he's hiding Le Bihan from us somewhere. I'll have Dubois go through his real estate holdings; maybe he owns some secluded cabin that would serve as a suitable hideout."

"Will that do any good?" Adel merged onto the main road then accelerated.

"After today, he knows the police aren't treating this as a simple hit-and-run. He'll get him as far away as possible. Maybe by tomorrow he'll be sipping coffee in a café in Marseilles or on a ferry to the UK."

"Let's hope we can get to him first."

Le Mascaret

Sandrine arrived early at the police station the next day. Her first stop was Inès Boni's office, who was always at her desk before Sandrine.

"Did you have any luck with Dr. Hervé?"

"Oh yes. But you're not going to like it."

"Did he run the tests I suggested?"

"Yes. But your suspicions weren't confirmed. He couldn't find any traces of the pain medication Auguste Barnais has been taking. Her stomach also showed no signs of other pills."

"What about cannabis?"

"Same story there. All tests came back negative. I'm sorry."

This was unexpected. Given the deceased's erratic driving, Sandrine had been convinced drugs would be present in Camille Barnais' system.

"But he's sending the samples for a more thorough analysis to a lab in Rennes. They might find something there."

"My gut tells me it's something straightforward. Something the perpetrator could easily get a hold of and administer to her without her noticing."

"Commissaire Matisse has completed the paperwork. The case has moved up the priority list, and the doctor has agreed to conduct the autopsy this morning. Who knows, maybe he'll make a discovery that will help us make progress."

"Your optimism is appreciated. But nothing will come of it, except to confirm that Camille Barnais was a healthy woman who could have lived many more years."

Inès took a dainty cup from the espresso machine, placed it on a saucer and handed it to her.

"Then at least a little something to lift your spirits." She added a Breton butter biscuit. The office manager must have brewed the espresso when Sandrine had entered the open office.

"Thank you very much. That's exceedingly kind, and I could definitely use a pick-me-up." She tore open a packet of sugar and poured its contents into the cup.

Sandrine hung her leather jacket and helmet on the coat rack on her way to her desk. As a precaution, she had decided to take her motorcycle this morning to avoid the awkwardness of having to give de Chezac a lift.

"Dubois," she called out, and her colleague looked up from his newspaper, placing his half-eaten croissant on the crumpled bakery bag.

"We need to dig into Albert Chauvin. I want to know if he owns any sort of accommodations, no matter how small or dilapidated, where Jori Le Bihan could be hiding."

"I'm on it, but it'll take a while; the guy is slippery as an eel. Most of his assets are run through a network of shell companies or relatives. It's about time we book him; he has enough notches on his belt. Hopefully, we can pin something on him."

"Maybe this time he's overstepped his boundaries. No one's ever been killed in his previous shady dealings."

"I'd be delighted to slap the cuffs on him." Dubois powered up his computer. While it was booting, he poured himself coffee from a metal thermos.

"Capitaine Perrot," Inès called out. "Phone call. Commandant Renouf from the Avranches office."

"That was quick."

She hadn't expected to hear back from her colleague so soon. Inès routed the call to her extension, and Sandrine picked up.

"Good morning, Commandant. Any news? ... Are you sure? ... Alright ... I'll need an hour. Let's meet at the barrier to the bridge."

She gulped down the now-cold espresso, rinsed the cup, and returned it to Inès.

"I've got to go; I'm not sure if I'll make it back to the office today. Let Commissaire Matisse and Brigadier Azarou know I'll be in Le Mont-Saint-Michel. We have a missing person – hopefully not another body – but he's definitely connected to the accident. While I'm gone, Azarou should apply for a search warrant for the Barnais' boat. If de Chezac gives him any more trouble, I'll try to get the family's permission. Meanwhile, Dubois will handle Chauvin, Le Bihan, and the co-driver."

"Will do. Is it someone from the family?"

"No, it seems the priest, the family's friend has gone missing. At least, nobody has seen him since last night."

She donned her jacket, grabbed her helmet, and left the office.

Instead of taking the prettier, winding route along the bay, Sandrine opted for a detour via Pontorson – a small town just over the Normandy border, where the priest lived. As she entered the town, she slowed to a crawl and followed the main road to the turn-off for the abbey. This was the path Père Martin would take on his bicycle when going to Le Mont. Daily, as Léon suspected. An average cyclist would need about 40 minutes for the journey. Even if the man was past eighty, he still looked spry. He surely wouldn't need much longer than that.

She assumed he'd avoid the busy main road and opt for one of the parallel narrow side streets. Maybe there'd be some trace of him there. The roads were tight and hard to navigate; a cyclist could easily be overlooked by a car in the dark, and bike lanes were a rare sight here. Someone from the local gendarmerie who knew the area would do a better job scouting the road for the priest. *Renouf must have already arranged that.*

The patrol car was parked in front of the gate to the bridge. She stopped and flipped up her helmet's visor.

Renouf rolled down his window.

"Going solo today?"

"It's mutual. After all, we both wanted to get some work done."

"Fair point. Follow me."

He started the engine and activated the remote for the gate. They drove carefully over the bridge. Today the water was significantly higher than on Sunday and still surrounded the northern part of the mountain. Last night, the tide must have transformed Le Mont into a true island, a phenomenon that occurred only a few days each year.

The rear section of the bridge and the plaza had been cleaned of the sediment left by the sea and now was glimmering wet in the sun. Everything was ready for today's onslaught of tourists. Commandant Renouf stopped next to a red crawler vehicle with a trailer from the fire department, which was parked in front of the city wall.

"Park your motorcycle here and put your stuff in the car. My colleagues," he glanced at two armed police officers who nodded in greeting, "will keep an eye out. A high tide is expected again today, and this area will be completely underwater by eight at the latest. But we should be long gone by then."

"Thank you." Sandrine chose to stow her leather jacket in one of the side cases and secured her helmet to the frame with a bike lock.

"Père Martin lives in Pontorson with his nephew, who reported him missing this morning. He didn't come home last night," Commandant Renouf explained.

"Doesn't he often stay with the Barnais family?"

"He does, but he has always called in to let his nephew know, so as not to worry him. The priest is quite elderly, after all."

"Do we know if he left the place yesterday?"

"He usually parks his bicycle at the Centre des Monuments. That's where we found it, so I assume he didn't head home."

"Who saw him last?"

"I haven't had a chance to talk to everyone yet. What I do know is this: After we left the inn yesterday, he had dinner with Auguste Barnais. Mushroom stew." He looked up from his notepad. "Later, they both went to Saint-Aubert Chapel on the northern side of the mountain to pay their respects to the departed." He flipped the page. "Around 6 p.m., Monsieur Barnais headed back, leaving the priest, who wanted to stay a bit longer, in the chapel on the north side. No one has seen him since. I assume he planned to spend the night on the mountain."

"What makes you say that?" asked Sandrine.

"A high tide was expected to peak around 9 p.m. Even some time before that, this area becomes an island. The window of opportunity to get back to town with dry feet after their prayers was closing fast."

"Have you checked the chapel?"

"Not personally. The tide only started receding two hours ago. It'll be a while before we can get there on foot." He knocked on the side of the tracked vehicle. "The firefighters couldn't resist taking their little gem out for a spin. The chapel was locked, and peering through the tiny window in the door, they didn't see anyone inside. They didn't want to break down the door based solely on a hunch."

"I get it. Who has a key?"

"The parish priest. He promised to leave it at the bookstore for us so that we can take a look inside the chapel."
"Then we should go get it."
"First, let's grab a coffee. We have some things to sort out."
"Sure, pick a place."

Sandrine took the paper cup filled with coffee and followed the policeman to an upstairs table in the brasserie overlooking the bay. It was still early, and hardly any tourists had ventured this way yet. By noon, finding a free table would be a tall order.
"These investigations are starting to get complicated," Commandant Renouf began. "One dead body in Saint-Malo and a missing person in Le Mont-Saint-Michel. You're with the Police Nationale, and I'm with the Gendarmerie Nationale – it's hardly a recipe for a seamless collaboration."
"Plus, I'm from Brittany and you're from Normandy, which only complicates things further," Sandrine added.
"The Bretons are already a handful, but the Malouins ..."
Evidently, the residents of Saint-Malo had a reputation in Brittany for thinking they were something special. *Ni francais, ni breton, malouin suis*, she thought, recalling the saying she'd heard from Inès earlier today. The policeman wasn't entirely wrong.
"And you're not even a true Breton," he continued, "You're a Parisienne, which is significantly worse." Commandant Renouf stirred his coffee, shaking his head with humorous drama.
"Let's not forget the two investigating judges we're saddled with."
"That's the icing on the cake. At least Madame le Juge Bonnard is tolerable."
"I can't say the same for de Chezac."
"Understood. I wouldn't want to work with him either."
"So, how do we get this ship to sail smoothly?"

"We could handle the cases separately and keep each other updated."

The man sought eye contact, and Sandrine understood he was testing the waters, or more precisely, trying to see how to keep the hypothetical ship on an even keel.

"We both know that the death of Camille Barnais and the disappearance of the priest are connected. Solve one case, and the other solves itself."

The policeman nodded, waiting for her to continue.

"We could either make life difficult for each other or set aside ranks, origins, and jurisdictions for a while and act like two cops with common sense pursuing a shared goal," Sandrine proposed.

"Sounds tempting. Are you able to see yourself not as the lead investigator, but as an equal part of a small team?" Renouf questioned.

"My ambition isn't to boss people around. I want to catch the people responsible for Camille Barnais' death." A sly grin spread across her face. "If you take care of the paperwork, you can have the glory of cuffing the culprits."

"You're too kind," he declared. "But I hate writing reports. Besides, I'm retiring next year, so I'm more than willing to forego the fame of an arrest."

"Feeling's mutual. We can sort out the details once the criminals are behind bars."

"So where do we start?" Renouf inquired.

"With the accident in Saint-Malo. Someone wanted to prevent Camille Barnais from boarding that yacht."

"A fender-bender causing property damage would probably have been enough to disrupt her schedule. But wouldn't that just have delayed her visit to the boat?"

"She was expected on Rue de Dinan. One of her rental properties had a burst water pipe. Whoever orchestrated the accident likely assumed she'd prioritise the more urgent water damage over picking up a few personal items."

"That sounds plausible. But who could be behind it? It must be someone who knew she wanted to go to the boat and also had access to it. So, someone from the family," Renouf reasoned.

"I agree. My bet would be on Michel Barnais. He tried unsuccessfully to deter his mother from going to the harbour. When I left the hotel, I saw him on the phone. He seemed quite agitated," Sandrine divulged.

"Circumstantial evidence, but no concrete proof," Renouf stated. "I think I can convince the judge to subpoena Michel Barnais' phone records. Then we can see who he's been in contact with."

"I'm fairly confident you'll find Albert Chauvin's number there. One of his men was behind the wheel of the car involved in the accident," Sandrine added.

"Any other connections between them?"

"We suspect they were involved in some shady deals, mostly involving stolen or counterfeit car parts. I don't see how that ties into the boat."

"Perhaps they expanded their business ventures," Renouf suggested.

"Who knows? I fear we won't find that out anytime soon," Sandrine conceded.

"What else do we have?"

"We've been able to track a good portion of the drive from the city limits to Quai Saint-Vincent on video. The woman seemed to struggle with controlling the car," Sandrine informed.

"Alcohol would have certainly been noticeable during dinner. So, drugs?"

Sandrine nodded, pleased that the man seemed to be on the same wavelength as her.

"That's what I assumed. In the Barnais' household, getting hold of an opioid isn't exactly a challenge. Her husband is battling advanced cancer. I'm sure his treating physician has prescribed him painkillers like Oxycodone, Fentanyl, or something similar. However, we didn't find any traces of such substances in her stomach," Sandrine explained.

"Was the woman addicted to drugs?" Renouf asked.

"Not as far as I know," Sandrine replied.

"Then something like Oxy would have knocked her out long before she reached Saint-Malo. That stuff hits hard and fast, and don't get me started on the effects of Fentanyl," Renouf pointed out.

"Apparently Auguste refuses to take opioids until the pain becomes unbearable. He prefers cannabis, I hear," Sandrine added.

"That could make more sense," Renouf mused, massaging his cheek thoughtfully. "If she ingested it orally rather than smoked it, the effects would kick in much later. She probably didn't notice anything unusual when she left. Maybe she accidentally drank some tea or nibbled on his cannabis cookies."

"That was my thought as well, but all the cannabis tests came back negative."

"So, what now?"

"Dr. Hervé is sending samples to the lab for further examination, but that will take some time."

"Shall we still operate under the assumption that she was either drugged or accidentally ingested something?"

"I can't think of another explanation for her erratic driving," Sandrine admitted. She recalled that the Barnais couple were friends with Suzanne Leriche's hippie parents. They both likely had experiences with cannabis. "I'd rule out an accident. Someone must have slipped something to her, probably during lunch. Camille dined with the family, but no one else complained of any signs of poisoning. The drug couldn't have been in the food or wine," Sandrine mused. "The chocolate truffle!" she suddenly exclaimed.

Commandant Renouf looked at her quizzically.

"The only thing she consumed that no one else did was a chocolate truffle she swiped off her younger son's plate. She even teased him about his sweet tooth," Sandrine explained.

"Then perhaps he was the intended target, not his mother," Renouf suggested.

Jean had suspected this himself, Sandrine recalled.

"It was his car, he was planning to head to a commercial printers in Saint-Malo to pick up menus, and under normal circumstances, he would've been the one to eat that spiked chocolate truffle. Yes, he could've been the target, making our theory about something being on the boat she wasn't supposed to find completely incorrect. Even then, I'd still point a finger at Michel Barnais," Sandrine theorised.

"If she managed to make it to Saint-Malo, the dosage couldn't have been very high. Then the intent was to incapacitate Jean Barnais, not necessarily remove him from the picture entirely," Commandant Renouf pondered, finishing his coffee and pulling a cigarette from the pack. "But why?"

The waitress cleared the neighbouring table, glancing disapprovingly at the cigarette. She seemed to consider reminding him of the smoking ban but decided against it. A police officer should know better.

"Sibling rivalry. Perhaps just a warning for Jean to stay out of Michel's affairs. We need to speak to Jean Barnais," he suggested, "and his brother as soon as he returns."

"I agree," Sandrine said, picking up her phone to call Adel. She spoke briefly with him. The search warrant had been signed by de Chezac, and the harbourmaster would notify them as soon as the boat arrived in the port.

"What's the plan?" Commandant Renouf asked.

"I'd like to speak with the family first," she said, rolling up the sugar packet and tossing it into the empty paper cup, where it stuck to the foam remnants. "But in Normandy, you call the shots. In Brittany, it's my territory." Sandrine intended to stick to their agreement.

The policeman nodded approvingly. "Fair enough. You handle Jean. The family knows you and seems to trust you. I'll take care of the priest." He glanced at his watch. "Reinforcements should be here by now. We have a dozen officers available to comb the area for him."

"Not much," she commented.

"It'll be enough. If Auguste Barnais wasn't lying and was indeed on his way back by 6 p.m., it's unlikely that Père Martin would be at the abbey. Tourist admissions close around this time, and the doors lock for the night at 7 p.m. That rules out most of the area."

"Who knows how long the priest was in the chapel?" Sandrine pondered.

"Not long, I would assume. The man has lived here for half a century; he knows the tides and the dangers. As I said, high tide is expected at 9 p.m., about two hours before that, say around 7 p.m., le Mascaret arrives."

"Le Mascaret?"

"It's the tidal bore – a large wave caused by the funnelling of a flood tide as it enters a long, narrow, shallow inlet. Especially popular among surfers and paddlers. And of course, tourists who are here on such a day to photograph and film the wave."

"And after that, the path back from the chapel to the town gate is blocked?"

"Unless you want to climb steep rocks or get your feet wet, yes."

"So we can assume that the priest either entered the town between 6 and 7 p.m. or spent the night in the chapel."

"But why didn't he call his nephew as usual when he stayed here overnight?"

Sandrine recalled her conversation with the family. Something had been weighing on Père Martin's mind. She was convinced that he must have observed something connected to Camille's death. It was imperative to find him. If he was still alive.

"Something must have happened to him."

"Get the key to the chapel. Siloë Bookstore is just a few steps up the Grande Rue. You can't miss it. In the meantime, I'll brief my team for the search. Later, we can both visit the chapel – perhaps we'll find a clue there about the priest's whereabouts," Commandant Renouf suggested.

"Agreed." Sandrine stood up, tossed her cup into the trash, and headed downstairs. Renouf said his goodbyes, tucked the cigarette he'd been toying with earlier into the corner of his mouth, and strode briskly down the street toward the town gate.

Her phone rang. It was Dr. Hervé.

"Your hypothesis about the woman's driving kept nagging at me. So, I decided to dig deeper."

"And?"

"I did find traces of drugs, specifically a cannabinoid."

Sandrine stepped into a narrow alleyway where it was quieter.

"Madame Boni claimed that all cannabis tests came back negative."

"She's absolutely right. What I found is synthetic THC, the active compound in cannabis. This synthetic stuff doesn't show up on standard tests, so it's difficult to detect unless you know what you're looking for."

"In the truffle?"

"It's usually an oily liquid that can easily be sprayed onto a truffle or any other object. This could be done in passing, without anyone noticing. Ingenious."

"Thank you for your effort; this helps me move forward."

"It's the least I could do. We don't want to appear sloppy

while you're investigating in Normandy. What would the local officials think of us?" Without waiting for an answer, he hung up.

So, they could definitively rule out that Camille Barnais had accidentally ingested any of her husband's cannabis supply. It had been intentionally applied to the truffle. She was becoming increasingly convinced that Michel Barnais was behind this. Given his past, he should have no difficulty obtaining such a substance. She texted Adel to pull up the man's file, to see if there was a connection to synthetic THC.

Sandrine entered the small bookstore on Grande Rue, which specialised in religious books, postcards, CDs, and various trinkets from Le Mont. The priest was supposed to have left the key to the chapel here.

"Sandrine?"

She turned around and found herself facing Blanche, who was shelving books.

"I didn't know you worked here."

"I just help out now and then, arranging books on shelves or placing devotional items in the cabinets."

Blanche picked up a rosary from an open box and offered it to Sandrine.

"Quite popular among the pilgrims who visit us," she said, smiling. "I assume I can't tempt you with one." She held onto it and placed the box on a stack of books. "Any updates?" Her smile faded, and her lips tightened. Curiosity and fear of what Sandrine might reveal flitted across her face.

She knows that the accident has something to do with her family, but she's not ready to admit it yet.

"Some, but none of it pleasant."

"My mother is dead; what could be worse than that?"

A man with a camera slung around his neck on a leather

strap squeezed past them and started rifling through the postcard rack.

"Let's step outside for some fresh air; we'll have more privacy there," Blanche suggested and signalled to a woman behind the counter that she was taking a break.

Blanche left the store, walked the short distance to the church, and sat down on one of the steps, away from the street.

"It's quieter here."

Sandrine sat down next to her. "We now believe that this wasn't an accident but rather a targeted attack."

"On Mother?" Blanche asked incredulously. "I don't know anyone who would wish her harm."

"I believe you. However, we're not ruling out the possibility that the person behind this was actually aiming for Jean and thought he would be in the car."

"Why would ... Oh, I see. He lent her his car and had talked about wanting to drive to Saint-Malo earlier. I understand."

"Who knew about his plans?"

"Everyone in the family, certainly some of the employees. Of course, the people at the printing press who were preparing the order. Jean also mentioned he was planning to meet with the harbourmaster later."

"Was there a problem with the yacht or the marina berth?"

"I wouldn't know. I never concerned myself with the boat. For a woman from Normandy, it's probably a glaring flaw, but just the sight of a ship makes me seasick. You couldn't pay me to get on one of those rocking tubs."

"Does Jean always have a chocolate truffle for dessert?"

"He has a sweet tooth. A little something after a meal is a must. Not a lot, but always something delectable. This week he's been working his way through a small pack of truffles – one with each lunch."

"Where does he keep them?"

Blanche hesitated. "What are you getting at? Why are the police interested in Jean's sweets?"

"We found traces of drugs. Camille must have ingested them during lunch."

"And we all ate the same thing, except for the chocolate truffle. That was meant for my brother." She took a deep breath. "So someone was trying to kill Jean?"

"The dosage wasn't high, definitely not lethal. But he would have felt its side effects: fatigue, probably nausea, and disorientation. Whoever prepared that chocolate truffle was aiming to prevent him from driving to Saint-Malo that day."

"For what reason?"

"Was he planning to meet anyone else other than the people at the print shop and the harbourmaster?"

"Not that I'm aware of, but you should ask him yourself. He's at the Auberge. Michel is there, too."

"He's back?" Sandrine asked, surprised. Adel had assured her on the phone that the boat was still out.

"Yes, he arrived just before breakfast."

Then he's the next person I need to speak with. He's unquestionably at the top of the list of those who had both the motive and the opportunity to tamper with the chocolate truffle.

"What about Père Martin?" Blanche inquired. "The priest said the police are looking for him."

"His nephew reported him missing. He didn't come home last night, and his bicycle is still at the Centre des Monuments, so he must be somewhere in the village. The Gendarmerie have already initiated a search."

"Nothing bad has happened to him, has it?" Genuine concern tinged her voice.

"Do you know anyone who'd want to harm him?"

"That old man?" She shook her head. "I have an interest in medieval history and the Church. Père Martin was mentally trapped in that era and, with his strict disposition, didn't make many friends. You've likely noticed that. He could be abrasive and condescending, but to wish him harm? No, I can't imagine that."

Blanche kicked away a pebble on the staircase. It skidded across the flagstones of the churchyard before coming to rest near the low wall.

"But then again, I thought the same about my mother." She stood up and brushed some dirt from the stairs off her dress with her hand. From a pocket, she pulled out a key and handed it to Sandrine. "For the chapel. The priest gave it to me."

"Thank you. What will you do now?"

"I'm going home to think about what you've told me."

"To the Auberge?"

"No, we have a house in the village. Over there." She pointed to a stone house with red shutters and a dark slate roof speckled with yellow lichen.

"Every family member still has a room there. Even though we lead our own lives, we spend a lot of time here on Le Mont. Especially now that Charlotte is overseeing renovations."

They said their goodbyes and Sandrine watched her go, her figure receding until it disappeared around the bend of Grande Rue.

"The boss is in the breakfast room," the young man at the Auberge's front desk said, pointing towards the staircase. "On the first floor."

A group of tourists must have already been on a mudflat hike and forgotten to clean their shoes. An employee was sweeping up clumps of dirt they had left behind from the blue carpet that covered the wooden stairs.

Sandrine entered the breakfast area. The staff was clearing away the last remnants of the buffet and cleaning the tables.

Plates and dishes clattered in plastic bins that a man was placing in the dumbwaiter.

A woman wearing an Auberge apron approached her. "I'm sorry, but breakfast is over."

"That's fine, I've already eaten," Sandrine lied. As usual, she had left home without breakfast. *An empty kitchen at least keeps you slim.* "I'm looking for Monsieur Jean Barnais."

"What's this about? Maybe I can assist you." Sandrine flashed her police badge, and the woman nodded.

"Please have a seat. I'll fetch the boss."

Sandrine chose a red leather sofa with a high back, positioned against a wall practically paved with black-and-white photos of the Auberge's famous guests. She recognised very few of the people in the pictures, which didn't surprise her. Her job left her little time to leisurely flip through magazines or newspapers. The faces of politicians she had committed to memory were usually from mugshots or police photos.

Jean emerged from the kitchen. He brought two small cups of coffee and a plate of cookies and chocolate truffles, which he placed on the table in front of her.

"Are the investigations making progress?" He sat down beside her on the sofa, and she eyed his bruise, which was slowly turning yellow-green.

"Does Michel have one of those too?" she asked, pointing at his injured eye.

"What makes you ask that?"

"I heard he's back from his trip."

"He is. But I'd be lying if I said I'd missed him."

"The yacht isn't in Saint-Malo."

"Where else would it be? And why are the police interested in our boat?" he said slowly, as if trying to buy time to ponder something. He seemed to be debating whether it would be wise to divulge it to Sandrine.

"We'll find out. And then our forensics team will thoroughly search it. The search warrant is in place." *Though only for the Saint-Malo district. Who knows what Jean might be hiding from us?*

"No warrant is necessary; the police have my permission to enter the *Émeraude* and look around at any time."

"Do you own it?"

"There's a family trust that manages some properties, some land, and the boat. I'm on the board, just like the rest of the family."

That should suffice for a legal search.

Jean reached for one of the chocolate truffles.

"I'd steer clear of those if I were you."

His hand froze above them and he looked at her, puzzled.

"Actually, these are now confiscated." She pulled a plastic bag from her pocket and dumped the truffles into it.

"Would you mind explaining why you're doing this? Or are you just a cunning chocolate thief?"

"First, I want to know what you were planning to discuss with the harbourmaster."

"Was I planning on speaking to him?" he replied, hesitantly.

"I can call him. This whole thing probably has something to do with that damn boat, or something that's on it or was on it."

Jean leaned back, and the leather creaked softly.

"Fine. The man called me because he had noticed some strangers lurking around the *Émeraude* on multiple occasions. He tried to confront them, but they took off as soon as they spotted him. He suspected they wanted to steal something."

"But?"

"I'm not sure. Since Michel has been back, he's been going out on it regularly. I'm too busy with work, and Father is happy that someone is looking after the boat. There's not really anything on it worth stealing."

"You planned on checking it out, and someone desperately wanted to stop you. The truffles on Sunday," Sandrine lifted the transparent bag, "were laced with drugs to incapacitate you. When that didn't work, your car was deliberately rammed."

"Drugs?" he asked, visibly stunned.

"Cannabis."

"But who would do such a thing?"

"Certainly someone who knew you'd eat one and had the opportunity to tamper with it."

"So, someone in the family." He sounded significantly less incredulous than Sandrine had expected.

"Or one of the employees."

"No. Definitely not."

"You're thinking of Michel?"

"He's the only one who could possibly have a vested interest in keeping me from inspecting the boat. Like I said, no one else has used it. And he tried to talk our mother out of collecting her belongings from there."

"But why?"

"No clue. Not in the slightest. There's nothing valuable on the yacht."

"Where can I find Michel?"

"At the house. Father isn't doing well."

"Then I'll make my way to him." She stood up. "And no more brawling," she warned him.

"The guy wanted to drug me and possibly kill me. How am I supposed to just let that slide?" Suddenly he froze. "Michel has our mother's blood on his hands," Jean stammered. The thought was so shocking that he'd only recognised the possibility at that exact moment.

"For right now, this is all pure speculation. There's probably a reasonable explanation for everything."

All colour had drained from his face as he stared at Sandrine.

"Michel always has a reasonable explanation for everything he screws up," he said, his voice almost toneless.

"Can I count on you not to do anything reckless?"

"Reckless? No, I won't do anything reckless. But I'd like to be alone for a moment."

She nodded and left him.

On the staircase, her phone rang. It was Adel. They had found Jori Le Bihan.

"I'm on my way," she said. Michel Barnais would have to wait. If she could get the driver to talk, she'd have an ace up her sleeve during Michel's interrogation.

It was just a few minutes from the Auberge to her motorcycle. On the way, she called Commandant Renouf and informed him she had to head back to Saint-Malo.

* * *

"Capitaine Perrot." Inès looked out of her office and waved at her.

"Has the hit-and-run driver been brought in?"

"He's in the interrogation room waiting. Adel assumed you'd like to lead the interrogation yourself."

"He assumed correctly. I'm heading there now."

"Commissaire Matisse wants to speak to you. Urgently." She stepped closer to Sandrine and lowered her voice. "Also, the new prosecuting judge is with him once again. He's practically a permanent guest."

"You haven't seen me," Sandrine entreated the office manager.

She was about to leave, but Inès grabbed her by the sleeve.

"I'd go if I were you. Not everyone here is as discreet as I am." Her gaze drifted to Brigadier Poutin, who was sitting at his desk, watching her over the rim of his coffee cup.

"He seems to get along better with de Chezac than you do. At any rate, Judge de Chezac has requested him for some kind of special surveillance."

"Fine. Then Le Bihan will have to wait a moment longer."

The door to the chief's office was open, so she decided against knocking. She gave the judge a brief nod.

"You wanted to see me, Commissaire Matisse?"

"Come in and have a seat with us."

"Back on the bike today?" De Chezac's eyes lingered on her leather pants, and the corners of his mouth turned downward disdainfully. "You should dress more appropriately for your rank. After all, you represent the police, not some motorcycle gang."

"Be that as it may," said Matisse, cutting Sandrine off before she could retort. "What's the status of the investigation?"

Sandrine took a seat and brought him up to speed.

"Then we can close the case shortly." De Chezac smiled smugly. "This Le Bihan will be heading to prison."

"I haven't interrogated the man yet, and as long as we can't prove that he deliberately ran Camille Barnais off the road, he might not be sentenced to prison for very long, if he's sentenced at all. Without more evidence, he can easily argue it was just a tragic accident."

It's all about closings cases as quickly as possible to you, isn't it de Chezac?

"Get me a confession, and we'll close the case." He closed the file in front of him and crossed his arms. It seemed unimportant to him how they would manage to extract such a confession from the man.

"We still have no trace of the priest."

"Do you think the two cases are connected?" Matisse asked.

"I'm certain of it."

"We have nothing to do with that clergyman. The man lives in Normandy and disappeared there. Let Madame le Juge Bonnard handle it; after all, it's her jurisdiction." He turned to

Sandrine. "Or do you think your colleagues from Avranches are incompetent?"

"Not at all."

"Well then, that settles it. Make this guy talk, write up the reports then we can get back to our daily tasks. Crime doesn't sleep in Saint-Malo. Quite the opposite. There's a lot of work piled up here." He stood up. "Don't disappoint me, Capitaine Perrot." Without another word, he left the office.

Only when he was out of earshot did she turn to Commissioner Matisse.

"If we don't fully investigate the attack on Camille Barnais, Le Bihan will get off lightly."

He leaned back, rocking gently in his chair.

"My hands are tied. De Chezac wants to close this case as soon as possible."

"He doesn't like working with Madame le Juge Bonnard."

"Shared laurels are half laurels, and he seems reluctant to share."

"There's clearly more to the accident than meets the eye. Are we going to let the masterminds of this crime go unpunished?"

"He's right about one thing: the missing priest isn't our concern. That's for the investigators in Normandy."

"And what about the boat that might be used for illegal activities?"

"That's clearly within our jurisdiction, coordinating with the coast guard if necessary. I'll give you until the end of this week to investigate further. By then, bring me something that indicates the accident was meant to cover up or enable another crime. Otherwise, you're off the case."

"Until the end of the week? That's not much time."

"More time probably won't help. Plus, I trust your work. If you don't uncover the connection by then, it's likely that none exists."

"But ..."

"We can't rely solely on your gut feeling. Not with de Chezac breathing down our necks."

"I understand. I'll find something by Friday. I'll start with the driver involved in the accident." She stood up and headed to the interrogation rooms.

"Where's Le Bihan?" she asked Adel.

"In interrogation room one, with his lawyer."

"He already has a lawyer? That was fast."

"You're not going to like her." He rolled his eyes and made a face.

"She probably won't like me either," she replied as she walked away.

"I have no doubt about that."

Sandrine looked through the window. "Damn."

"I told you."

"Why hasn't the bar association disbarred her? She should be sharing a cell with her friend." The lawyer Lianne Roche had been knee-deep in illegal activities surrounding a woman's death on the Breton Coastal Trail and had even tried to eliminate a witness.

"Treville didn't press charges. He suddenly couldn't remember who ran him off the road."

"That must've cost her a pretty penny." A private stash, one his wife knew nothing about, had probably come in handy for César Treville. His wife owned the camp-ground and kept him on a short leash, which wasn't surprising given the man's reputation as a womaniser.

Through the glass, she observed the two for a moment. They couldn't have been more different. Jori Le Bihan, a gaunt man with cheap-looking tattoos on his arms and neck, gazed anxiously at the door, while Lianne Roche intently studied a file. The meticulously groomed woman's suit surely cost more than what the guy earned as a security guard at Chauvin's in a month.

Sandrine reached for the door handle and swung the door open with gusto.

"Monsieur Le Bihan," she called out to the man, deliberately ignoring the lawyer.

The woman's expression darkened noticeably. She probably expected a hostile greeting, but Sandrine chose to ignore her. This would unsettle Lianne Roche, and the more she was able to disorient the lawyer, the better.

"I have no idea why you dragged me here," the man exclaimed immediately. "Whatever you want to pin on me, I'm innocent."

Sandrine sat down at the table, with Adel following suit. Years ago, he and Lianne Roche had been a couple. He didn't talk about it, but his demeanour suggested the breakup had been quite bitter.

"My client is not guilty of any wrongdoing," she started. "I demand that you release him immediately."

"She has to say that; it's what she's paid for," she explained to the man. "Pure routine and completely meaningless."

She would continue to ignore the lawyer for a while and assess the battlefield. She had no idea yet where to strike to make Jori Le Bihan crumble.

"She's quite good-looking, exclusive, and expensive. Way out of your league, Jori," she said with a touch of irony, as if discussing a prostitute with him. She could almost hear the grinding of the woman's teeth.

"The lawyer has ..."

"That's none of the police's business," she interrupted sharply. The man flinched in surprise.

"It's okay. Albert Chauvin is a generous boss who believes in your innocence."

Sandrine tried to sound understanding. She'd rather he saw her as the good cop and the lawyer as the bad one. Lianne Roche couldn't stop his nod of agreement. *Now we know who's paying the woman and who commissioned the accident. But proving it will be tough.*

"Who or how my client settles his bill is irrelevant for the purposes of this interrogation," Lianne countered.

Sandrine held Le Bihan's attention with a piercing gaze. He pulled out a handkerchief and nervously wiped his forehead. Stealing cars, peddling stolen goods, and petty crime were his forte. Perhaps he'd roughed someone up at his boss' behest, but he didn't have any killings on his record. He knew he'd botched the job. Anxiously, he crumpled the handkerchief in his right hand.

"I didn't do anything, I swear," he pleaded with her.

"Stay quiet," Lianne interrupted him. She knew the man wasn't the sharpest tool in the shed. Sooner or later, he would slip up and contradict himself. "I will now make all statements regarding the sequence of events," the lawyer declared assertively.

Sandrine decided to play this game a bit longer. The lawyer must hate being ignored by her. Lianne Roche was one of those alpha females. She wouldn't bother with the brigadier; she was looking for a confrontation with Sandrine. Against her, the woman wanted to win, no matter the cost.

"Did you steal the plumber Gerard Dupuit's car on Rue de Dinan Sunday morning?"

"Me? No."

"Shut the hell up," Lianne Roche snapped at him.

"Your lawyer is getting vulgar. Seems to me like a sign of how shaky her defence is. Don't you think?" Slowly and deliberately, Sandrine turned towards Lianne Roche, smirking condescendingly.

"You have nothing, Capitaine Perrot."

"At the very least we have a photo of Jori sitting in the stolen car."

"A distant acquaintance called my client and asked him to help out with some construction work. He was picked up by him. Monsieur Le Bihan had no reason to believe it might have been a stolen vehicle."

"Give me the name and address of the driver."

"I don't really know him that well. He goes by Jacques, that's all I know."

"Seriously?"

"On my honour. If I knew more, I'd definitely tell you," Le Bihan replied, a glimmer of hope stealing into his eyes.

"No big deal," Sandrine reassured him. "We have your phone records. After all, you haven't spoken to very many people."

His jaw dropped. The man truly wasn't bright. Chauvin must've realised this, or he wouldn't have hired such an expensive lawyer to get Le Bihan out of police custody.

"As I can see, you've only had two conversations during the period in question. One of the numbers belongs to Albert Chauvin – what a coincidence – and the other to a certain Chopard. Who, by the way, goes by Frank and not Jacques."

"To my client, he introduced himself as Jacques. Monsieur Le Bihan had no reason to distrust him."

"You followed Madame Barnais through Saint-Malo."

Sandrine sought eye contact, but the man looked down.

"Direct your questions to me. My client won't say anything further."

"Then explain this pursuit to us. To me, it almost seemed like police surveillance."

"Coincidence. Monsieur Le Bihan had no knowledge of who was in the car ahead of him."

"The old woman was weaving in and out; it was impossible to overtake her."

The lawyer shot him a stern look, and the man pressed his lips together. Chauvin probably made it clear that he'd better listen to her if he didn't want to get into trouble, otherwise a guy like him would never allow himself to be silenced by a woman. Sandrine believed him. She remembered the footage well. The effects of the drugs had already set in.

"I see no crime here. Monsieur Le Bihan wasn't in a rush, and there's no law against driving slowly behind someone. Therefore, I again demand that you release my client."

"At Quai Saint-Vincent, you suddenly accelerated and rammed into Madame Barnais' car." Sandrine continued addressing Jori Le Bihan.

"An unintentional accident. Barely more than a light brush," Lianne Roche replied.

"Unintentional?" She shook her head in disbelief. "Twice in a row? In both roundabouts?"

"It can happen when two bad drivers are involved. My client's friend panicked after the first contact. Understandably so, if the car was indeed stolen. Besides, word from the forensic department is that the woman was under the influence of drugs, which explains her erratic driving and irrational reaction after the minor brush."

Sandrine forced herself to appear surprised.

"How did you come by that information? The forensic results have not been released yet."

"Did you slip a few bills to an employee?" Adel interjected, validating Sandrine's obvious intentions.

"That's beside the point. Is my information incorrect?"

Sandrine smiled, knowing Lianne Roche had played a trump card she believed would end the game in her favour.

"All drug tests conducted so far were negative," Sandrine said with emphasis. "So I'd be interested to know where you got this information. Certainly not from the police or the forensic department."

At least the preliminary report available at the precinct didn't mention the latest tests conducted by Dr. Hervé.

She could only know this from the person who tampered with the chocolate truffle. Or from Albert Chauvin, her client. She had given herself away. A broad grin spread across Sandrine's face as Lianne Roche's expression turned to stone. It must have dawned on her that she played her trump card too soon, and perhaps to her detriment.

"I don't reveal my sources," she retorted defiantly.

"I take your allegations seriously and will instruct the forensic department to conduct additional tests."

She turned to Adel. "Can you ask Dr. Hervé to send the samples to Rennes for an extended drug screening?"

"It's good to know you're finally starting to take your job seriously," the lawyer remarked sarcastically.

"Clearly, someone in your circle knows more about drugs related to Camille Barnais than we do. Who could that be, if not the one who gave them to her or sneaked them in? A clue we definitely should pursue."

Sandrine could easily imagine the cogs turning inside the woman's head. Was she afraid that she had led the police to the drugs, and thereby to a lead at Le Mont-Saint-Michel? That would upset Albert Chauvin. Whether Le Bihan went to prison or not was of little concern to either the lawyer or her client. Their goal was to keep Albert Chauvin out of jail, and she might have jeopardised that with her premature statement. Sandrine wouldn't let on that they already knew about the drugs. Not until an official report from the forensic department arrived.

"Regardless. Monsieur Le Bihan is at most an inadvertent witness, dragged into the accident through no fault of his own, but by no means a perpetrator. I demand you release him immediately."

"Quite a compelling narrative, and perfectly rehearsed. Congratulations, I almost believed your story. However, there's a small detail your client misrepresented." She looked to Adel, who, with a smug grin, pulled a photo from the folder and placed it on the table before her. Lianne Roche stared at it. For a moment, she pressed her lips together, then regained her composure. Le Bihan had obviously lied to her as well that he had only been the passenger, and she had forgotten to check.

"Is that your client behind the wheel, or am I mistaken?"

Sandrine revelled in the silence and the suspect's gaze, which was fixed intently on the floor.

"The identity of his accomplice is known. It's just a matter of days before we catch him." She rapped her knuckles on the tabletop, and Le Bihan looked up at her, startled.

"It's simply a matter of who talks first, you or Frank Chopard. One of you will end up with a considerably shorter prison sentence than the other. Right now, you have the chance to be that person. Don't mess up this opportunity to save yourself."

"My client will not comment further on these allegations."

Lianne Roche effectively halted the interrogation. The photo had derailed her strategy, and now she needed time to regroup.

"He doesn't have to. We can already prove he was involved in a fatal accident. We're still working on proving intent, but we'll get there, I'm sure of it. There's no rush; your client is going into pre-trial detention."

"On what grounds? He has a job and a permanent address."

"Which is where we did not find him. Instead, we located him in a secluded house owned by his employer. We suspect he's a flight risk and might tamper with evidence. That's why he remains in our custody." She leaned forward, looking directly at Le Bihan.

"Why did Chauvin task you with this crap?"

The man's eyes widened, and he took a deep breath before shaking his head. Right now, he was more afraid of his boss than he was of jail. But Sandine knew he would soon give that a lot of thought. Jori Le Bihan was not the kind of man cut out to serve time on someone else's behalf.

"Furthermore, it's for his own protection," Adel remarked. "Perhaps his employer is trying to convince him to stay silent."

Le Bihan shot up. "He would ..."

Lianne Roche elbowed him sharply in the ribs. Sandrine's smile spread across her face. When the lawyer resorted to physicality, Sandrine knew she had her back against the wall.

"This interrogation is over. Monsieur Le Bihan will not make any further statements," she declared.

"As your client wishes." Adel turned off the microphone.

"He's already admitted enough to spend some time in jail," Sandrine said, even if it was a stretch. Once she had to reveal that Camille Barnais was indeed driving under the influence of drugs, a shrewd lawyer like this would effortlessly negotiate a probationary sentence for him. Unless, of course, they could prove he acted intentionally and under orders.

"Think carefully and listen to your attorney," Sandrine advised the man. She hesitated for a moment. "Perhaps she'll also tell you about how she wanted her last client, who sat here, to rot in jail just to get a hold of her assets."

Lianne Roche leaped up. Her chair toppled over, crashing to the floor. For a few moments, she glared at Sandrine with palpable hatred. Finally, she exhaled deeply, and her clenched fists slowly relaxed.

"This policewoman is trying to sow distrust between us. Don't pay her any mind."

Le Bihan's anxious gaze was glued on his lawyer, revealing that he'd paid quite a lot of attention to Sandrine. He wasn't naive enough to be unaware of where his attorney's loyalties lay, with him or in protecting Albert Chauvin.

"Discuss matters with your attorney. We'll meet again." She

nodded to the man and then left the room. The brigadier left the photo on the table and followed her out.

Adel cast a glance through the window into the interrogation room.

"You really shook them up. That witch probably thought she'd calmly walk out of here with her client. Instead, she revealed that her employer knew about the drugs in the chocolate truffle. Not her finest moment."

Lianne Roche must have really hurt him. Typically, Adel was the more composed and noticeably polite half of their small team, but to the brigadier, Lianne Roche was clearly like a red rag to a raging bull.

"It's surprising she didn't expect to be lied to by her client. That should be business as usual for a criminal defence lawyer."

"Do you really intend to put Le Bihan in pretrial detention?"

"I'd like to, but it's unlikely to happen. The new prosecuting judge won't go along with it. We can only hold him here for the 24 hours we're allowed by law. Judge de Chezac will hold a press conference declaring the case solved, and then he'll release Jori Le Bihan until the trial. Roche is right, the man has a job and a fixed residence. The judge won't buy my bluff about Le Bihan potentially destroying evidence."

"The search for Chopard is underway," Adel said. "Do you think we can get Le Bihan to testify against his boss?"

"Unlikely. He's too scared of the guy. He'll only talk to us in the presence of his lawyer from now on, and in front of her, he'll stay loyal to Chauvin. That man could cause him a lot more pain than we can."

"Capitaine Perrot." Inès descended the stairs towards them.

"Any news?" Adel asked. "Have they located Chopard?"

"Unfortunately, no. But Commandant Renouf from Avranches called."

Sandrine felt her throat tighten. There were only a few reasons why he'd want to contact her, and none of them pleasant.

"Did he leave a message?"

"Yes. They found a body, and he suspects it's Père Martin."

"Merde."

She looked around for something to kick, needing to vent her frustration, but found nothing suitable. The man had acted strangely, almost guilt-ridden, during their last meeting. *I should have talked to him. He knew something about Camille's death, and it cost him his life. Now it's too late.*

"Is he related to our case?" the office manager asked.

"I can't prove it, but I believe so. Would you be kind enough to call Commandant Renouf and let him know I'm on my way?"

"No problem."

Adel looked at her uncertainly.

"You're right, it's not my case, but it's directly related to Camille Barnais' death. I need to find out as much as possible before de Chezac throws a spanner in the works or Madame Bonnard pushes me out of the investigation."

"People from Normandy like to keep to themselves," Inès murmured as she climbed the stairs.

"Do you think Commandant Renouf might want to take over the case?"

"Unlikely. He's been respecting our agreement so far, otherwise he wouldn't have called. But I don't plan on giving him the chance to shut me out."

"Should I come with you?"

"That would be helpful, but the folks from Avranches might get skittish with too many of us Malouins showing up."

"We don't exactly have the best reputation over there. They think we're stuck-up."

"I'm classified as a Parisienne, which isn't any better."

"Considerably worse, actually."

"At least it's not like that here." She hesitated, noticing Adel's deliberately casual avoidance of her gaze. *So, it's the same here too.*

"I'll get going then. Keep on Chopard's tail and try to find out where that damned boat is."

Sandrine parked her motorcycle beneath the monastery and walked back to the squad cars in front of the main gate. An ambulance driver sat behind the wheel, blowing cigarette smoke out the window. Eighties pop music played on the radio.

"Capitaine Perrot?" A firefighter in a black uniform with yellow reflective stripes approached her.

"Yes?"

"Commandant Renouf instructed me to take you to Tombelaine."

"Where is that?" She was unfamiliar with the place.

"We can't see it from here. It's Le Mont-Saint-Michel's sister."

"Sister?"

"There are two tidal islands. Tombelaine is about two to three miles north in the bay and is much smaller than Le Mont-Saint-Michel."

"How do we get there? With that?" She glanced at the red firefighting vehicle with continuous caterpillar tracks; she had noticed it the day before. But today, it was missing its trailer. Sludge dripped from the broad rubber tracks, and splashes stained its sides. The man must have transported Commandant Renouf and the forensic team to the island.

"Precisely." He gave a gentle pat on the closed door, the way one might pat their favourite horse. *And the way I occasionally pat my motorcycle or my trusty Citroën.*

"Let's get going then."

The firefighter opened the door of the towering vehicle.

Sandrine placed a foot on the track, gripped the frame, and pulled herself up. The seat was snug and not particularly comfortable. One wouldn't have to be too large to feel cosy in the cabin.

The man started the diesel engine and drove off. Sun-dried mud flew in chunks behind them as they left the concrete area and picked up speed.

"Cool machine," she commented. "Must be fun driving this around."

"Better than a roller coaster. Only I wouldn't have to clean those afterward." He grinned, aiming for a tidal channel that lay across their path. "Hold on!"

The vehicle tilted forward, water spraying sideways as they crossed the stream, only to ascend the opposite slope shortly after.

"I see what you mean. Ever fear getting stuck in the mud?"

"This tracked vehicle was specifically purchased for the tidal flats around Le Mont-Saint-Michel. A five-cylinder diesel engine with 163 horsepower. I can get through anything here, as long as I don't get caught by the tide. On the road, this beauty can theoretically reach over fifty miles per hour, but in the tidal flats, much slower, and if the water rises to the doors, it drops to three. The tide flows into the bay at over sixty miles per hour. I can't outrun that."

"We'll need to hurry at the crime scene then."

The man glanced at his chunky wristwatch. "It's almost 3 p.m. Half an hour to low tide. Enough time to look around Tombelaine and comfortably return. With the trailer, I can fit up to sixteen people, and there aren't that many out there. But whatever the forensic team doesn't capture now will definitely be gone or ruined by tomorrow. If there's anything to find at all."

They circled around Le Mont and the silhouette of the island emerged ahead, jutting out of the shallow tidal flat.

"Tombelaine is about 800 feet long and about half as tall as

Le Mont, standing at about 150 feet." The man seemed to enjoy playing the tour guide for her.

Sandrine gave him an encouraging smile. "Does anyone live on the island?"

"Louis XIV suspected his Finance Minister Fouquet of planning a rebellion against him there. Understandably, he didn't take kindly to that and ordered all buildings on Tombelaine demolished. Since then, the island has been uninhabited. Nowadays, it's a bird sanctuary and a popular destination for tidal flat hikers. After all, it's pretty hard to miss."

Sandrine kept her eyes on the approaching island, pondering what could have led the priest there. He surely hadn't ventured across the tidal flat of his own accord, especially right before the tide the previous evening. Soon, she discerned the outlines of the police officers. She counted just under a dozen people.

They parked at the edge of the island, and the engine's rumble faded.

"I'll wait here for you," the firefighter said. "I can't stomach the sight of a corpse. Especially not that of a priest."

"It's hard for me, too, but it unfortunately comes with my job."

She opened the door and climbed out. The sun blazed from a brilliantly blue sky, and the ground's top layer was mostly dry, save for a few puddles here and there. Any evidence from the previous night would be non-existent now, erased by the tide.

Commandant Renouf was in conversation with a man in disposable overalls and signalled her over.

"Capitaine Perrot, glad you could make it, even under these unpleasant circumstances. May I introduce you to Monsieur Deschamps, our forensic examiner from Cherbourg?"

"Pleased to meet you."

The man stood almost a head shorter than her and looked fragile, prompting her to shake his hand very gently.

"Likewise."

"Any information on what happened to Père Martin?"

"Come with me." The forensic examiner led her to the edge of the island. The cloth they'd used to cover the body fluttered slightly in the rising wind. A portion of the black cassock peeked out from beneath.

Sandrine lifted the cloth. The priest's eyes were open, fixed on the horizon. Nothing remained of the intense gaze he'd given her in the inn, scrutinising her with hostility. Now they were still and lifeless, like two glass orbs. Green algae speckled his grey hair and beard. There was no doubt; it was Père Martin.

"When did he sustain these injuries?" She gestured to the abrasions and cuts on his cheeks and forehead.

"At first glance, I'd say all the external injuries were inflicted post-mortem. The cause of death appears to be drowning. The receding tide dragged the body, pushing it here against the rocks where it got caught, hence the abrasions. We're fortunate he isn't floating somewhere in the English Channel by now."

"Sometimes fate does favour the police," noted Commandant Renouf.

"Any other signs of foul play?" Sandrine replaced the cloth over the priest's face.

"You're wondering if he had been held underwater and drowned?"

"Something like that."

"So far, I haven't noticed any indications of that. My guess is he was careless, strayed too far from Le Mont, and was caught by the tide. The autopsy will provide more details."

"Thank you, Monsieur Deschamps. This helps." She rose and took a few steps away. Renouf followed her.

"What's your take on this?" the policeman asked.

"Death by drowning seems plausible."

"But? Something's bothering you about it, isn't it?"

"The man lived his entire life by the bay. He knows the tides like the back of his hand. How could the tide surprise someone like him? It doesn't make any sense to me," Sandrine responded.

"You mentioned he seemed notably distracted during your last encounter. Perhaps he was lost in thought and wasn't aware of his surroundings. After all, he is over eighty."

"Do you believe that, Commandant?"

Renouf pulled out his pack of Gauloises, noticeably thinner since morning, lit one up and took a deep drag. Leaning his head back, he exhaled a plume of smoke into the air.

"It would certainly simplify the investigation. An accident, as occasionally happens around here. Maybe even a suicide. Who knows? We could close the case by tonight and treat ourselves to a nice dinner. What do you think?"

Sandrine scrutinised him thoughtfully. *Was he testing her or was it a genuine suggestion?*

"You don't strike me as someone who chooses the easy route," she replied.

He took another deep drag, then snuffed out the cigarette in a metal tin once used for candy.

"You're right about that. I can't quite buy the idea of an accidental death. Suicide seems unlikely, but I wouldn't rule it out until I learn more about the background."

"And murder?" She posed the question they had both been dancing around.

The policeman hesitated. "Not much points in that direction, but I wouldn't deem it impossible. However, I'll wait for the autopsy results before investigating along those lines."

"Would you do me a favour?"

"If it's within my power, of course."

"Please order a comprehensive drug test. In Camille Barnais, we found traces of synthetic THC which she likely ingested unknowingly."

"Any other findings from the examination?"

"Nothing that advances our case."

"I'll let the doctor know, but I'm not concerned about the forensic team. They operate smoothly without our input."

"If you say so," Sandrine replied hesitantly. She knew all too well about the backlogs in the labs. Pressuring and waiting for results was a regular part of her job.

"Just look at the doctor."

"Monsieur Deschamps? What about him?" She turned towards the man who was squatting next to the corpse, dictating into a voice recorder.

"He's friends with your Dr. Hervé. They often compete in Pétanque with their respective teams. Word has it that these French bocce matches can get quite intense."

Sandrine waited, wondering where he was leading.

"He's from Normandy, and your man's a Breton. Dr Deschamps won't let a Malouin conduct a more thorough examination than he does. Père Martin will receive an exceptionally detailed and meticulous treatment, and it won't end up on the overtime sheet. You can count on that."

"Good. I'll inform Dr Hervé then."

"No need. The two medics have already spoken." He stepped closer to her. "It's a matter of honour where the decisive clue will be found: in Cherbourg or in Saint-Malo."

"Brittany against Normandy. Isn't that a bit childish?"

"For a Parisienne? Certainly. But not for the locals around here."

"What would happen if the Parisienne solves the case? Will she be tarred and feathered?"

Renouf winked at her. "And chased out of the region with torches and pitchforks."

Sandrine wondered how much of that was said in jest. "Hopefully, this rivalry proves productive and doesn't become an impediment. Let's head back. I want to take a look at the chapel. That's where the man was last seen," she suggested. "Or do we need to stay here?"

"I'll gladly accompany you. My team will continue searching for a while longer, but I don't hold out much hope for useful clues. The body was washed up here; the crime scene, if there even is one, is somewhere else." He looked towards the mainland. "Somewhere between here and Le Mont is where it must have happened."

The firefighter stopped on the north side of the island, letting her and Commandant Renouf out. On a rocky outcrop, which jutted defiantly into the bay, stood the Chapel of Saint-Aubert, a chunky stone structure with a lichen-covered slate roof. The path to the chapel was via stairs carved into the rock. The building wasn't particularly large, perhaps holding three dozen people if they didn't mind standing close together.

"Do you think he'll bring us luck?" Renouf gestured to the statue of the saint, who was peering down at them from the roof's gable.

"I wouldn't count on it," she replied.

Sandrine grabbed the door handle and shook it until it rattled; it was locked.

"At least Père Martin locked the door when he left."

"Or someone else did," said Renouf. "At least, no key was found on him."

"It might be somewhere in the mud."

"True, but unlikely. Men of the cloth are said to have deep pockets." Renouf chuckled softly.

She hadn't heard that saying before. Had the policeman just made it up on the spot?

She retrieved the key she had gotten from Blanche Barnais

from her pocket. The door was old, pieced together from cracked boards affected by the salty sea air, but the lock was a modern cylinder type. She was relieved to have the key, even though she didn't peg Renouf as a cop who would struggle with the idea of lock-picking. At least not as long as they were on the right side of the law.

The door creaked open, and they entered the chapel. The air was cool, tinged with a faint scent as if someone had recently burned incense inside. To her knowledge, no Masses were held here, and the only visitors she knew of were Auguste Barnais and Père Martin. Why would either of them light incense?

"Romanesque, 12th century," Renouf said, almost reverently. "Dedicated to Bishop Aubert of Avranches."

"This is home turf for you then," she quipped.

She took a couple of steps into the room. Even without her knowledge of the priest's death, the atmosphere in the dim chapel felt oppressive. Light streamed in through the single narrow arched window, illuminating a depiction of Jesus placed in front of the altar at the chapel's far end. The floor tiles were arranged in a brown and white chequered pattern, worn uneven from the shoes of the faithful who had visited this place over the centuries. There were two small benches against the wall. Had Auguste Barnais and Père Martin sat here and prayed together?

"What could've happened here that led to the priest's death?" Sandrine mused, speaking more to herself than to Renouf.

"We don't yet know if what occurred in this chapel is related to his death," he replied.

Her gaze settled on a slim metal box, hardly bigger than a deck of cards. It lay behind one of the candlesticks on the altar. Sandrine picked it up and examined it for a moment. "This is definitely not from the 12th century. It feels out of place here."

"What did you find?" Renouf stepped beside her.

She pointed to the lens. "A mini-projector. I have one like this at home."

"Why would anyone need such a device here?" He looked around. "I'd be surprised if there's even electricity here."

"I can't think of a reason either." She carefully placed the projector into an evidence bag, which she always carried with her for such occasions. He was right about the lack of electricity. The projector likely operated on an internal battery or could be connected to a laptop using a cable.

"Best to ask the parish priest. He should know."

"Or whoever's behind the priest's disappearance left it here by mistake." Renouf leaned in to examine the device. "Given its small size, it could easily be overlooked."

Sandrine handed him the bag. "Another one for the lab in Cherbourg."

"Let's go to see Auguste Barnais; perhaps he can tell us something about it."

She locked the chapel door and together they descended the staircase. The city gate was just a short walk away.

"Père Martin didn't hint at anything when you met him yesterday?" Renouf asked again.

"He was unusually quiet but also seemed nervous and avoided eye contact with me."

"The man was notably conservative, even for a Catholic priest. Strong-willed and liberated women probably made him uncomfortable, especially those who carry weapons."

"At our first meeting, he didn't hesitate to imply that women should be at home by the stove, rather than dealing with criminals."

"Perhaps you set him straight."

"I believe he noticed or observed something connected to Camille's death that deeply disturbed him. The priest, who never missed a chance to throw in a Bible verse, bit his lip to keep from speaking."

"If you're right, his knowledge might have been his undoing. However, that would imply a member of the family or an employee of the Auberge was involved in the accident."

"At the moment, that's what I'm assuming," Sandrine said.

"Anyone specific in mind?"

"The only one who tried to stop Camille from visiting the boat was Michel Barnais. If the attack was originally intended for Jean, he'd also be at the top of my list of suspects."

"Then let's knock on the door." Charles Renouf turned his head toward the family home. The slate-roofed house extended over a retaining wall. Two of the dormer windows were open. Someone was home.

Blanche opened the door for them. "I presume this visit isn't for me again."

"We need to speak with your father," said Renouf.

"Come in, both of you. He's in the living room with Michel."

So, he really was back from his trip. But where was the yacht? Certainly not in the port of Saint-Malo.

The men looked up as Blanche led them in. Shelves filled with books dominated the room's side walls. The small windows let in enough light for them to see the two clearly. Auguste sat in one of two identical leather armchairs. Michel stood before him, looking down with irritation. They had been arguing. Up to now, she had only seen how joyful Auguste was about his son's return to the family fold. *What could have happened?*

"Any updates?" Michel Barnais' tone was sharp and demanding.

"You're back from your trip?"

"As you can see."

"The boat isn't at the port of Saint-Malo. Where did you leave it?"

"What does that have to do with your investigations? My mother didn't have a boating accident."

"But she wanted to board it and two men used force to prevent her from doing so."

"Why would someone do that? That's nonsense," he snapped at her.

Commandant Renouf stood beside her, eyeing Michel Barnais. "I hope you had a pleasant day at sea. Where did your journey take you?"

"That's utterly irrelevant."

"We're investigating your mother's death and Père Martin's disappearance. It's up to us to decide what's irrelevant." His tone hardened, and Michel Barnais' expression darkened.

"Since you insist on knowing, I was in the Channel Islands and returned an hour ago. If what's being said is true, the priest disappeared while I was at sea," Michel said.

"We haven't accused you of being involved in his disappearance," Renouf replied. "In fact, we're not even assuming that anyone was involved."

"And what am I being accused of?" The red spots on his cheeks darkened.

"We're not accusing you," Sandrine said. "Not yet."

"Then don't come here asking these insolent questions."

"Michel!" Auguste banged his cane on the wooden floor. "The officers are just doing their job. There's no need to be rude."

For a moment, Michel Barnais held Sandrine's gaze. His eyes narrowed, and the creases on his forehead deepened. He took a deep breath and turned to his father.

"I'm sorry. I'm just on edge. First, mother's accident, then Père Martin's disappearance, and now the police show up at our home, harassing our family with their insinuations."

"In truth, we haven't insinuated anything," said Sandrine. "But we would like answers now. Where is the *Émeraude*?"

"In the Bassin de la Rance, at Pointe du Ton, if you must know."

"Why there and not in the Saint-Malo marina?"

"The radio was acting up, and by the end of the trip, it had completely broken down. A friend has a workshop at Pointe de Ton and will fix it in the next few days. It will be anchored there until then."

"I hope you won't object to us inspecting the boat," she said, looking at Auguste.

"What's the meaning of this?" Michel snapped. "I thought you weren't accusing me of anything?"

"It's just a routine investigation. Besides, if there's nothing on board that could incriminate you, as you've assured us, there should be no issues."

He glanced at his father and then turned back to Sandrine.

"Do what you must, but you won't find any evidence related to my mother's death on there."

"We assume as much, but it's our duty to check. It's tedious, but necessary."

Michel Barnais shrugged, shooting her a hostile look. She had doubts herself about finding anything incriminating. The man had had plenty of time to dispose of anything that linked him to his mother's death or any illegal activities. By now, any evidence would be at the bottom of the English Channel.

"Is that all? We have other business matters to discuss," he said tersely.

"One more question. Do you also discuss business matters with Albert Chauvin?"

He froze, and it took a few seconds for him to regain his composure.

"I don't recognise that name." It was a lie, one she could easily prove, but she decided to save that for an official interrogation.

"It's said that you often associate with Monsieur Chauvin."

"Then whoever said that is mistaken."

"The man is a fence, and you have a record this thick." She held her thumb and forefinger a few inches apart. "Dealing in counterfeit car parts is just one of the charges against you."

"Slander and false accusations, none of which have ever been proven." He pulled his wallet out of his back pocket and retrieved a business card. "I consider our conversation over at this point. I'd appreciate it if you refrained from any further harassment. If the police have any more questions, contact my attorney."

He took a step forward and tripped over an upturned edge of the carpet. Angrily, he kicked at it. "It's about time to toss out this old thing," he snapped. "Might as well do it myself."

He thrust the card into Sandrine's hand and pushed past her. The door slammed shut behind him.

'Lianne Roche, Attorney at Law', was printed in golden letters on the card. She sighed. The woman had her hands deep in the gang's operations. It shouldn't have surprised her that she was also representing Michel Barnais. She just wondered if in this case too, Albert Chauvin was picking up the tab, just like with Le Bihan.

"Please excuse my son. He can be quite temperamental, and his mother's death has deeply affected him. He's only recently returned to his family, and then such a tragic turn of events," Auguste said, defending him.

"These are uncomfortable questions, but I have to ask them," said Sandrine.

"I understand. You're trying to track down my wife's killer. It's your job. But it won't bring Camille back, and I doubt I'll live to see the outcome of a trial." His voice sounded fragile yet clear. At that moment, he must have been pain-free, as far as that was possible in his condition. "Perhaps it will help the children move past their grief."

"I'm truly sorry."

"That's the fate we all face. The old must eventually step aside and make room for their children. At least I lived to see Michel return to us, which lets me accept my illness with calmness and inner peace. The Auberge will pass into his hands, as is the tradition in the family."

She looked at the painkillers on a dresser. Several packets. One was open.

"Who has access to these pills?"

"Blanche already informed us that someone slipped drugs to Camille. I blame myself for leaving these around. Anyone who has a key to the house can take some without notice. So all family members and a few long-term employees."

"We now know that it was a cannabinoid. You shouldn't feel guilty or blame yourself. Your medications were not involved."

"Cannabis? Camille hasn't smoked a joint in ages. Not since she was pregnant with Michel."

"According to our forensic pathologist, she didn't smoke anything."

"Then she accidentally ingested the cannabis?"

Sandrine had intentionally omitted the fact it was synthetic THC. From Auguste's reaction, he clearly suspected it might have come from his stash. *A cookie or some of his tea. He has no idea the chocolate was tampered with or who is responsible.*

"It was a synthetic cannabinoid. A presumably oily liquid that was sprayed onto the chocolate truffle that Jean had set aside for himself."

"There's such a thing? And who?"

"We don't know yet," Renouf said. "But I'm sure we'll find out."

Auguste Barnais' gaze shifted back and forth between Sandrine and Commandant Renouf. Almost imperceptibly, his eyes widened, and his hands gripped the walking stick tighter. *He knows someone who has or had possessed the substance. He has a hunch about who might be behind his wife's accident.*

Sandrine didn't ask. The man would never reveal it, not now at least.

"Have the police found Père Martin yet?" he asked, abruptly changing the subject.

"We just came back from Tombelaine. I'm sorry to inform you that hikers found his body. It seems he drowned," replied Commandant Renouf.

"Just yesterday, we were both in the chapel, praying and remembering Camille. And now he's also dead. It's been almost forty years since he married us." Auguste looked out over the bay. "We have many shared memories. What a sad fate. And yet, he knew the dangers of the sea better than anyone."

"When did you part ways?"

"I leave my wristwatch here when I go to church, so I can only estimate. Père Martin wanted to stay in the chapel for a while, and I had to get back to the hotel. The kitchen was opening for dinner, and we were fully booked. I was back here around half-past six."

"Did you see him again after that?"

"No. We talked about his wanting to be on his way back before the tide cut off the path. This morning his nephew called." He gently tapped the end of his stick on the floor. "If only he had stayed the night here."

"We still don't know exactly how the accident occurred. Since he was alone, we'll probably never fully understand what happened."

"The sea has swallowed many and never returned them. At least his body was found and can be given a Christian burial," said Auguste softly. "He had a long and fulfilling life in the service of the church. That's more than most of us can claim."

"Did he act in any way unusual last night?" asked Sandrine.

"Not at all. He was, as always, a man of God. We prayed and talked about death and life thereafter."

"It almost seemed to me during our last encounter that Père

Martin knew something about your wife's accident and was struggling whether to reveal it or keep it to himself."

"If that was the case, he chose to keep silent. He didn't disclose anything to me, and I was the closest person to him in this family." His head drooped slightly to his chest, and he sighed heavily. Perhaps the pain was returning?

"I am tired," he said. "Let's continue this tomorrow."

"Of course. Just one more question. We found a mini-projector in the chapel. Do you know anything about its origins?"

"A what?" asked Auguste.

Renouf held up the plastic bag containing the device.

"I've never seen such a thing. We have one or two projectors at the hotel, but they're much larger. I'm sorry I can't be of more help."

"We'll figure out how the device got there. It's probably completely irrelevant."

They said their goodbyes and left the house. They hadn't learned much. But their suspicion towards Michel Barnais was intensifying. Just then, Sandrine's phone vibrated. It was Adel.

"Excuse me." She stepped aside. "What's new? ... This helps ... I'll text you the boat's location ... We'll meet there tomorrow morning. See you then." She quickly typed a message into her phone, informing Adel where the *Émeraude* could be found.

"Good news, I hope," said Renouf.

"I think so. We received an anonymous tip about the whereabouts of the second driver involved in the accident."

"Do you have an idea where the tip might have come from?"

"Perhaps." At the moment, only Albert Chauvin's secretary came to mind. She could have overheard a conversation between her boss and the two men. *Would she be willing to testify against Chauvin? Probably not.*

"Do you want to be there for the arrest?"

"My motorcycle isn't that fast. My assistant is already on his way."

"Do you have a moment for me?" Charlotte emerged from the house.

"I should be going now. The evidence needs to go to the lab." Renouf nodded his goodbyes and headed down Grande Rue.

"I hope I didn't drive him away."

"Not at all."

"I heard Père Martin drowned." Sadness was reflected in her gaze. Sandrine didn't know if the woman had liked the priest, but he had been part of the family.

"Yes. The tide must have caught him off-guard on his way back. Does the water here really rise that quickly?"

"Come with me, I want to show you something that might be helpful."

Sandrine followed Charlotte, who climbed the fortress wall and briskly headed north.

"Come on, we have to hurry or you'll miss it," Charlotte called back as she squeezed past a group of tourists. She stopped at the last tower of the fortification and turned to Sandrine.

"This is the Tour du Nord. There aren't as many onlookers here as at the city gate or on the bridge to the mainland." She winked. "Most are afraid of getting trapped once the water spills over the square."

Sandrine glanced at her watch; it was just before seven. The sun was low behind them, and Le Mont cast a long shadow over the mudflats. By evening, the spring tide would turn Le Mont into an island.

"The tide starts soon?"

"That's why we're here. Father told me you found Père Martin." She took Sandrine's arm and pulled her to the parapet. "He must have left the chapel around this time and walked across the mudflats."

The tower was on the north-east side of the island. From

here, the chapel was out of sight, but she could oversee the bay and the Normandy coast up to Avranches.

"What are those people doing?"

Far below them, a group of people with surfboards and narrow kayaks stood on the dry mudflat.

"They're waiting for Le Mascaret to ride its current. The tidal wave isn't very high, maybe up to the knees, but it's said to be as fast as a galloping horse, which is probably an exaggeration."

"Over forty miles per hour."

Charlotte nodded, clearly impressed. Sandrine silently thanked the kind firefighter who had given her the chance to show off some insider knowledge.

"Le Mascaret is only visible during spring tides. If you're out there and see it coming, it will catch you. Nobody can run that fast, especially not on the mudflats, and certainly not through the tidal creeks that criss-cross the bay to escape it."

"What could the priest have been looking for out there? He knew the risks."

"I have no idea. He was well-informed about the tides. He would never have willingly headed towards Tombelaine during a spring tide."

"How well did you know Père Martin? Something must have been distracting him."

"He was a friend of my father. I haven't spoken to him much in recent years. Michel often went to confession; the rest of us aren't as faithful. But you're right, he seemed unusually distracted, as if he was preoccupied with a troubling thought."

"Any idea what it might have been?"

"Not in the slightest."

That would have been too convenient.

"Look! Over there."

Sandrine shielded her eyes with her hand. "A white line. What is that?"

"That's Le Mascaret. What you're seeing is the foam crest as it breaks."

Crowds gathered tightly on the bridge. In the mudflat, the surfers and half a dozen canoeists readied themselves for the tidal wave's arrival.

"People can actually surf on this?"

"It's certainly not Hawaii, but yes. The wave carries you ahead. At the Gironde, it's taller because the river course keeps narrowing. Here, it remains consistent across the width of the mudflats."

Sandrine leaned against the wall. The white crest of the wave approached quickly. *She's right, you can't run from Le Mascaret. Especially not from the billions of cubic metres of water following it.*

The wave split and circled the island. People on the bridge cheered on the surfers who let themselves be carried by it. It flowed past Le Mont-Saint-Michel and dissipated along the coastline. As far as Sandrine could see, water covered the mudflat.

"The plaza is currently still about a foot above the water level, but you should probably get going. It may be another half an hour before the sea floods the road and the bridge's end. You won't be able to leave here without getting wet."

"Good idea." She definitely didn't want to be stuck on Le Mont for the next four or five hours until the ebb tide revealed the passage to the mainland again. "What's the quickest way to my motorcycle?"

"Where did you park?"

"In the parking lot beneath the Abbot's building."

"That's easy. Just continue along this path. It leads directly to the parking lot below the abbey. It won't take you more than ten minutes."

"Thank you."

She bid her farewell and marched along the wall, turning left onto the path that took her to the east side of the town. At the end of the long staircase at the foot of the abbey, her motorcycle was waiting for her.

Sandrine mounted it and drove off as a police officer directed her through. The first waves were already spilling over the road, and tourists were queued up in long lines at the bus stop.

An hour later, she drove down the driveway to her cottage. Rosalie stepped out of the main house and waved to her as Sandrine parked the motorcycle in the garage and walked over.

"I'm in the middle of preparing dinner, would you like to join me? You're on a case and probably haven't had anything decent to eat all day."

"You know me too well." She smiled gratefully at her best friend. "When have I ever turned down an invitation from you?"

"Then come on in, the oven is already hot."

Sandrine followed her into the rustic kitchen. Rosalie had likely heard the motorcycle and quickly turned on the oven.

"You're like a mother to me." She adjusted a chair and sat down at the tall table, crafted from sun-bleached driftwood.

"Nonsense. I've been writing all day, now I'm famished and there's nothing more boring than eating alone."

"I'm not good company when I'm on a case. It's hard for me to switch off."

"I'm a good listener, and besides, I'm quite familiar with murder and mayhem."

She was certainly right about that. Her detective novels featuring Commissaire Hugo Delacroix were selling like hotcakes and had garnered numerous awards. The short, yet cunningly crafted love scenes certainly played a part in that.

Rosalie fetched a baking tray from the cupboard and placed it on the table. "I know what you mean though. Until a book is finished, I keep mulling it over in my mind. You're working on the accident at Quai Saint-Vincent?"

"How do you know that?"

"Word of mouth travels swiftly from Saint-Malo to Cancale." She unrolled a sheet of parchment paper over the tray. "Plus, you're on the front page." Rosalie walked to the dresser and fetched the daily newspaper. "Here."

She pointed to a picture and Sandrine pulled the paper closer. In the foreground stood Antoine de Chezac, and in the background one could see the crane pulling the SUV out of the water. Sandrine was clearly recognisable next to Commissaire Matisse.

"De Chezac. Your nemesis is now in Saint-Malo. What a mess." Rosalie put a hand on Sandrine's shoulder. It felt comforting to feel her genuine sympathy.

"You can say that again."

"You never get a break, do you?" She pulled Sandrine into an embrace, holding her tight for a moment. "I hope you at least had a pleasant day with Léon."

"How did you ..." She stopped mid-sentence. Keeping anything secret from Rosalie was nigh on impossible. For someone who claimed to be engrossed in writing all day, she always seemed to be remarkably informed about local goings-on.

"I happened to run into him in town."

Rosalie had never made a secret of her wish to see Sandrine in a stable relationship, and Léon seemed to be the perfect candidate in her eyes. Sandrine sighed at the thought. A job in the police force and a relationship often clashed, as she had recently experienced on Sunday. She had had to cut a pleasant day short and watch a dead woman being pulled from the water. *No man would put up with that for long. And I don't want the constant guilt of having to work long hours on important cases.*

"He is lovely, but a committed relationship is far too complicated for me."

"Nonsense."

"Hugo Delacroix flits from one flower to another, just like a hummingbird. Maybe I'd like that too."

"Hugo is a playful scamp; you're a grown woman. There's a difference."

"I wish it were that simple." She gazed at Rosalie. "You look troubled," she said, changing the subject. "Tell me what's going on if you want to."

"If Camille Barnais had turned onto Rue de Dinan, she'd probably still be alive," said Rosalie. "I've been writing crime novels for twenty years and my gut feeling tells me that something was on the boat that she wasn't supposed to see. Maybe it's still there."

Sandrine had often received excellent advice from Rosalie in the past and knew that she could keep a secret. As her friend placed slices of bread on the baking sheet, Sandrine told her about the case.

"If there was evidence on the yacht, it will have been removed."

"You always speak highly of your forensic expert. What's his name again?"

"Jean-Claude Mazet."

"Just trust that he and his team will find something."

"That would be nice." She was more sceptical in this respect than Rosalie. If she were in Michel Barnais' shoes, she would have either cleaned up the boat thoroughly or completely sunk it in the English Channel.

"Do you have a suspect?"

"All signs point to a man, but I don't have enough yet to pin him down."

"You'll get there," Rosalie encouraged her while mixing

crème fraîche, cream, and grated Comté cheese in a porcelain bowl.

"What puzzles me also is the death of the priest. He drowned – either an accident, which I don't believe, a murder or a suicide. There are no signs of murder at the moment. The body had no external injuries that could have occurred before death. There were also no bruises that could indicate he was held underwater. Perhaps there will be some clues from the forensic pathology."

"Very few priests condone suicide. Grave sin," murmured Rosalie, spreading the cream mixture on the slices of white bread. Then she added ham, another piece of white bread, and cheese on top.

"The man knew the tides too well. It doesn't add up. Especially since my prime suspect has an ironclad alibi. He was with the boat in the Channel Islands. Too far away to kill someone in Le Mont-Saint-Michel at the same time."

"Then the question remains, what could drive a stiff-necked and deeply religious priest to commit suicide?" asked Rosalie.

"He must have been desperate. I would assume conflicting and mutually exclusive values."

The oven door clattered as Rosalie opened it, sliding the baking sheet inside.

"He knew something he wouldn't even confide to Auguste. And the two had been friends for decades." Pensively, she watched the cheese melt. She hadn't eaten anything since breakfast with Commandant Renouf, and her refrigerator was empty. Rosalie was her saviour, as she'd been so often before.

"Perhaps he'd made a promise he felt bound to."

Sandrine straightened up and looked over at her friend. "'That's it."

"A promise? Was he so close to the suspect that he felt obligated to him?"

"It's not about the suspect. It's about the church."

"Over the millennia, they've killed many, but not nowadays."

"It's not a promise, but a vow. The confessional secret. Père Martin must have heard something about Camille Barnais' death in the confessional. Maybe he didn't recognise it at first, but it became clear to him later." Hence the change in the priest's demeanour between their first and last meeting.

"All you have to do is find out who in the family regularly goes to confession. And you'll have the one who has the priest on their conscience." Rosalie smiled contentedly, like a reader who believed they had figured out the ending of the crime novel that had them captivated.

What had Charlotte said today at the bookstore? Only Auguste and Michel went to confession; the rest of the family were less faithful. All the evidence reliably pointed in Michel Barnais' direction. Yet, during the crime, he was supposedly sailing the yacht on the English Channel. Either he had commissioned someone else or he moored the boat nearby and returned unnoticed to rid himself of the problem. His trust in the priest's discretion might have been high, but only the dead keep secrets forever.

Rosalie switched on the oven's grill function, and Sandrine stepped outside to make a call.

Adel picked up after the second ring.

"Is there a way to verify if Michel Barnais was really out with the boat?"

"I'll have to check. Dubois might know; he's a sailor himself. What are you thinking?"

"Perhaps he moored it earlier at Pointe de Ton and returned without being seen to deal with the priest."

"It's a possibility," he replied thoughtfully. "When we inspect the boat tomorrow, Jean-Claude can access the navigation system. After that, we'll know more."

"But we'd only know where the boat was. Maybe he wasn't on board at all and lent it to someone for the trip."

"That's also true. Who might that have been?"

"I wish I had a specific suspect in mind. So far, it's just jumbled thoughts that don't make much sense."

"It will come."

"Thanks. I'll let you have your evening then."

"Kind of you, but..." He hesitated to continue, which was unusual for him.

"What's going on?" she prodded.

"Probably nothing, but I can't shake this feeling that something's happening at the precinct. Something they're trying to keep you and, likely, me out of."

"Any idea what?"

"Not in the slightest, except that Poutin is involved."

Sandrine had never been fond of that man. Anything that could harm her professionally, he would back with gusto. Hadn't Inès hinted that he got along famously with de Chezac? The snobbish prosecutor would only tolerate a man like Poutin if he saw some advantage in it. What that was, she couldn't discern.

"We'll face it when the time comes," she tried to reassure him.

"De Chezac has requested him for a special task."

She whistled softly. What could he be up to? "There's nothing we can do. We'll play it by ear," she said and bid Adel goodbye.

"Trouble?" Rosalie asked as she pulled the finished Croque Monsieurs out of the oven. A delicious aroma of warm ham and melted cheese filled the kitchen.

"I don't know yet. But nothing capable of spoiling my appetite."

"That's good then. All this would have been too much for just me."

Sandrine sat down at the table, and Rosalie placed a Croque Monsieur on her plate.

"Odd name, when you think about it," she said and cut into it. The cheese oozed thickly between the slices of white bread.

"Interesting story, actually."

Rosalie sat next to her at the table and poured them both a glass of cider.

"It's said that the owner of the Parisian café Bel Age in the 1930s was the first to top slices of white bread, instead of baguette, with ham and bake it. A guest reportedly asked what type of meat it was, and the chef replied 'meat of the gentleman'. Hence, Croque Monsieur. He apparently had a sense of humour and was alluding to rumours of cannibalism associated with his café."

"Cannibalism?" She lifted the top slice of bread with her fork and examined the ham.

"People talk a lot when they're bored. But today, I could only get regular ham from the store. They were out of 'Monsieur'." Rosalie laughed, taking a bite.

"Glad to hear it," said Sandrine. "'Tastes fabulous." She took a sip of cider. *Maybe I should learn to cook. No, not as long as Rosalie is here.*

The Émeraude

Sandrine parked her car at the station the next morning and continued with Adel. It took them less than half an hour to get to the spot where the sailing yacht should be moored in the Bassin de la Rance.

"This must be it," the brigadier remarked, driving past a smaller shipyard towards the shores of the Rance. By a boat dock, she spotted a vessel that matched their description.

"It says *Émeraude* on it," Adel pointed out. "That's our boat."

He pulled to a stop at the end of the dock. A man stood with his back to them at the helm, while another was working quickly to untie the ropes.

"They're trying to make a run for it!" shouted Sandrine, flinging open the car door and darting out. The boat's engine roared to life, and the man on the dock tugged at the rope holding the boat in place. He managed to release it, tossing the loose end carelessly into the river before leaping aboard. The propeller churned the brackish water, making it frothy. The man at the helm turned to face her. It was Albert Chauvin. He clearly recognised her.

"Stop!" Sandrine yelled, charging forward. The wooden planks echoed loudly under her sprinting feet. Behind her, she heard the brigadier's hurried steps. *He's not going to make it in time.*

With a determined yell, she leaped off the dock. Stretching her arms out in front of her, she just managed to land on the back of the boat. The man who had untied it greeted her with a forceful punch to the ribs, sending her crashing onto the deck. She screamed in pain, gasping for breath. Instinctively, she drew her legs up. The man towered over her by at least half a head and had shoulders as wide as a wardrobe. With all the strength she could muster, she kicked his shins. Judging by his howl, she'd struck true. The man's feet slipped out from under him. He flailed, trying to maintain his balance but to no avail. Sandrine kicked out again, sending him toppling overboard. His fingers tried to grip the boat's edge, but they slid off, and he plunged into the waters of the Rance. Chauvin, still at the helm, cursed loudly, reaching for a baseball bat that rested against the boat's hull. He advanced, intent on finishing her off. Without hesitation, she pulled her gun from its holster, aiming it squarely at his head.

"Stay where you are and drop the bat," she commanded.

He lifted the baseball bat, a smirk on his face.

"You really think you have the guts to shoot me in the head? After all, you're one of the good guys," he taunted, taking another step towards her. Just one more step and he'd be within striking distance.

"That's true. I don't like to kill, not even a piece of trash like you," she said through gritted teeth. Sandrine lowered the gun's barrel, moving it from his forehead, down his chest to his groin. "But I won't hesitate to blow your balls off. At this distance, it's a sure shot. You'll live, and I can claim the gun went off accidentally. That'd be the end of any little Alberts from you."

He froze in place, clearly taking her threat seriously.

"Don't mess with me, you bitch."

"Drop it! Now!"

His eyes darted from his baseball bat to Sandrine's gun, still aimed at his groin. Realising he had a lot more to lose than gain, he dropped the bat, which rolled off the boat into the water. One less piece of evidence.

"What's this all about?" he snapped at Sandrine.

"This boat isn't yours. What are you doing here?"

"A friend lent it to me. We were planning a simple fishing trip and then we get ambushed. Of course we'd defend ourselves. We had no idea you were police."

"Which friend?" Sandrine straightened up and leaned against the cabin wall, pain shooting through her left side. Chauvin's burly friend had landed a solid hit on her upper torso. She hoped no ribs were broken. But they were definitely bruised. By now, the thug had reached the pier. Adel pulled him out of the water and handcuffed him. He limped, and she could hear him swearing with each step. Then she turned her attention back to Albert Chauvin.

"Spit it out. Who lent you the boat?"

"Why, Michel Barnais. He owns it."

"The same Michel Barnais who claims he's never heard of you?"

"Well, not everyone's honest when speaking to the police. Maybe good old Michel had something to hide. Who knows?"

"You do business with him?"

"Not at all. It's just a casual bromance."

"Take us back to the pier."

"I'm not sure I can do that. You threw the Capitaine overboard." He sneered at her, probably correctly guessing that Sandrine had no idea how to operate the yacht and that she was simply relieved to be sitting down, not having to move.

"No worries, those guys will handle it." She pointed to a coast guard boat approaching them. Adel had requested backup that morning, in case the *Émeraude* was anchored out in open water.

"Shit!"

Chauvin took the helm, turned the boat around and headed back to the dock. Two patrol cars and the van from Mazet's team pulled up on the shore.

"You'll never been able to pin anything on me."

"This isn't about stolen car parts anymore; we're investigating a murder which means we scrutinise things much more closely."

Cursing, he slowed the boat, but they were moving too fast and crashed into the dock. Sandrine barely managed to keep her balance.

The man tossed a rope to Jean-Claude Mazet. Finally, they were securely tied to the pier and Adel and a uniformed police officer jumped aboard.

"Take him away," he said, nodding towards the patrol car. "And the other one, too. Lock them both up in a cell at the Saint-Malo police station."

"We didn't do anything. You can't just arrest us," Chauvin protested.

"Assaulting a police officer should suffice."

"She threatened to shoot my balls off. You should lock her up too; she's a menace."

Chauvin struggled against the grip of the officer holding him.

"You threatened my colleague with that baseball bat. I'm not sure why she hesitated to shoot you."

"I don't see any bat. Do you?"

"It was clearly visible from the shore. Now, off you go."

"My lawyer will give you hell," he vowed as he was led away.

"Nothing's more overrated than the fear of lawyers," Adel called after him. Sandrine holstered her gun and extended a hand to him.

"Could use some help here."

"That bastard really got you," he remarked, pulling her up. A sharp pain made her gasp. Adel was right, the hit had been spot on. The man knew his way around a brawl.

"It's hard to jump aboard a yacht and fend off an attack simultaneously. He knows his craft and landed a solid hit."

"The ambulance will be here soon."

She looked at him, surprised. "It's not that bad. Probably just a bruise." She hoped this was true, even though every breath hurt.

"It's not for you. But we do have a broken shin though. You got him good, too." He pointed towards the pier where the attacker sat, one leg stretched out.

"I didn't think I kicked him that hard." The man could dish it out, but seemed to have real trouble taking it. "What a wimp."

A grin spread across Adel's face. "He didn't know who he was messing with, otherwise he would've been more cautious."

Sandrine beckoned Jean-Claude Mazet.

"Have a thorough look around. For some reason, everyone was supposed to be kept off this boat. There must be something here that can give us a clue as to why."

"If there's something to find, we'll find it."

"I'm very confident about that."

"I have something for you," Adel called out.

Sandrine turned towards him, but too quickly. Her ribs protested, and her mouth contorted in pain.

The brigadier held up a folding chair, jumped onto the pier, and set it up.

"Take a seat, then you won't be in our way."

"Very kind of you." She climbed off the boat and carefully settled into the chair. "That's better," she murmured. She'd be sitting here for a while, overseeing her team.

One of the uniformed officers approached and handed her a steaming thermos cup.

"It's chilly this morning. Something warm will do you good."

"Thank you," she replied, surprised.

"It's still untouched."

"I don't want to drink up your coffee."

"After seeing you throw Chopard, that scumbag, into the water, it's worth more than a cup of coffee to me." He winked at her conspiratorially. "Though I probably shouldn't say that as a cop."

So, the hefty guy was the sought-after Chopard, the one who was in the van with Le Bihan that had rammed Camille Barnais. Now she regretted not kicking him harder.

"The man deserved it," she said.

At that moment, an ambulance appeared on the road between the workshops. Some workers standing in front of the buildings, gazing curiously their way, stepped aside to let it pass. One of the officers directed the paramedics to Chopard, who, still handcuffed to the railing, sat at the end of the pier. Chauvin was hunched over in a police car, glaring at her. Sandrine had no doubt who he'd call as soon as he was at the precinct. Lianne Roche seemed to be the lawyer for the entire gang. She would advise the men to refuse to make a statement. Unlike Le Bihan, Chauvin was smart enough to follow that advice. They wouldn't get a word out of him.

The coastguard's dinghy docked at the pier and an officer nimbly climbed up the ladder.

"It seems you didn't need our help. You managed to handle those guys without a hitch." There was respect in his voice. He must've watched as Chopard went overboard.

"If you hadn't shown up, that guy wouldn't have given up so quickly. And I must admit, I have no idea how to handle a boat.

I probably would've destroyed the entire pier trying to dock then sunk the yacht."

The man laughed and nodded. "It's not that easy the first time. I wish the weekend Capitaines from Paris had similar insight."

Jean-Claude appeared in the narrow doorway leading inside, holding something black encased in a transparent cover aloft. "I found something," he shouted.

"What's that?" Sandrine asked.

"Looks like a cell phone."

"They often put them in condoms to keep them dry," the coast guard officer explained.

"Who does?" Sandrine asked.

"Refugees trying to get to England but who don't have entry visas. There are always makeshift villages around Calais with refugees trying to get across somehow. Many attempt to sneak onto trains or the backs of lorries, but the border patrol has become quite vigilant. Human smuggling via boats has surged recently. It's not far from Calais to Dover, just three or four hours. It's a lucrative business."

She looked at the *Émeraude*. Had Michel Barnais been using it to smuggle refugees?

"But from here? That's quite a distance, all the way across the English Channel. Is it worth it?"

"The route from Calais to Dover is much shorter but is closely monitored by the English coast guard. The boats the smugglers use there aren't suitable for the journey from Saint-Malo, but a yacht like this one is. There's only a slight chance it would get checked. The crossing is, accordingly, expensive. It's worth it."

No wonder Chauvin had a hand in this.

"That's why Camille wasn't allowed on the boat," Adel said. "The refugees Michel wanted to smuggle were already on board."

"The cell phone alone won't be enough evidence," Sandrine replied doubtfully.

"It won't be pleasant, but check the toilet. Usually, the chemical toilet is emptied and cleaned before a longer trip," the coastguard officer suggested.

Jean-Claude made a face. It was clear who would be tasked with that job.

"How many people can you fit on board?" Sandrine asked.

"The boat is about 45 feet long. I'd guess it has three or four cabins. That'd be a maximum of eight people for a comfortable private cruise."

"There are four cabins," Jean-Claude confirmed.

"Then I'd say double, or even triple that number. Twenty people on board, crossing the English Channel, would likely lead to full toilets." He smiled, obviously enjoying schooling the landlubbers in some nautical knowledge.

"Thank you for your assistance. This could help advance our case." Sandrine realised it might only be enough to pin the smuggling on Michel Barnais, but not Chauvin, if Michel kept quiet.

"Seems like you don't need the coastguard's help anymore. We'll take our leave; there's plenty more for us to do." He looked across the Rance to his ship. "In the summer, tourists flood the coast. They have no idea what we deal with daily."

"Maybe someday you'll get the chance to share some stories with us," Sandrine remarked.

"I'd be happy to." The man said his goodbyes and boarded his boat. Moments later, the outboard engine roared to life, and he made his way back to his ship.

"Nice guy," Adel commented, watching him go. "But what a tough job. Just looking at boats makes me queasy."

"A Breton who gets seasick?" Sandrine chuckled but immediately regretted it. Every movement of her upper torso was agonising.

"A Breton by migration, not by birth," he corrected her. "My family would need several more generations before we can call ourselves Bretons."

"Welcome to the club."

Sandrine's phone rang, and she answered the call. It was Suzanne Leriche, inviting her for a walk on the walls of the old city.

"I'd usually love to, but I'm a bit banged up at the moment. How about some coffee? Sitting in the sun without moving sounds perfect right now." Suzanne had a remarkable knack for understanding people and was familiar with the Barnais family. Perhaps a helpful hint might come out of their conversation.

Adel parked near the Office de Tourisme by the Porte Saint-Thomas, within sight of the spot where Camille Barnais had met her end.

"You'd be better off going to the hospital. That guy hit you pretty hard. Plus, we need to document it properly if we want to press charges."

"Don't look so worried, I'm fine. I've been through worse. By tomorrow, I'll have a decent bruise that'll photograph well." Sandrine enjoyed working with Adel and trusted him, which was rare for her, but she got irked when someone tried to mother her.

"Your ribs could be broken; you shouldn't take this lightly."

"I'd feel it if they were," she tried to reassure him, though judging by his sceptical look, she wasn't very convincing. "I'll go to the hospital tomorrow for a check-up. I promise."

"If necessary, I'll drag you there myself. In handcuffs if need be."

"You're like the mother I never had." Sandrine blew him a teasing air kiss and opened the car door. With her face turned away from him and her jaw clenched, she pulled herself out of the seat. She'd never wince in front of him. She wouldn't put it past Adel to drop her off at the nearest ER without her consent and ensure she didn't bolt. *As if any doctor could help me better than just getting a good night's sleep.* And that's precisely what she planned to do tonight.

Keeping her back straight and walking as upright as she could, Sandrine passed through the city gate leading to Place Chateaubriand in front of the Hotel de Ville. *He's probably watching me.* Only once she was sure to be out of sight did she allow her shoulders to slump, letting out a muted groan. Her ribs ached with every breath. Of course, Adel was right, as usual. But she couldn't afford to waste time in a hospital. Matisse had only given her until the end of the week, and then he'd pull her from the investigation. She felt she was close to cracking the case. The puzzle pieces were right in front of her; now it was up to her to piece them together to make sense of the events.

Suzanne Leriche sat at one of the few available tables beneath a dark sunshade stretched in front of the Hotel France & Chateaubriand. She waved as soon as she spotted Sandrine.

"Ouch." Without thinking, Sandrine had raised her arm to wave back.

"You look kind of worn out," the psychologist greeted her.

"It's been a rough day." Sandrine leaned on both armrests of the chair to ease herself into a sitting position. "A good night's sleep and I'll be right as rain."

Unlike Adel, Suzanne didn't press the subject, trusting Sandrine's self-assessment of her current condition. She probably was one of those women who showed up to work no matter how bad they felt.

"A challenging case?"

Shuffling her chair closer to Suzanne, Sandrine lowered her voice, even though the chances that the family sitting at the neighbouring table was eavesdropping were slim – they were too engrossed in their smartphones.

"Slippery as an eel. Every time I try to get a grip, it slides right through my fingers."

A waiter brought Suzanne a quiche and a bottle of Badoit water.

"I have an upcoming appointment, so I ordered a small bite," she apologised. "I highly recommend the quiche."

"Espresso. As much as the cup can hold. With two packets of sugar." A dose of caffeine was what she needed; she'd skip the food.

"Lunch is the most important meal of the day," Suzanne teased, her eyes twinkling.

"I thought that was breakfast." Something she had also skipped today.

"That too. And dinner, especially."

"You'd get along with Rosalie."

"The writer?"

"And cookbook author, on the side at least."

"I'd love to come over for a meal," she said, smiling at Sandrine. "But that's not what's currently on your mind, is it?"

"Confidentiality?" Sandrine asked.

"Absolutely. Compared to me, a grave is like a chatterbox. It's part and parcel of my profession," Suzanne Leriche emphasised.

"How would I silence a Catholic priest?" Sandrine was curious if the psychologist would arrive at the same conclusion as her.

The woman pondered for a moment. "I'd confess to him. The seal of confession is unbreakable."

"But what if it means he betrays a friendship that spans decades?"

"Technically, you can't call it betrayal. A priest doesn't have a choice. Church law forbids him from disclosing anything from confession. It's not open to interpretation."

"That's my theory as well. He sits across from his close friend, looks him in the eyes, and sees the depth of his suffering – all the while knowing he has the means to help."

"Auguste and Père Martin?"

Sandrine nodded. "The priest must have discovered something connected to Camille's death. Whoever was responsible for her death confessed to him to ensure his silence. That's my current hypothesis."

"The priest is dead, isn't he?"

"Yes. Drowned off the coast of Le Mont-Saint-Michel." She remembered his eyes, which had lost their shine. The windows to his soul had shut.

"What do you suspect?" Suzanne interrupted her recollections.

The waiter placed a bulbous cup in front of her. The espresso was topped with a light-brown foam layer, and the aroma of strong coffee wafted up to her nostrils. She tore open the sugar packets, poured them in, and stirred pensively.

"I ruled out an accident; Père Martin knew the dangers of the tides too well. Either someone, ultimately not trusting the sanctity of Confession, silenced him, or he was so internally conflicted that he ended his life."

"Suicide?" Suzanne Leriche shook her head dismissively. "Never."

"Why do you discount it?"

"I didn't know the man very well, but from the few times we met, he struck me as a dogmatic and staunchly conservative priest."

"That sounds about right," Sandrine said, placing the tiny espresso spoon on the saucer.

"I'm going out on a limb here," Suzanne began, "and I might be wrong."

"I'm intrigued."

"The internal conflict might have gnawed at him, but his loyalty seems very clear to me: firstly, the laws of the Church, then his faith, and only after those, his friendship with Auguste Barnais."

"The Church before faith?"

"Absolutely," she asserted. "The rules of his Church moulded him into the man you met. To question them would be to question himself. A very painful process, one the priest wouldn't contemplate." She raised her hands, palms up. "That's my personal assessment."

"So, you rule out suicide?"

"It would be a mortal sin, likely even worse than breaching the seal of confession. I'd completely discount such an act for him."

"That leaves only one possibility." Sandrine leaned her head back, closed her eyes, and relished the warmth of the sun on her face for a moment. The chatter of neighbouring tables and the passing tourists faded away. *She's right. He wouldn't take his own life; someone else must have intervened.*

Suzanne Leriche speared a piece of broccoli from her vegetable quiche. Sandrine briefly contemplated ordering some food for herself after all, but she was expected back at the precinct.

"You're familiar with the Barnais family?" Sandrine asked the psychologist.

"I really only knew Camille and Auguste. They often visited my parents."

"Considering what you've told me about your parents, it's hard for me to picture Auguste there. He seems a bit too traditional."

"In a hippie commune?" Her laughter was light and endearing. "Camille was my mother's friend, from their school days.

Auguste would come along just for her sake. It was clear he genuinely loved her, even I could see that as a child."

"I only briefly met Camille. She seemed to be quite the free spirit."

"Absolutely. She was exceptionally lively. In the Barnais family, it seems acceptable to sow one's wild oats in youth before joining the family business. At any rate, Auguste seemed to enjoy our gatherings. He and my father often spent hours mushroom hunting, which they'd later enjoy by the campfire." Her peaceful gaze suggested she remembered those days fondly.

"He still seems to have a penchant for mushrooms." Sandrine recalled the side dishes that accompanied the rack of lamb. *Didn't he prepare a mushroom stew for himself and Père Martin, the evening the priest died?*

"I can imagine. How is he doing?"

"The death of his wife was devastating, plus the prospect of his own impending death. In spite of this, I'm surprised by how composed he remains."

"Everyone grieves differently. Auguste is deeply religious; perhaps he finds solace or even meaning in that. Who knows?"

"Thank you for taking the time, but I must go now. Someone's waiting for me in a cell at the precinct."

"Good luck. I hope the interrogation brings some clarity."

"We'll see." But she was rather sceptical. Albert Chauvin was a cunning crook who had never been convicted. *He probably won't say a word, and we'll have to let him go.*

Inès Boni approached her as soon as she entered the office, handing her a note barely larger than a business card.

"You have an appointment at the hospital tomorrow morning."

"So, Adel spilled the beans?"

"Of course. After all, an attack on a police officer must be properly reported."

The office manager looked around to see if they were being watched, which they weren't, and grinned broadly.

"You broke that guy's shin. Well done."

"I was just defending myself."

"Absolutely. And if you're going to do something then do it right." She nodded emphatically with each word. "In any case, he's now in the hospital with a cast on his leg, and there's a cop outside his door. I hope he goes straight to jail."

"We'll see." Sandrine wasn't particularly hopeful. Auto theft and hit-and-run weren't enough to keep someone in custody, and the beating he had given her would secretly amuse de Chezac. The guy would likely be released on bail soon.

"Where's Adel?"

"Still in forensics. He'll be late, and I'm supposed to send Dubois with you for the interrogation."

Sandrine waved it off. "I can handle it on my own."

"That would be against regulations. The guy already tried to go after you with a baseball bat." Inès stepped a little closer. "Would you really have ... shot the guy's ... genitals?" Adel had clearly left no detail out.

"I was sure it wouldn't come to that. In any case, they seemed more important to him than his brain," she said tersely. "I have to go now. Let's see if I can get anything out of him."

"His lawyer's already arrived, not five minutes after Chauvin. He won't say a word."

Inès signalled Dubois, who packed his half-eaten baguette into his lunch box, neatly folded his newspaper, and got up. Sandrine wondered who he would listen to more: her, his boss, or Inès. Probably Inès. *And she's right about Chauvin. We can't pin anything concrete on him.*

. . .

Dubois opened the door to the interrogation room and allowed her to go in first. Chauvin and Lianne Roche were already waiting in the sparsely furnished space. The icy stare the lawyer shot her rivalled the cold light from the overhead lamps. Sandrine ignored them both, taking a seat opposite them, and turned on the microphone. She quickly and mechanically rattled off the standard lines about the current time and those present while Dubois took a seat next to her.

"What's with this charade?" The lawyer launched her offensive as soon as Sandrine looked up from the microphone.

"We've been seeing a lot of you around here lately," Sandrine countered. "You seem to have an impeccable reputation in certain circles."

"I'm good at what I do. Something that can't currently be said about you. Otherwise, you wouldn't be picking on innocent people."

"Are you an innocent man?" She directed the question to Chauvin.

"Of course," the woman replied on his behalf. "There was no adequate reason to threaten my client with a weapon, drag him here in handcuffs, let alone the matter of his companion's broken shinbone." She leaned forward, locking eyes with Sandrine. "To me, this clearly looks like a case of excessive police force."

"Your client ignored our order to stop, tried to evade the police and threatened an officer with a baseball bat. He's facing quite a list of charges." Sandrine would have loved nothing more than to slap the woman, but she kept her cool, ensuring her voice remained calm and factual.

"Monsieur Chauvin had borrowed a yacht from an acquaintance and was about to set out for a pleasant day at sea. He didn't hear your orders because, tragically, he's deaf in his left ear. He only noticed you when you ran across the dock and jumped onto the boat. He feared you were about to attack and rob him, especially after witnessing you assault his companion."

"Monsieur Chauvin knows me, and I clearly identified myself as a police officer. His companion was the one who attacked me."

"And you threatened him at point-blank range with a loaded and unsecured gun."

"You're forgetting about the baseball bat again."

Lianne Roche leaned back, smoothing the jacket of her grey business suit.

"What bat? I don't own one. Or did you find one on board?" Chauvin blurted out.

"You're well aware that it fell overboard. Two officers can attest to that, and the brigadier has one of those modern dashcams mounted on his dashboard. You'd be surprised at the quality of images they capture nowadays." She was bluffing, and from the slight smile on the lawyer's face, she knew it.

"Then it would also show that you threatened to ... shoot me."

"Stay calm," his attorney instructed, and he kept his mouth shut, even though he looked like he had plenty more to say.

"Then let's wait and see what kind of sharp footage we get." Lianne Roche shrugged. "Who wouldn't pick up a weapon in such a situation? And nothing more than the yacht owner's baseball bat was at hand."

Sandrine turned to Chauvin. "The boat was used to smuggle people into England. Quite the lucrative endeavour, as my coast guard colleagues have informed me."

"My client had no knowledge of this. When he went out fishing, no one was aboard."

"Was your human cargo already aboard the *Émeraude* on Sunday? Was that why Camille Barnais couldn't board the boat?" Sandrine crossed her arms. "Le Bihan and Chopard really messed that up, didn't they?"

The attorney placed her hand on his shoulder. He shot her a smug grin and leaned back in his chair.

"What part of this can you prove? Nothing, I'm afraid."

"Michel Barnais must have been furious. You murdered his mother."

The grin on his face faded, anger flashing in his eyes. But he wouldn't let her bait him into a hasty response.

"I have no idea what you're talking about," he spat.

"We're handing the case over to the prosecuting judge. They'll determine if and when charges will be brought against you." Sandrine turned off the microphone.

"De Chezac?" Lianne Roche's mouth twisted in disdain. There was apparently one point where they were in agreement. "It's unlikely we'll be summoned here again," she said to Albert Chauvin. "The man won't start his first case in his new job with such flimsy accusations."

"That's up to him," Sandrine replied tersely. She forced her hands onto the table, resisting the urge to clench them in frustration. The woman was right. De Chezac would bury the case. The man wouldn't touch anything that wasn't rock solid.

The lawyer stood up and gestured for her client to follow.

"I assume we can both leave the police station now."

"Of course. We know where to find Monsieur Chauvin."

At the door, the attorney paused and turned to Sandrine.

"As you know, I also represent Monsieur Barnais. If you wish to question him, please contact me first. I'm sure we can find a suitable time in the near future." Without waiting for a response, she left the room.

Sandrine remained seated until the door clicked shut behind them.

"What a jerk," Dubois said earnestly.

"Not nearly as bad as the woman." As soon as she was able to resume her training, she had quite a lot to vent. She already felt sorry for the punching bag. *Who knows when I'll be able to walk properly again.*

"That fishing trip story was a lie."

Sandrine turned to Dubois. "That much is clear, but what are you getting at?"

"Did you see that guy's shoes? Nobody goes sailing in black leather shoes. They'd be ruined quickly if they got wet."

"The white blotches," she said, whistling softly. She had noticed them but hadn't given them much thought.

"Saltwater. He must've been at sea recently. They got wet and then dried. Salt is tough to get out."

"That means he must've accompanied Michel Barnais. I pegged him as someone who sits behind his desk like a spider, pulling the strings."

"When there's enough money at stake, even the most cautious comes out of the woodwork."

"Do you know anyone from the police in Guernsey?"

"I do. I'll call them right away. Maybe someone saw our friend on board the *Émeraude*."

"Thank you. That was very observant of you."

"It's my job." Still, he beamed. Her praise seemed important to him.

Adel stood by the window, looking down at the street. "You let that guy go?"

"What was I supposed to do? We can't prove he committed any crime. Mere suspicion isn't enough."

"At least Chopard will be behind bars soon. Maybe we can get him to talk."

"Doubtful. He'll keep his mouth shut and lay all the blame on Le Bihan. Your old girlfriend will make sure Chauvin stays free."

"Lianne isn't my ..."

"It's alright. Any good news?" Sandrine settled into her desk chair. The faux leather creaked, and the backrest gave a slight bounce. She cast a longing glance towards Inès Boni's office, where the espresso machine was, but the office manager was nowhere to be seen.

"The Coast Guardsman was spot on. Michel Barnais has been smuggling people across the Channel and dropping them off in Devon or Cornwall."

"How do you know?"

"The cell phone. Marie managed to crack the pin. Several numbers were in the call log. One of them is linked to a line in Casablanca. My old stomping ground."

"I thought you were from Beziers?"

Adel glanced at her for a moment, then nodded.

"That's where I was born, but my family is originally from Morocco."

"How does that help us?"

"I figured it wouldn't hurt, so I called, claiming I'd found the phone."

"They believed you?"

"Why not? I sound trustworthy."

"You do."

"The owner's name is Mehdi Faras. According to his cousin, he called from the UK yesterday. But he didn't specify from where exactly or chose not to disclose it."

"Good job. Michel Barnais has some explaining to do."

"There's more. Faras attacked a truck driver who found him in the back of his vehicle and threw him out. He also tried to make a crossing in a boat that the coastguard intercepted."

"So, someone desperate to get to the UK. I don't know what they expect. Lousy weather, and the food is an acquired taste. They aren't exactly welcoming to outsiders these days either, if they ever were."

"Apparently, he has relatives living near Manchester. Inès

has requested investigative assistance. Faras could be a key witness against Michel Barnais and Albert Chauvin."

"We'll see. What does he stand to gain testifying against them? He'd only be cutting off a smuggling route for other migrants and be seen as a traitor. I wouldn't expect too much."

"I also spoke with Commandant Renouf. He believes there's enough evidence to request a search warrant for Michel Barnais' apartment from Judge Bonnard."

"She'll grant it. I have no doubt about that." Unlike de Chezac, she believed the judge wouldn't show any favouritism to local well-known individuals.

"He thinks so, too. Anyway, he wanted to know if you're interested in being there."

The man was keeping up his end of their cooperation agreement, which she appreciated.

"Of course. I'll head over there right away."

She stood up and stretched. The pain from the bruise was subsiding.

"You can't be serious?" Adel looked at her in disbelief. "Driving in your condition is out of the question."

"How else am I supposed to get there? In a patrol car?"

"I'll drive you, of course!"

"Alright, you can drop me at the car park or the shuttle bus station," she conceded. She wasn't in the mood for a long discussion. She'd probably return in a patrol car anyway. A bit of rest in the passenger seat wouldn't hurt.

The phone rang, and Adel picked it up. It was Commissaire Matisse, who wanted to speak to Sandrine.

To her surprise, she found de Chezac in her superior's office again. Soon, he'd be bringing his own chair. Matisse gestured at her to come in; Sandrine took a seat at the conference table.

"You were injured this morning?" Matisse sounded

genuinely concerned, but she didn't need another person insisting on getting her medical attention.

"It's not a big deal."

"Then we can begin," the prosecuting judge decided, the last person from whom she'd ever have expected or even accepted sympathy.

"As I see it, the investigation didn't yield anything concrete. A car theft and hit-and-run with a fatality."

"Michel Barnais smuggled refugees to the UK on his boat. They were already on board by Sunday. He wanted to prevent his mother from boarding the yacht and discovering them. That's why he called Albert Chauvin. His people were supposed to involve Camille in an accident, but things went south."

"But what part of that can we prove? Nothing. A few calls that the involved parties can easily explain. There's no credibility." He closed the folder he had been flipping through and dropped it on the table. "I'm closing the investigation. Le Bihan and Chopard will be charged with car theft and hit-and-run resulting in death. Chopard additionally for assaulting a policewoman." He looked at Sandrine. "Unless he beats us to it and files a complaint against you for assault."

"I wouldn't put it past his lawyer," Sandrine agreed.

"Be that as it may, Renard Dubois can handle that. Surely a more suitable job can be found for the head of the department."

"The death of Camille Barnais and that of Père Martin are related ..." she began, but the prosecuting judge interrupted her.

"The case is now in the hands of our colleagues from Normandy. It's none of our business. Madame le Juge Bonnard will be able to maintain order in her domain. In any case, we're out."

De Chezac seemed to seize any reason not to collaborate with the prosecuting judge from Avranches. The woman had set boundaries for him, something he resented.

"Commandant Renouf has a search warrant for Michel Barnais' apartment and asked me to be present. We might find something supporting our investigations into human smuggling." It wasn't strictly the truth but was close enough.

"And when is this search supposed to take place?" Judge de Chezac looked at her with surprised curiosity.

"I should head over soon."

"Perfect. Do it as a sign of goodwill for future collaborations. Our Norman colleagues should have no reason to complain," he said, much to her astonishment.

From the corner of her eye, she noticed the commissaire's raised eyebrows. Both expected more resistance from de Chezac. Why would the man entertain this if he wanted to bury the case?

"And tomorrow, you're taking the day off," de Chezac continued. "That's an order. I don't want to see you here at the precinct. Rest up, and come back when you feel fit again. Dubois and Azarou are perfectly capable of handling the paperwork."

She looked to Matisse, who had the final say on the duty rosters in his precinct, but he seemed to have no objections. The two men were probably right; she should take a day off, but the feeling of having been sidelined gnawed at her. "I better be on my way then," she said, taking her leave and exiting the office.

She met Commandant Renouf and several uniformed officers at the Barnais family's apartment building.

"I'm sorry I'm a bit late."

"Not at all. We've just entered the apartment."

In the two high back chairs sat Auguste and Blanche Barnais.

"Hello, Sandrine," the woman greeted her. "I already

informed your colleague that Michel isn't home. But he doesn't seem to believe me."

Judge Amélie Bonnard entered the room at that moment. Clearly she, too, didn't want to miss the search.

"We need to inspect your brother's room. Whether he's present or not doesn't matter." So, she had caught the tail end of Blanche's conversation with the authorities.

"Is this about the investigation into my mother's accident?" Blanche directed the question at Sandrine, not at the prosecuting judge overseeing the search. Judge Bonnard gave her a nod.

"It's about your boat. Michel was smuggling people illegally into the UK. That's why he wanted to keep your mother from boarding the *Émeraude* to fetch her belongings. The people were already on board, therefore his intentions would have been exposed. Camille would have put a stop to it instantly."

"Michel a smuggler? I don't believe it," Blanche responded, though not sounding entirely convinced. She was probably all too familiar with her brother's criminal past. Auguste sat silently in his chair, gazing out of the window, as if the search didn't concern him.

"We have clear evidence."

"As I said, I haven't seen him since breakfast."

"Do you know where he might be?"

"He doesn't make a habit of sharing his personal life with me." She didn't sound like she regretted that fact.

"And you, Monsieur Barnais, can you tell us anything about your son's whereabouts?" Judge Amélie Bonnard asked. Without taking his eyes off the window, he shook his head slightly. They wouldn't get anything out of him. He would protect his heir at any cost, Sandrine presumed.

"Leave my father alone; he's been through enough these past few days," Blanche told the prosecuting judge.

"Of course. If Michel contacts you, please let him know we'd like to speak with him."

"I will. Though I can't recall the last time he called me."

Commandant Renouf stepped into the doorway, signalling for Sandrine to follow. As she left, she noticed that the corner of the rug wasn't raised any more. "A new carpet?" she asked Blanche.

"We have several identical ones in the house. Antique heirlooms. People tripped over the other one frequently, so Michel replaced it. It was about time."

"Understandable."

She remembered how Michel had tripped over it and lost his temper. It seemed he was already behaving as if he was the master of the house. And the rest of the family silently accepted it.

Michel's room was coolly and practically furnished, more like a hotel room, devoid of any personal touch. Only a bottle of Cognac and a used glass on the shelf, as well as a basket half-filled with dirty laundry, testified to someone regularly staying there. A few decorative items, probably from Camille, stood out of place in the room, and the picture of the sunset behind Le Mont hung slightly askew on the wall. Michel Barnais' home was clearly not in Le Mont-Saint-Michel. Sandrine decided she would call Adel and task him with finding out where the man truly resided.

"All clean," one of the officers reported. "Except for the laptop, there's nothing of significance here."

"Let's see what we can find on it then." The prosecuting judge sat down at the antique desk, which seemed so out of place for Michel Barnais, and turned on the laptop. To Sandrine's surprise, it booted up without asking for a password.

There's a first time for everything. She had never encountered a criminal who didn't use password protection.

With a speed that Sandrine hadn't expected from the woman, she navigated through the files.

"This is the last file that Michel Barnais opened." She looked back at Sandrine, who stood behind her. "Curious?"

"If I weren't, I would be in the wrong profession."

"It's a video file." Amélie Bonnard highlighted it and pressed the enter key. A video began to play shortly after.

"What on earth is this twisted stuff?" Renouf leaned forward. Flickering flames, animations of devils and tormented souls played across the screen. Human screams and music, which made the hair on Sandrine's neck stand on end, echoed from the speakers. The prosecuting judge turned the volume down.

"It's a documentary on the ten circles of hell. Or at least a segment from it." Blanche Barnais stood in the doorway, observing. "It was recently broadcast on Arte."

"Your brother watches Arte?" Renouf couldn't hide his surprise.

"Not likely." Blanche stepped into the room. "The recording is mine."

"Yours?" Judge Amélie turned in her chair to look up at the woman. "An ... unusual taste."

"Not really, at least not for a historian. Last year, I organised an event at the monastery. The subject was Dante Alighieri's *Divine Comedy*. We enhanced certain passages with corresponding video sequences projected onto the walls. This one pertained to the antechamber of Hell and its nine circles. It had quite the dramatic effect. The audience loved it."

"How could your brother have accessed the recording, and what did he want with it?" Sandrine found it hard to believe that Michel Barnais had any interest in culture.

"My room is never locked. The videos are on an external

drive without a password. He could've copied them at any time," Blanche replied. "But what he wanted with it ...?" She shrugged. "I doubt he's ever read Alighieri. Who knows if he's even heard of him."

"We need to take the laptop." Judge Bonnard closed the lid and handed it to one of the uniformed officers.

"If you're authorised, I can't stop you."

"We are." Amélie Bonnard stood up. "If your brother contacts you, please let him know we need to speak with him," she emphasised once more.

"I'll relay the message if I see him."

The judge said her goodbyes and exited the room, Renouf and the officers following. Only Blanche and Sandrine remained.

"What happens now?" Michel's sister asked.

"It's incontrovertible that he used the boat to smuggle people into the UK. He'll have to face trial for that."

Blanche went to the window and looked out. The sun shone on the roofs of the houses below, illuminating the yellow lichen on the slate tiles. From this vantage, the town seemed deserted. On the vast expanse of the bay, only a few hikers moved, and the closely packed houses obscured the view of the crowds in Grande Rue.

"What does he have to do with our mother's death?" Sandrine didn't miss the slight quiver in her voice. Unsurprisingly, the past few days must have taken a toll on her.

"Michel got involved with some very unsavoury characters who didn't want their operation exposed. They probably intended to cause a minor accident to dissuade Camille from boarding the *Émeraude*. They surely didn't mean to kill her. But under the influence of drugs, she must have panicked."

"Somebody must have warned them that she was heading to the boat."

Sandrine stayed silent. The answer was obvious.

"Father was so relieved when he found his way back to the Auberge," said Blanche softly. "But Michel has torn the family apart. Mother was Father's pillar. He fought against his cancer for her. Now, he no longer has a reason to live. Michel's taken them both from him." She turned to Sandrine. "Do you think he's also behind the death of Père Martin?"

"I can't say. He was on the boat when the priest died."

"That's what he claims, at least."

"Do you have doubts?"

"Perhaps he ordered one of his associates to do the job, just like with Mother."

"That's possible, but we have no evidence to support that." The phone records for Michel Barnais hadn't arrived yet. They would shed light on whom he had spoken to. A call to Albert Chauvin wouldn't surprise her much.

"Thank you for your help." Blanche turned and hugged her tightly.

"Ouch!"

Blanche instantly released her grip and took a step back. She looked at Sandrine in surprise, noticing her gingerly touching her ribs.

"It's nothing serious. Just a bruise. One of your brother's friends wasn't too pleased about being arrested."

"Let me see. Bruises can be tricky."

"It's really not necessary."

"No arguments."

"Alright then." Sandrine lifted her T-shirt slightly. The spot where Chopard had hit her was turning shades of blue and yellow.

"Come with me." Blanche turned and headed for the door. Adjusting her T-shirt, Sandrine followed her into an adjacent room. Blanche opened a drawer and retrieved a small jar.

"This will help. It's the Barnais' family remedy. We practically grew up on this. With the steep stairs here, it's easy to get a bruise."

"Thank you." Sandrine took the small jar and tucked it into the back pocket of her jeans. "I do have one more request."

"If I can help, sure."

"Could I get a copy of the video? The judge took the laptop, and I'd like to watch the film again."

"Of course. Come to my room."

Blanche booted up her computer, fetched an external hard drive from a drawer, and plugged it in. Moments later, she handed Sandrine a USB drive.

"It has two different connectors and should fit into your phone."

"Thank you."

"You can't possibly drive in your condition. That bruise must be incredibly painful."

"I'll have someone pick me up."

"Nonsense. You're staying here."

"That's very kind of you, but ..."

"One of our guests cancelled, so we have a vacant room. You'll sleep at the Auberge. No arguments." Her voice had the assertive tone of a schoolteacher who wouldn't tolerate any nonsense; Sandrine eventually nodded in agreement. *I should take a day off anyway. Might as well stay here and explore the island.*

"Thank you. I'll pay for the night, of course."

Blanche waved it off. "The cancellation came in way too late. The room's already paid for."

"Thank you."

"We always welcome friends here." The woman glanced at the clock. "But now I need to go. I have a meeting with Charlotte at the monastery."

Sandrine said farewell and headed to the Auberge. Some rest would do her good.

Sandrine sat with her feet propped up on the windowsill, comfortably settled in an upholstered chair in front of the open window. Her trousers, socks, and shoulder holster were laid out on the wide bed, covered by a red and white patterned bedspread, while her weapon was securely stored in the room safe. The ointment warmed her bruise, alleviating the pain, but it had a terrible smell. *I won't be going out today.* The idea of dining alone in a crowded restaurant wasn't enticing enough to dress up again. She would spend the rest of the evening enjoying the view from her window and ordering a small snack to her room.

From the third floor of the Auberge, she watched the shuttle buses stopping at the end of the bridge, disgorging new day-trippers. By now, the tide of tourists had shifted. More people were leaving Le Mont-Saint-Michel than arriving. Most paused to photograph the place and the monastery. Those who were staying overnight pulled their rolling suitcases behind them, making a beeline for the town gate.

The sun was already low on the horizon, and a breeze billowed the curtains printed with colourful diamonds. The fresh scent of the sea wafted in. Sandrine pondered what had ever drawn her to life in Paris. The thought of returning to the bustling city seemed utterly absurd at that moment.

She reached for her phone resting in her lap and played the video again. It was a short clip, no more than two or three minutes. What could someone like Michel Barnais want with it? The idea of seeing him at a reading of Dante Alighieri's *Divine Comedy* was beyond Sandrine's imagination. Perhaps it wasn't meant for his personal enjoyment but to serve as a message to someone else. Maybe a warning to the priest about where he'd end up if he broke the seal of confession? Did Père Martin fear hell? Most likely. She put the phone back in her lap and grabbed the coffee mug that sat on the dresser beside her. By now, it had gone cold, but that was nothing new in her line of work.

Creating and sending that video sequence seemed too intricate and decidedly too cerebral for a criminal like Michel Barnais. She pegged him more as someone who'd resort to threats or use brute force. His brother's black eye was testament to that. Even if he hadn't admitted where it came from, it was pretty obvious. It was Blanche and Charlotte, the family members versed in church history, literature, and the necessary tech skills, who were capable of devising and crafting such a message. But how did it end up in Michel's possession?

It's not your case anymore, you've been pulled off it, she reminded herself. She despised leaving the investigation to prosecuting judge Amélie Bonnard and Commandant Renouf. Not that she doubted their ability to solve the case, but because she'd always had a hard time walking away from a puzzle she hadn't solved yet. *That's probably why I have issues with de Chezac.*

A knock on the door jolted her from her thoughts. Aside from Blanche and the receptionist, no one knew she was staying the night at the Auberge Saint-Michel, and she hadn't ordered room service yet.

"Yes?" she called, draping the jacket that was hanging over a chair onto her bare legs.

Léon peeked in.

"Hello. Ready for a visitor or am I intruding?"

"Not at all, what a pleasant surprise. Come in."

He stepped inside and looked around. "Nice place. Are you on vacation or are you now investigating the Auberge?"

"More of a forced vacation. De Chezac sent me off for an extended weekend. How did you know I was here?"

"As I was paying my condolences to the family, Blanche mentioned you were staying here. She also told me some thug did quite a number on you." His gaze roamed over her face and then down to her legs peeking out beneath the jacket as if searching for evident injuries.

"It's alright. He managed to land one on my ribs before he lost his balance and went overboard." She conveniently left out the part about the guy ending up in the hospital with a broken shin.

"Is it still hurting a lot?" He knelt beside her on the floor, putting them on the same eye level, which Sandrine appreciated. She never particularly enjoyed having to look up at someone.

"Childbirth is worse."

His eyebrows shot up momentarily before a smile tugged at his lips.

"Did you hide a child from me, otherwise how would you know that?"

"My mother told me. Every time I got into mischief."

He audibly inhaled through his nose.

"Did Blanche give you some of her miracle salve?"

"Yes. It has quite a pungent smell, but…"

"It works," he finished her sentence. "I've had the pleasure of using it a few times myself."

"You might want to keep your distance then."

He ran his fingers through her hair. "It would take more than a little thing like that to keep me away."

Sandrine wrapped her arm around his neck, pulling him closer. She tilted her head and gently pressed her lips against his. His lips were soft and warm. Léon reciprocated the kiss, and what started as tender turned passionate. He lifted her up and carried her to the large bed.

She let out a brief groan as he moved her.

"I'm sorry."

"It's not too bad. I'm just glad you're here."

"That's more than I was expecting." He chuckled and carefully placed her on the edge of the bed. Sandrine reclined, pulling him towards her.

Léon's phone buzzed. The mattress shifted as he leaned over the edge, searching for it in the pocket of his trousers that lay on the floor. He answered the call and climbed out of the bed. Sandrine opened her eyes. It must be late; outside was cloaked in darkness, save for the beams from floodlights mounted on the city wall, directing their glow towards the bridge.

She bunched up her pillow, sliding it beneath her head; she watched Léon who had taken a seat in front of the window. In the dim light seeping in from outside, she could only vaguely make out the contours of his face. Today, she had gone further than she'd intended, but it had felt right. No regrets. But also no expectations. *Neither of us is looking for a lifelong partner.*

"Did something happen?" she asked.

He covered the microphone and turned to her. "Just go back to sleep, everything's fine."

And who calls you in the middle of the night? She held back, swallowing her query. *We aren't a couple. It's none of my business who he speaks with.*

"Since you're already awake, what's the name of that lawyer you can't stand?"

"Lianne Roche, why do you ask?"

"It's for an acquaintance."

Sandrine sat up in bed, suspicion dawning. Her police instincts were now fully alert. If he needed someone like Lianne Roche, he was surely in trouble. *What is he hiding from me? Is his business not as clean as he always claims?*

He finished his call and placed his phone on the bedside table. For a moment, he gazed pensively out of the window, seemingly processing the information he'd received. It didn't look like a call from a buddy wanting to reschedule a barbecue. *But if he plans to keep it from me, that's his prerogative.*

He got up and returned to bed.

"Do you have to leave?"

He shook his head slightly.

"Definitely not. I've been looking forward to this night for too long to leave over a trivial matter. Plus, the breakfast at Saint-Michel is top-notch." He turned to face her. "We've never had breakfast together."

There was an occasion when he had stayed at her place in Cancale, albeit he only slept on the couch. But Adel had fetched her for a crime scene before he could discover just how empty her fridge usually was. *Any hotel breakfast is better than what I offer at my home.*

"I'm not trying to pry. It's none of my business," she remarked, lying on her side. The salve had worked wonders; the pain had subsided, though lying on it wasn't such a good idea.

"I'm sorry. There was a minor issue at the club, and Simone wanted to update me. There's no need to rush back. She's handling things perfectly. The woman is a control freak and likes to have a plan for every situation, hence the lawyer inquiry. I really doubt we'll need her."

"She double-crossed her last client. Stay away from her; she's pure poison."

On the other hand, she was currently doing an outstanding job keeping Albert Chauvin out of prison.

"As I said, Simone is overly cautious."

"Are you sure you don't need to go back?" she asked, though she'd regret it if he did.

"Absolutely certain."

She moved closer to him. "I'm glad." She hadn't felt the warmth of another person in a long time; she realised how much she had missed it.

Michel Barnais

"Not again," murmured Sandrine, pulling a pillow over her head.

"This time, it's your phone."

"I'm off today," she growled toward the phone, but it was relentless and continued to ring. Before she risked waking the neighbours, she grabbed it.

"Hello?"

"Capitaine Perrot?"

It was Commandant Renouf. When a police officer calls, any hopes of sleeping in are dashed.

"What can I do for you?"

"I hear you're staying at the Auberge Saint-Michel."

"That's correct." *How does he know that?* "Today's my day off."

In truth, she had been practically forced to take leave, and not by Commissaire Matisse, but by Monsieur Le Juge Antoine de Chezac who had closed the case. But she didn't feel like spelling that out for Renouf. The irritation still lingered deep within her.

"A very pleasant hotel indeed," she said, gently pushing

Léon's hand off her thigh when he tried to touch her. Now wasn't the time for that.

"We've found Michel Barnais."

"That's excellent news. I assume you don't particularly need me for the interrogation. The evidence is more than enough to put him behind bars for a long time."

"This might be more complicated than you think. In fact, I'm standing next to his body right now."

She kicked off the covers and leaped out of bed.

"Where?"

"Five minutes from your room, if you take your time. At the foot of the abbey church, near the parking lot. Forensics from Cherbourg are on their way."

"Thank you for letting me know." Tucking the phone between her ear and shoulder, she began to put on her trousers. *Where are those darn socks?*

"I didn't know if you'd still be interested in visiting the crime scene."

"Of course, I'm already on my way." She paused. "Why wouldn't I be interested?"

"Word has it that Monsieur le Juge de Chezac pulled you off Le Mont-Saint-Michel and is about to close the Camille Barnais file."

She pursed her lips. The man was clearly well-informed about the goings-on at the Saint-Malo police station. Had de Chezac already called Amélie Bonnard to hand over the entire case to her? Most likely.

"I'm on my way," said Sandrine.

"I didn't intend to ruin your day, but I thought it might be of interest to you."

"Don't worry, it is."

"It's just before six now. Your partner can keep on sleeping. By the time you return, the breakfast room at Saint-Michel will be open. Perhaps it will still turn out to be a pleasant day after all."

She resisted the urge to ask how he knew about Léon's presence. It was a relatively small town and not much remained a secret here.

She darted into the bathroom, squeezed a dollop of toothpaste onto the tip of her index finger, and brushed her teeth as best as one could without a toothbrush. She quickly got dressed and retrieved her service weapon from the room safe.

"Expecting trouble?" Léon asked with a hint of mockery.

"I don't think so. But the staff have the master code for the safes. I'd like to avoid one of them fooling around with it and accidentally injuring themselves or someone else."

"What's going on?"

"My case just took a dramatic turn."

"I thought there wasn't a case anymore and you're essentially on forced leave to recuperate. Your boss is quite generous. I assumed he didn't like you."

She hesitated for a moment.

"He doesn't. It did surprise me that he wanted me there during the search of Michel Barnais' apartment."

"And a day off. A Friday, so a long weekend. It seems to me he values your commitment to the precinct."

"Nonsense. He'd rather have me out on the street writing parking tickets. He probably just wanted me out of his sight for a while. I have no clue what he's up to." *But it has something to do with Poutin, that much I did catch.* She pulled on her light jacket, which somewhat concealed her weapon.

"What are you getting at?" she asked Léon.

He stood up and gently pulled her close.

"I'm just concerned about you."

She wriggled free from his embrace. Nothing killed her mood for romance and sensuality quite like a dead body waiting for her.

"If you think I need a man to protect me, you're barking up the wrong tree."

He held up his hands in a placating gesture.

"Far from it. I know what you did to the guy on the boat." He kissed her cheek in farewell. "Would you even accept help if you needed it?"

"Of course," she said. "You can fill up my plate at the buffet later." She touched her ribs and grinned. "After all, I'm injured."

"I'll wait at the breakfast room until you're back. Call and place your order."

"It won't take long," she said. More out of habit than conviction.

Sandrine closed the door behind her and descended the creaking staircase. Exiting through a side door of the Auberge, she found herself on the narrow path leading to the parking lots where Commandant Renouf awaited her.

Clouds obscured the rising sun, and a fresh wind blew in from the sea. Sandrine rubbed her upper arms as a shiver ran through her. When she was tired, she felt the cold more acutely. The thought of her warm bed made her regret her decision to inspect the body.

A police officer stood at the end of the path behind a police tape, demarcating the crime scene and intent on keeping onlookers at bay. She waved to Commandant Renouf, and he signalled the uniformed officer to let her through. The man lifted the tape, and she ducked under it.

Renouf tossed his cigarette butt on the ground and stamped it out. He must've been pulled out of bed significantly earlier than she had. From Avranches, it would take him at least half an hour to get to Le Mont-Saint-Michel.

"I'm genuinely sorry for disturbing you, but I assumed you'd want to see the crime scene, even if it's no longer your case," he apologised once more.

The human trafficking from Saint-Malo was definitely her case. Michel Barnais' death was likely connected to it. Therefore, it was her concern. The fact that the man had been killed in Normandy didn't particularly interest her. Perhaps Renouf and Bonnard saw it differently, but she wouldn't be pushed aside. Not by de Chezac anyway. *I wonder if Matisse will have my back?*

"That's absolutely right. Depending on what happened here, we may need to re-evaluate events," she said.

Renouf left the "we" in Sandrine's statement unaddressed. The question of jurisdiction would keep de Chezac and Bonnard busy for a while. With some luck, they would be closer to the culprit by then.

"Doctor Deschamps is already here, examining the body."

"From Cherbourg?"

"He happened to be in Avranches when the call came in."

"What happened here?"

"At first glance, it appears Michel Barnais fell from the abbey, hit the rocks, and rolled almost to the base of the slope. He ended up resting among the bushes."

She tilted her head back, looking up. Above them, the monastery towered majestically into the sky.

"He must have fallen from there." Renouf pointed to a wall behind which they could see the upper body of a person. The commandant probably had one of his people temporarily secure the potential crime scene.

Sandrine estimated that the wall was 120 to 130 feet above the location where the body was found. Surviving such a fall would be miraculous. The thought of having to deliver the news of another death to the family weighed heavily on her heart. She could leave it to Renouf or Bonnard, but that would be cowardly. *But first, I need to be sure about what happened here.*

"Suicide, accident, or foul play?"

"I'd rather wait for the doctor's findings and the forensic results before I make any assumptions."

"You've been in our line of work for a long time. Usually, an initial gut feeling would be quite accurate," Sandrine pressed the seasoned officer.

"His human trafficking ring was exposed, and we were hot on his heels. The man was practically already behind bars. But I can't imagine Michel Barnais being the type to kill himself over this. What's the worst that could have happened to him? A few months, maybe a year in prison? Someone like him would serve that easily." He pulled a pack of Gauloises from the breast pocket of his uniform shirt and took one out, placing it between his lips without lighting it. "An accident seems just as unlikely. What could have happened? Was he cheerfully balancing on the wall, slipped, and fell? Highly doubtful."

"Someone gave him a push." Just like Père Martin. However, her theory that Michel was behind the priest's death was currently collapsing like a house of cards, and she couldn't pull another suspect, who benefited from the deaths of both men, out of thin air.

"I'd like to take a look at the body."

"Come with me." He rummaged in his jacket pocket for a pair of disposable gloves and handed them to her.

At the end of the rocky cliff, among some medium-height bushes, lay the body, which someone had covered with a dark blue tarpaulin. A bit farther, and it would have slid under a blue container where the renovation debris was collected. Doctor Deschamps held a Dictaphone close to his mouth, speaking into it. He greeted her with a curt nod. Sandrine knelt beside the body, looking up at the forensic doctor.

"May I?" she asked, reaching for one end of the tarp.

"It's not a pretty sight."

She took that as permission and lifted the cloth where she expected the man's head to be.

"Oh," she murmured.

She barely recognised Michel Barnais. His face was covered with scratches and abrasions that made identification based on appearance difficult. His clothing was relatively clean but torn in several places. She tried to recall if these were the same clothes he had worn during their last meeting. When she had seen him, he had always been carefully dressed and surely wouldn't wear the same outfit for two days in a row without changing. *That gives us a hint as to how long he's been dead.*

"Evidently he fell from the abbey grounds. There's blood on the rocks. I assume it's his, but I'll have to confirm that."

"Your theory?" Sandrine asked the doctor.

"I'm a medical professional and I work with evidence, not theories. That's your domain."

"There must be something you can share to help us."

"Wait for the autopsy. The man is a priority and will be on my table later today."

"I'm sorry."

"It's okay, it's just most detectives think we medical professionals can simply conjure answers out of thin air."

"You're right about that. I'm a pest. Doctor Hervé usually tries to avoid me or offers his initial assessment just to get rid of me."

"'That's what Christophe does?" blurted out Deschamps. "I mean, Doctor Hervé."

"I can be very persistent. I inherited it from my mother, or so my father says. But yes, he gives me some details just for a little peace and quiet. I wish I was as often right in my investigations as he is. Of course, I understand that you want to be thorough."

The doctor knelt beside her.

"I don't want to pre-empt the autopsy, but you can assume that he was already dead when he fell down the slope. I can give you the exact time after the examination, but I'd estimate it to be yesterday evening."

"Too little blood," she agreed with him.

He pointed to a rough cut across the left cheek. A sharp-edged stone had torn the flesh, but the wound hadn't bled, implying his heart wasn't beating when he fell. Someone must have hoisted the body over the wall and given it a powerful shove.

"Thank you, this gives us more insight."

"But one wound stands out." Using the tip of his ballpoint pen, he circled a spot on the back of the deceased's head. "Blood flowed here. You can see the matted hair and the blood-soaked shirt collar."

"So, that's the blow that killed him?"

"I can't say for certain. But if I were an impatient detective trying to pit two doctors against each other, I'd assume so."

Out of the corner of her eye, she noticed a hint of a smile on the man's lips. He seemed pleased to have seen through her ruse, even if it was a little late. She had the information she needed to proceed with her investigation.

"Thank you. I'll now await the results of your autopsy."

"The report will be sent to Commandant Renouf. I'm sure he'll let you take a look." He couldn't resist that jab, but Sandrine didn't hold it against him; he had been of great help. She let go of the cloth and stood up.

"Are there signs of a struggle up there?" she asked Renouf.

"We don't know yet. The body was only recently discovered, and we're waiting for the forensic team. I don't want to accidentally trample over any potential evidence." He glanced at his watch. "They should be here within the hour. I don't want to stumble around a possible crime scene. Nothing's moving from up there. Until then, access to the monastery for tourists is closed."

Sandrine stepped back to get a better overview of the location where the body was found. "Who discovered him?"

"The truck driver who came to pick up the container and drive it to the landfill. That was around five o'clock. He arrived early, hoping to be on his way home before the shuttle buses start, but Michel Barnais had once again parked his car in a way that the truck couldn't load the roll-off waste container. The man decided to take a breakfast break, during which he found the body."

"I guess that ruined his appetite." Looking at Michel Barnais' battered face, her own anticipation for breakfast waned, even though she had seen her share of gruesome corpses.

She looked at the blue waste container. A familiar piece of fabric peeked over the back edge. So this was where Michel had dumped the old carpet he had been so upset about. The container was meant for construction waste, not household trash. Maybe he wanted to annoy Charlotte, who was supervising the renovation work. But his time as the master of the Barnais household hadn't lasted very long.

"Do you think he was killed up there?" she asked Renouf.

"Hard to say. The construction workers finish up around five o'clock and the last tourists leave the abbey about an hour later. After that, it's pretty quiet in the monastery, and not many people pass by here either. He must have been thrown down either in the evening or after midnight."

"He didn't strike me as someone interested in historical buildings. What could he have wanted up there?"

"He might have had a rendezvous. Once the abbey gates are closed, it's a secluded spot. Maybe there was an argument and now he's down here. Or someone wanted to silence him," Renouf speculated.

"Chauvin? I could imagine him getting rid of someone who knew too much, just to avoid prison and save his business.

Without Michel Barnais' testimony, we wouldn't have anything on him."

"Then we should speak with the man."

"Don't worry, we will. But I'm afraid we won't get much out of him. The guy owns junk yards and dismantles cars. Surely he'd choose another place to dispose of a body. At least, that's what I'd do if I had access to multiple car crushers." She remembered the premises well. Finding a body there would be like searching for the proverbial needle in a haystack, especially if the deceased was inside a car now shaped like a metal cube.

"You're suggesting we should cross him off our list of suspects?" Renouf sounded disappointed. He'd surely have preferred a Breton killer over a Norman.

"For Michel Barnais' death: yes." She stepped closer to the man. "It had to be someone from here. An island inhabitant. Definitely a perpetrator who knows Le Mont intimately."

"How do you figure that?" He sounded dismissive. The theory of a murderer from the criminal underworld was clearly more appealing to him than accusing one of Le Mont-Saint-Michel's residents.

"First, the obvious: the murder took place here. How do you get a body to such a crowded place? The only way in or out is the bridge. And the place is teeming with tourists late into the night. It's an extremely high-risk venture, one I wouldn't take unless there were compelling reasons. But I don't see any."

Renouf nodded reluctantly. "It could be someone who blended in with the tourists, or a visitor of Michel Barnais."

"And this visitor had access to the abbey outside of its open hours? That seems unlikely to me." Sandrine was convinced: the murder had been committed by someone close to the victim.

"Michel might have taken him there to discuss his shady dealings in private."

"Can you think of a more appropriate place? Besides, Michel Barnais had only recently returned to the Auberge. We need to find out if he had a key to any of the entrances to the abbey. I'd be surprised though."

He looked around, then the policeman moved closer to her.

"You're aware of what you're suggesting?"

"I'm afraid so." At least two members of the Barnais family had access to the abbey at any given time. Charlotte supervised the renovations. Blanche organised events and assisted in the souvenir shop. Auguste's life was closely tied to the abbey; she would be very surprised if he, too, didn't know how to access the monastery at night.

"Do you seriously believe the murderer is from the family? Do you think the twins could have struck down a strong man like Michel?"

"Women can kill too. It wouldn't be the first time."

"What motives could the siblings possibly have to kill their brother? No, I think that's far-fetched."

"You might be right," Sandrine replied evasively. There were plenty of reasons, and since confronting the family with Michel's illegal activities involving the boat the day before, there were even more. But she pushed the thought aside.

Renouf looked at her in disbelief. "You're fibbing."

"Excuse me?"

"You don't believe for a second that I might be right." He pulled out a lighter from his pocket, lit his cigarette, and took a deep drag. "I see what Matisse sees in you. You won't rest until you've turned over every stone multiple times, without any doubts or reservations. I'm not surprised that some careerists despise you."

"Who might that be?" It was a rhetorical question; of course, de Chezac despised her.

"There's no need for both of us to stand around here waiting for the forensic team. Why don't you go to the Auberge?" He glanced at his watch. "The breakfast room is open. I'm sure the breakfast is excellent, and your friend will miss your company. I'll join you once we're allowed into the crime scene."

"You know everything that goes on on this island, don't you?"

"Much, but sadly not nearly all. Otherwise, we wouldn't be wondering who has this man's blood on their hands."

The allure of hot coffee, fresh baguettes, a generous serving of scrambled eggs, and Léon's company was too tempting to pass up, so she bid him goodbye. She hadn't planned on Léon staying the night; it had just happened in the spur of the moment. *No idea what he expects from me or how things will proceed between us.* Sandrine feared she might let his hopes down; she wasn't one for a serious relationship.

"One more thing."

She had already walked a few steps away but stopped and looked back at the policeman.

"Madame Bonnard will arrive soon. It would be appropriate if she breaks the news to the family. She will be leading the investigation."

"Of course. She's in charge of this area." Delivering death notices wasn't something she was eager to do, but she resolved to be present. That was the least she could do for the family.

Sandrine was descending the stairs to the Auberge when her phone rang. It was an unknown number. "Hello?"

"Capitaine Perrot, it's me, Inès."

"Are you at the office?"

"No, not yet. There's a lot going on in the police station."

Sandrine glanced at the clock. It was a quarter to eight; Inès should have reported for duty by now.

"Moreover, I'm not at the precinct, but in the car in front of Intermarché. This is my personal phone."

She stopped and leaned her hip against the railing. Something must have happened if Inès had left her office to call her. Something someone didn't want her to know.

"So, spill the beans. What disaster took place during my absence?"

The young woman hesitated, exhaled audibly before continuing. "Technically, I shouldn't even be talking to you," she began.

"Who would forbid you to do so?"

"De Chezac."

Now it was her turn to take a deep breath. Was the Paris incident repeating itself here? Was he trying to pin something on her to push her out of the police force?

"Last night, I was with friends at Équinoxe when the police suddenly stormed in. De Chezac had a raid carried out. With the personnel from the National Gendarmerie. From ours, I only saw Poutin."

She remembered the call Léon had received but had downplayed.

"I wasn't aware he intended to do that." And even if she was, she wouldn't have warned Léon. Why should she, after all? He had assured her his dealings were clean.

"Exactly. No one here knew, not even Matisse. He's livid but can't do anything about it."

"The club is within city limits. The National Gendarmerie has no jurisdiction."

"Technically, the raid was carried out by us, that's why Poutin was present. The Gendarmerie was just called in for backup."

"Well, if there was any evidence that warranted such an action, it's within a prosecuting judge's authority to issue a search warrant and order the raid."

"I wanted to warn you because ..." Inès paused for a moment, probably considering how much she should reveal. "After all, you and Léon Martinau are friends."

"We are, but I have nothing to do with the club. In fact, I'm hardly ever there."

"There's a rumour going around that they found drugs in his office. Enough to charge him and strip him of his license," she blurted out. "I'm sorry."

"You don't have to be. Thank you for giving me a heads-up. Now I know what's waiting for me on Monday." *Policewomen who are friends with drug dealers don't have a future in law enforcement. Merde, merde, merde,* she cursed internally, kicking the side wall with each word. *I bet de Chezac is already on the phone, gossiping with Deborah Binet. I can already picture the front page of the local news.*

"I wish I had better news."

Inès sounded so dejected that Sandrine tried to console her. "We'll get it all cleared up. I'm glad you trusted me enough to inform me. I'm sure Léon has nothing to do with drugs."

"It's the least I could do."

"Where's Adel?" She changed the subject. She would think more about the raid and its implications, but only after she had calmed down.

"At Doctor Hervé's. After that, he planned to drive straight to you. He doesn't know what's happened yet."

"I'll fill him in as soon as he gets here."

"Take care." Inès hung up. She probably wanted to be back at her office before she was missed.

Sandrine sat down on one of the staircase steps. The sun wasn't high enough yet to warm her, and the coldness of the stone seeped through the fabric of her trousers. *Did I misjudge him so badly? Léon was certainly no saint, but a dealer?* She refused to believe that.

"Let's see what he has to say about it," she murmured, pulling herself up using the railing. She typed a message on her phone, letting him know he could expect her for breakfast.

. . .

Léon was waiting at a table in the breakfast room. The heap of scrambled eggs, sausages, and bacon piled up on his plate didn't suggest a guilty conscience or any concern about the raid. *Maybe he's tougher than I could ever imagine. After all, I haven't known him for that long.*

"I didn't expect you to show up at all." He stood up, attempting to kiss her cheek, but she turned away.

"Did I do something wrong?" Léon glanced at his plate. "Did I start too early or is it too unhealthy?"

"Neither." She poured herself some coffee and sat down next to him.

"So, what is it then? Maybe I can make it up to you." He pulled out his most innocent boyish grin.

"You lied to me," she said; it came out harsher than intended.

"About the phone call?"

"Didn't you think I'd be interested in a police raid on the club of the man I spent the night with?"

"I wanted to keep you out of it. It's enough that I'm in trouble with your colleagues. Why would I drag you into it?"

"There's a small but significant difference between dragging someone into something and informing them. Plus, I've been involved for some time now. Everyone at the precinct knows we're friends."

He pushed the plate aside. His appetite seemed to have vanished.

"It was a wonderful evening. Our first night together, and I didn't want to ruin it." His shoulders slumped and his smile faded. "Seems I ruined it anyway," he said, remorsefully.

"You could say that. My office manager called me this morning. From her car, because she was making sure no one was eavesdropping. I was caught off guard. A warning would have been very helpful."

He looked at her in astonishment. "We frequently get visits from the police. They check IDs looking for minors or for weed, then usually leave without finding anything. There's never been any trouble. The Équinoxe is clean."

"Why did you ask about Lianne Roche?"

"Simone, my deputy, was concerned. Things went really weird this time. Instead of searching people in the club, they ransacked the office and asked some strange questions. Especially the new prosecuting judge. Such a high-ranking official has never been present at a raid before."

"What questions?" Her alarm bells started ringing. Maybe it wasn't about Léon and the club. Perhaps his friendship with her was the reason for the police visit. De Chezac might have targeted him to hurt her.

"About drugs in the club and ..." He paused and reached for her hand, but she pulled it away. "And about you."

"What could Simone tell them about me? We've only met once or twice and never talked."

"They were extremely curious about our relationship, how often you're at the club, whether you're giving me any insider information, and all that kind of nonsense."

"So the prosecuting judge suspects I'm a criminal?" She was left breathless. Even for de Chezac, these were outrageous accusations.

"They suspect that of me as well, but they're mistaken," said Léon, which wasn't particularly reassuring to her.

"It's not just a suspicion," she replied without thinking.

"What do you mean?"

She leaned forward and spoke more softly.

"They found drugs in your office, apparently a significant amount."

"Nonsense. I don't have any drugs."

"They're being held as evidence at the precinct, from what I've heard."

"Simone didn't mention anything about that." He reclined in

his chair and crossed his arms over his chest. "Totally impossible," he murmured in disbelief.

"Look at me," she demanded and waited until she could look into his eyes. "Are you dealing at the Équinoxe?"

"No, absolutely not." The lines on his forehead deepened, but he maintained eye contact with her. Her intuition told her he didn't know about the drugs. *Would you accept that if you hadn't slept with him?* She pondered for a moment, then nodded to herself. *Yes, I would.*

"I believe you, but you know what the accusation means for you?"

"That someone is trying to set me up. No idea who."

"Maybe Simone. Or doesn't she know the combination to your safe?"

Two children noisily stormed into the breakfast room, and Léon fell silent. The little ones raced to the buffet and snagged sausages with their fingers from the warming dishes before their parents appeared and claimed a table by the window.

"Yes, she obviously knows it, but I trust her. She's been working with me for years, and there's never been an issue," Léon responded.

"Someone planted the drugs in your place. We need to find out who."

"Recently, I've banned a few people I suspected of dealing. Nothing else out of the ordinary has happened."

"Do you think they could have smuggled the stuff into your office?"

"I always lock up. Other than Simone and me, no one has access to the keys."

She took a sip of her coffee. It was hot and strong, aiding her thought process.

"Maybe you aren't the actual target," she ventured cautiously.

"Then who is? I'll be the one facing a drug possession charge. This could easily cost me the license for the Équinoxe."

Or a few years in prison.

"It might be revenge against me, and you're just a means to an end."

"Do you suspect someone specific?"

"A few come to mind. The first one that strikes me is Albert Chauvin. He blames me for the loss of his lucrative smuggling operation." In fact, her initial thought had been of de Chezac, but the idea that a prosecuting judge would use a friend of hers to hurt her, just because she'd wounded his vanity, seemed too absurd; she quickly dismissed it.

"Chauvin." Léon sounded contemplative. "The guy's certainly capable of it, even if I haven't seen him in the club for months. He's never been involved with drugs before, but he knows a ton of people who are. Getting hold of some stuff to plant on me would likely be no trouble for him."

"I was planning to pay him a visit anyway. We'll see what I can find out."

"I wouldn't want to be in his shoes."

"You should be more concerned about saving your own skin."

"I won't let our first breakfast together be ruined, not by a scoundrel like Chauvin." Léon pulled his plate closer, grabbed a sausage, and took a bite. "Very tasty."

His mood was contagious, and she headed to the buffet. A hearty breakfast would help her power through the day. At least the bruise isn't hurting any more. *I should stock up on that smelly miracle remedy.*

Léon said his goodbyes and set off for Saint-Malo. The staff began clearing the buffet, and Sandrine poured herself one last coffee. By now, the forensic technicians must have arrived. She glanced at her phone. No message from Renouf. Her fingers drummed on the black-lacquered wooden table. Patience was never one of her strong suits.

Just then, Charlotte entered the breakfast room. Judging by the dusty stains on her dark jeans, she seemed to have come straight from a construction site. She scanned the room, and as soon as she spotted Sandrine at her table, she marched over. She dispensed with pleasantries.

"Michel is dead?"

She pulled a chair over and sat down, never taking her eyes off Sandrine. It was pointless to deny it, so she nodded.

"Who told you?" *Maybe Renouf or Bonnard.* "I promised to wait with the news until the judge arrived. She's responsible for the district and the investigations."

"What happened to him?" Charlotte ignored Sandrine's question. "Gustave found him this morning, at the foot of the cliff, near the parking lots. The police must know what happened."

"Gustave?"

"The truck driver. He comes once a week to pick up the rubble."

"How did he recognise Michel?" She herself had hardly recognised the man, the facial injuries were so severe.

Charlotte picked up one of the unused knives, twirling it between her fingers, likely as a way to calm herself.

"My brother wasn't exactly the kind of person who was considerate of others. Gustave had to fetch him several times because his car was blocking the waste container. Michel usually took his time and they often argued loudly." She hesitated. "You don't think Gustave had anything to do with his death, do you?"

"If everyone's already aware, I can tell you the little I know."

A server approached, placing an unsolicited espresso in front of Charlotte.

"My condolences," she murmured, then retreated. News travelled at lightning speed in this small town.

"There's absolutely no indication that the driver was in any way involved in your brother's death. He must have died yesterday evening or at some point during the night."

"I never would have expected that of him."

"What?"

"That he would take his own life, of course."

"Michel fell from the abbey to his death. That's all we know at the moment. Whether it was suicide or an accident is still under investigation." She couldn't reveal more without compromising the case. In particular, she left out the details about the fatal injury on the back of his head and the fact that a violent crime was also being considered.

"What was he doing in the monastery?" Charlotte looked perplexed. "He never cared for the abbey. And after visiting hours, there are only a handful of nuns and monks left up there."

"We're not sure but we're very curious about how he gained access. The visitor's entrance was locked."

"There are smaller entrances. Anyone familiar with the place can get in at any time. Or they might never have left the abbey in the first place. Hiding when they close in the evening is literally child's play. We've seen it happen many times. Especially by people wanting to take photos undisturbed. But Michel? What could have brought him to the abbey? Was he planning to end his life, or was it another one of his shady deals?"

"That's the question. We need to find out what he was after. Maybe he had a meeting, but with whom?"

"I have no idea. Since he left on that boat trip, I've only seen him briefly. I'll ask Blanche, maybe she overheard something. She was in the house all day yesterday." She stressed the words 'boat trip' distinctly. She seemed to strongly disapprove of her brother's criminal activities. Perhaps she also resented the fact he'd dragged the family into it, jeopardising their good reputation. And even their lives.

"I assume Madame le Juge Bonnard is already at the scene." She avoided using the word 'crime scene.' "She'll want to speak with the family later."

"We want to speak with her too," Charlotte replied. Her composure remained intact, revealing not her grief, but her revulsion towards the death of her brother. "We need some answers at last."

Sandrine reached for Charlotte's hand.

"You and your family have my deepest sympathy. I can hardly imagine how hard it must be to cope with what has happened in the past few days. First, your mother, then Michel."

"Thank you. I know you genuinely mean that." She squeezed Sandrine's hand in return. "Father is taking it the hardest. To lose the two people he held dearest, our mother and his eldest son, in such senseless ways within days ..." Her voice trailed off. The restraint she'd displayed began to crumble, and her eyes welled up with tears.

"No one can easily brush aside such a tragedy. Take some time off."

"Blanche and I will stay in Le Mont-Saint-Michel for a while. She can work from anywhere, and I spend most of my day up in the abbey anyway. The rest of the time, we take care of Father. Jean is managing the inn; it's in good hands with him."

Unlike his brother.

"I meant time off from work."

Charlotte let go of her hand. "Just sitting around would drive me mad. The job distracts me a little." She picked up the delicate cup and stirred the espresso, which by now must have turned cold. She didn't seem to have any intention of drinking it. Her heart was probably racing enough without the caffeine.

"Camille made my father feel needed, and the return of his heir assured him that the Barnais family tradition would not die out. Now he's lost both in a violent manner within days. I fear his will to fight the cancer died with them." A tear trickled down her cheek. She wiped it away with a napkin. "I'm sorry." Charlotte was clearly not the type to cry in front of others. "I have to go. Blanche is waiting for me." She signalled the waitress over.

"Claire, could you please open the bar for Madame Perrot later?"

"Of course."

"You'll need a room for your discussion. The police station at the city gate is too small, and you'll hardly find a place to speak undisturbed. Not with all the tourists coming into town. If you're looking for us, we're all at home. You know the way."

They stood up, hesitated briefly, but then embraced. Sandrine gave Charlotte an encouraging squeeze.

"Thank you," the woman whispered in her ear before leaving the room.

At the exit of the Auberge, she encountered Adel, who looked around curiously. He nodded politely to the woman at the reception, then noticed Sandrine and approached her. Today, he had chosen a white polo shirt and sneakers to go with his beige cotton trousers. She hoped he wouldn't have to crawl through any dusty chambers in the abbey, but she couldn't help but smile at the thought.

"I see you're taking it easy," he greeted her.

"Given the circumstances."

"Finding your first body before breakfast can be hard to stomach."

He didn't mention the raid at Léon's or how it might affect her career. Since he knew about the corpse, it meant that he had already spoken to Inès. But he never pried into her personal affairs without being asked, something she deeply appreciated about him.

"What's the update on our case?" she asked.

"I thought we were off the case."

"At least until the end of this week."

"It's Friday already. Time's almost up."

"All the more reason to hustle."

Adel reluctantly pulled out his notebook. "Dr. Hervé already called you about finding drugs in Camille Barnais. According to Dubois, there's only a small market for the stuff in Saint-Malo. From what he's heard, Michel Barnais had a hand in it."

"So, we're thinking he sprayed it on the chocolate truffle."

"Not just that. It took a while, but we finally got Michel Barnais' phone records. Around the time his mother left here, he was on the phone with Albert Chauvin."

"And then Chauvin called Chopard," she surmised.

"We can't prove that. I can't access his phone records. De Chezac is stonewalling. He thinks the evidence is too flimsy."

"As much as I hate to admit it, he's right. We had to let the man go. Since Michel, his partner, is dead, it's unlikely we'll be able to pin anything on him. Any evidence the forensics team finds on the boat could be from that supposed fishing trip; we can't prove otherwise."

"Do you think he's behind Michel Barnais' death?"

"Renouf entertained the idea. He'd rather suspect a killer in Brittany than here in Le Mont-Saint-Michel."

"What about you?"

"Chauvin's not the type to get his hands dirty. Le Bihan is small fry, and Chopard, who I'd believe capable of murder, is out of commission. Even for someone like Chauvin, it's not easy to find someone he can trust quickly enough to take care of his problems."

Her phone buzzed. Renouf was waiting for her at the abbey entrance.

. . .

Tourists crowded the elongated staircase that ran alongside the towering monastery wall leading to the abbey's entrance, waiting to be admitted. Many grumbled about the delay, double-checking the entry times printed on their tickets. A man in shorts and a billowing T-shirt voiced his displeasure as Sandrine squeezed past him. At the entrance gate of the Châtelet, the fortified entrance to the monastery flanked by two tall towers, a uniformed police officer waved them over. Sandrine cast a wary glance at the portcullis, a heavy latticed iron gate which opens and closes vertically, hanging above her; she quickly stepped away from it.

"You need to head up to le Gouffre; Commandant Renouf is awaiting you there."

"Up where?" Adel inquired.

"The passage, of course. The Benedictines called it le Gouffre, the Abyss, due to the staircase leading into the abbey's interior being exceedingly steep."

"Odd name," the brigadier commented.

"You might change your mind once you've made it to the top," she replied. The officer in uniform grinned and waved them through. Disgruntled murmurs rose from the waiting crowd behind them, but Sandrine didn't glance back; her gaze was fixed on the daunting staircase ahead. It certainly lived up to its name, rising sharply ahead of them. Flanked by the towering buildings, it would remain in shadow until noon.

"I see," Adel muttered. "At least it's not too hot yet. The forecast predicted over eighty-six degrees."

"They're waiting for us." Sandrine led the way. Beyond the Abyss was a somewhat less steep, yet considerably longer staircase – the grand internal staircase – bordered by the foundations of the church and the abbot's residence, leading to an open space in front of the abbey church's western side. Commandant Renouf stood with the prosecuting judge, Madame le Juge Bonnard looking down over the parapet. Directly below them, nearly in a straight line, was where Gustave had discovered Michel's battered body.

Amélie Bonnard turned to face her. She didn't seem surprised to see Sandrine there. Renouf had likely already informed her of Sandrine's presence. She wondered if he had omitted the part about her boyfriend or embellished it as a light-hearted anecdote.

"I'm truly sorry to see that your vacation had to be interrupted," Madame le Juge said in greeting.

"May I introduce you to my assistant, Brigadier Chef Adel Azarou? He brought me the forensics report from the yacht and the forensic pathology report on the Camille Barnais case. Sadly, no findings that would advance our current investigation."

Madame le Juge Bonnard extended her hand in greeting to him; Renouf settled for a collegial nod.

"Antoine de Chezac informed me yesterday that he's closed the Camille Barnais case. Why are you still working on it?"

"Commissaire Matisse has given me until the end of the week to tie up a few loose ends. My assistant was kind enough to keep me updated so that I can prepare some paperwork for Monday."

"I've heard you were injured. I hope it's nothing serious." *She's spoken with Matisse. What might the two of them have been plotting?*

"Just an ordinary bruise, which barely hurts at all now."

"In your line of work, you must endure quite a bit. But I hear you're a tough nut to crack and excellent at pushing back."

Sandrine scrutinised the older woman. What was she alluding to: the blow she had taken from Chopard or the way she was treated by de Chezac?

"It's manageable," she replied evasively.

"And what did the forensic examination reveal?" Renouf,

having had enough of their small talk, redirected his attention to the case.

She nodded at Adel, and he summarised Doctor Hervé's report in a few sentences. Most of it he already knew from her. Except for the THC in Camille's blood, the doctor had not found any abnormalities.

"Drugs, then," Madame Bonnard mused. "Just like with Père Martin."

"Do you already have a report from Doctor Deschamps?" She wasn't particularly surprised at how quickly the examinations had been conducted. The forensic expert from Cherbourg didn't want to be outdone by his colleague.

"He sent it this morning."

"Synthetic THC as well?"

"Naturally his Breton counterpart called him and pointed it out, but nothing was found. However, a high dose of psilocybin was."

Sandrine noticed Adel's inquisitive look.

"Magic mushrooms," she clarified for him. "Not particularly common in this region."

"But easily obtainable," Renouf interjected.

"Now that we have this additional information, we can probably rule out an accident or suicide. He was a staunchly conservative Catholic priest, not a hippie," Madame le Juge Bonnard concluded. "Someone drugged him and drowned him."

"Michel Barnais was familiar with drugs and occasionally dealt with them. I suspect he was deeply involved in both cases," Renouf agreed.

"We can confirm that," said Adel. "He's come to the attention of the narcotics division multiple times. He definitely had access to synthetic THC. I'll follow up to see if he also dealt with magic mushrooms."

The commandant looked over at the two forensic technicians who were scanning the ground.

"Any evidence that can help us?" Sandrine asked.

"There are no signs of a struggle or footprints, which I would have found surprising on the gravelly ground anyway. Hundreds of tourists walk through here daily. This spot by the wall is a popular photo stop. On a clear day, you can see to the west all the way to Cancale and Pointe du Grouin, and to the east as far as Avranches."

"Bloodstains?" Bonnard inquired.

"According to Deschamps' assessment, the wound must have bled heavily. But no blood was found here. The man was killed elsewhere, transported here later then thrown over the wall."

Sandrine whistled in astonishment. That was unexpected. She looked back at the staircase they had ascended.

"Michel Barnais was a tall and rather robust man, weighing at least ninety kilos. Who would be capable of dragging such a behemoth up the outer staircase, the Gouffre, and then the grand inner staircase, only to throw him down from here? It doesn't make sense at first glance. It would have been much easier to leave him down there," Sandrine remarked.

Madame Bonnard furrowed her brow and looked questioningly at Renouf, but he merely shrugged. "Plus, there's the risk of being discovered."

"Maybe someone wanted it to look like a suicide?" Adel suggested.

"It's possible. But then that person would have had no knowledge of forensics. Deschamps ruled out suicide immediately." Sandrine walked to the wall and looked down. Light-coloured rocks jutted out above the sparse vegetation. The likelihood that the body would be stopped by any bushes or shrubs on the way down was low. The killer's intent wasn't to hide the deceased. The sea would have been a much better hiding place for that. They had found the priest's body through sheer dumb luck, whereas Michel Barnais' corpse could hardly have been placed more conspicuously.

Why would someone throw a body onto these rocks? To break a few bones? That's it!

She turned to the others. "Do you remember the body? The face looked quite battered."

"Yes," Renouf agreed. "He was barely recognisable. Do you think it wasn't Michel Barnais at all, but someone else dressed in his clothes?"

"Definitely not. But whoever threw him over the wall intended to badly mutilate him."

"To cover up another wound?" Renouf speculated. "Like the blow he received to the neck?"

"Exactly. His face, his entire head was smashed. This elaborate act aimed to conceal and obliterate the fatal injury."

"Deschamps wasn't fooled by that." Madame Bonnard straightened up; the woman seemed to grow a few centimetres taller with pride in her Norman forensic expert.

"The good doctor knows his craft," Sandrine affirmed. *Gaining a few points in her favour wouldn't hurt if I want to stay on this case.* "We should keep quiet about having seen through this ruse. It might make the perpetrator cocky," she suggested.

"Or the perpetrators. The murders of Père Martin and Michel Barnais are too different. Also, it would be exceedingly difficult for one person to bring the body up here."

Sandrine agreed with Amélie Bonnard. They couldn't rule out the possibility of dealing with multiple perpetrators.

"The stairs I've just come up; I definitely rule them out as a transport route," Adel said. "How else do you get a body into the abbey?"

"Through the ossuary," Renouf said. "The old monks' cemetery, the final resting place for human skeletal remains. Follow me. I'll show you. I should have thought of this sooner."

The commandant set off, motioning for one of the forensic technicians to accompany him. The path led them across the abbey, past the cloister, until they reached a smaller hall. Behind a column stood a bulky wheel, about ten to fifteen feet in diameter. The man stopped in front of it, patting the wood with an open hand.

"In the Middle Ages, the monks used these wheels to haul up the building materials for the monastery. Above the wall, a sled was connected to the wheel with a sturdy rope. It worked like a kind of giant crank. However, this one is just a replica and dates from the period after the Revolution. The abbey was then used as a prison, and in this manner, they brought up food supplies."

"Do you believe someone remembered it was here and used it to hoist up the body?"

"In theory, it's possible, but that," he pointed to an iron grate in front of the window through which the heavy rope ran, "makes it rather unlikely. Still, we have to examine everything here for clues."

"Isn't that a waste of time?" Judge Amélie Bonnard inquired.

"Here? Probably. But not over there."

He led them to another window, obscured by columns and a fence. They stood before a modern cargo hoist.

"This one is used by construction workers to haul their materials, the monks for their food, and the souvenir shop for their books and knick-knacks. A strong wire rope, to which the cargo basket is attached, leads downward," explained Renouf.

Sandrine leaned out the window. The steel cable ran down the steep side of the abbey and ended at a small station at the base of the hill. Also just a few steps away from the parking lots.

"The engine and controls are down there. The basket has a diameter of a little over one foot and is secured with a railing. The tricky part would be getting the body to the station unseen. The rest is child's play. You can lower the cargo basket and place the body inside. The railing would prevent it from falling out. Up here, you'd need a second person to receive the basket. The path to the platform isn't too far and is significantly less strenuous than the inner staircase. There's probably a wheelbarrow or something similar at the construction site that one could use."

"So there *were* at least two people involved in the act," said Madame Bonnard.

"Maybe not in the act itself, but certainly in the cover-up," Sandrine replied.

"And it must have been someone who can get hold of the key for the cargo hoist's controls. That significantly narrows down the number of suspects."

And it brings the twin sisters back into focus. Charlotte definitely has a key, and probably Blanche too, who organises events up here and sells her books in the souvenir shop.

"I've informed the family of our upcoming visit. Let's not keep them waiting any longer." Madame Bonnard turned to Sandrine. "Would you like to join us?"

"I'd be happy to. However, they already know that Michel is dead."

"I expected as much. In such a small village, nothing can be kept secret for very long."

On the way back, Adel approached her.

"I'd rather skip this visit. These people are stressed enough without us showing up in a large law enforcement contingent. It would better if I head to Saint-Malo. Let's see if anything has happened at the police station." He still didn't mention the raid, which loomed over them like the proverbial elephant in the room. The brigadier was obviously waiting for her to bring it up on her own. Sandrine slowed her pace, and they fell a few feet behind Bonnard and Renouf.

"You know about the raid at Équinoxe?"

"I only heard about it this morning. I never thought that Poutin could hide anything from his colleagues. Especially not from Dubois. They've been working together for decades and are close friends outside of work."

"De Chezac believes he can get to me through Léon. That seems to be worth a lot to him."

"I'm still surprised he'd stoop so low as to do something like that."

"Our new prosecuting judge can be very charming and persuasive."

"They say Poutin found drugs in the club. A significant amount."

"Léon insists that Équinoxe is clean. He has no idea where they came from; maybe someone planted them. Just like Brigadier Poutin, someone who actually wants to harm me. Being friends with a criminal doesn't exactly cast me in a good light. Even if they can't pin anything on me, my career is over."

Adel stopped and looked at her with a serious expression.

"Do you believe him?"

Sandrine pondered for a moment before replying.

"I do. Léon is such a bad liar, I would have noticed."

"I trust your judgment of people. Besides, we've been in several interrogations together; you have an excellent instinct for when a suspect is lying."

"Thank you." *But I don't sleep with them.*

"Do you have someone in mind?"

"I haven't been in Saint-Malo long enough to have many enemies yet. Right now, apart from de Chezac only Albert Chauvin comes to mind. He's the only one who might want to associate me with drug trafficking to tarnish my reputation. It could help him in case I have to testify against him in court."

"Do you think he's cunning enough for that? I seriously doubt it."

"If he isn't, his lawyer certainly is."

He remained silent until they reached the bottom of the stairs.

"Lianne is definitely capable of something like that. In the case of the dead woman on the customs path, you put her in quite a difficult situation. She hates losing, and she's exceptionally vengeful and vindictive. She could easily be behind it."

"Could you look into it?" Sandrine asked. "Discreetly?"

"Of course."

"It would only make Léon's situation worse if I got involved in the investigation."

"No worries. Inès assured me she's got your back. The rest of the team does, too."

"That's so heartening. But I don't want any of you risking your careers because of me. Understood?"

"*Oui, mon capitaine,*" Azarou teased. Sandrine didn't notice his playful grin.

"It won't take too long with the Barnais family. Could you wait and drive me to Cancale?"

"Of course. But don't you have a room here for the weekend? Relax a bit. We'll take care of Lianne and Chauvin in the meantime."

"Well, a toothbrush and fresh underwear aren't something to sneeze at. The overnight stay was unexpected. I might come back to the island this afternoon. Some distance from the precinct will do me good. Right now, I'd probably struggle to bear Poutin's smug grin."

Blanche opened the door for them and led them into the living room. Charlotte sat at the table. Jean stood by the window, leaning against the sill with his arms crossed, casting a reluctant glance their way. It was evident that he didn't want any of them in the house.

Madame le Juge Bonnard and Renouf expressed their condolences, while Sandrine observed Michel's siblings. Blanche appeared paler than usual and spoke in a quiet, tear-strained voice. Jean remained tight-lipped, but his animosity radiated freely throughout the room.

"Will your father be joining us?" Judge Amélie Bonnard inquired.

Charlotte waved dismissively.

"Our doctor left shortly before you arrived. Father has taken his pain medication. He's asleep now. These events have taken a toll on him. He needs time to process these tragedies. Probably more time than he has left." And her gaze clearly conveyed the idea that he shouldn't waste any of it with the police.

Sandrine nodded sympathetically. Cancer was ending Auguste's life in the foreseeable future. It was likely they wouldn't get another chance to question him. She understood the siblings' desire to protect their father from further distress. She vividly recalled the sparkle in his eyes when Michel had entered the room. The joy of his son's return had been short-lived and ended tragically. She couldn't imagine how they could possibly console the man.

"So, I presume you've already heard about what happened to your brother?" the prosecuting judge asked.

"People say he threw himself off the rocky walls beneath the abbey church." Blanche's voice trembled as she fidgeted with the damp handkerchief in her hand.

"He was found this morning at the base of the walls, next to the parking lot. It seems he fell from the west side of the abbey. We can assure you that he didn't suffer." Amélie Bonnard's voice was calm, almost business-like. Delivering bad news was part of her routine.

"That's a real pity," Jean interjected sharply.

"What are you implying?"

"Michel was responsible for our mother's death. He beat me to it; otherwise, I would've thrown him off the cliff myself."

"What makes you think he was involved in your mother's death?"

"His cronies rammed the car Mother was driving, ensuring she wouldn't board that damned boat and expose his criminal operations. He informed them that she was on her way and which car she was driving. Those thugs were waiting for her. Mother had no chance of escape, and he's to blame for that." As he spoke, his fists clenched. His knuckles were scraped, and scabs were beginning to form.

Perhaps some of the injuries on Michel's face came from there.

Madame le Juge Bonnard seemed to be following the same line of thought.

"Your hands look like you've been in a recent fight. May I ask with whom?"

"That was some time ago. This is from that," he said, pointing with his index finger to his eye, which had turned a bluish-yellow hue. "Sandrine can confirm that I already had this black eye during our last meeting. She asked me about it."

"That's true. I remember that well," she affirmed. *But your hands were unscathed then. Those scrapes are fresh. Who did you fight with? Probably Michel again. DNA traces on his brother's face wouldn't be conclusive. They lived together; there could've been a transfer at any time.*

"Do you both think that's what happened with your mother?" Amélie Bonnard turned to the twins. Blanche avoided her gaze, looking down at the table, while Charlotte maintained eye contact.

"The evidence suggests as much, or are you telling me the police aren't investigating in that direction?" Charlotte looked towards Sandrine.

"We can't prove it, but it does seem likely. Now that he's dead, he can't confess," Sandrine replied.

Jean snorted loudly.

"Of course it was him. It's obvious. Ever since he came back here, he's been deceiving our father. Michel knew he was going to die soon and showed up for one reason only: to secure his inheritance. He didn't care about the Auberge. As soon as he could, he would have sold it."

"Well, that won't be happening now, will it?" Judge Bonnard remarked.

Sandrine felt relieved that the prosecuting judge raised this, sparing her from having to.

"Thankfully not. The Auberge has been in the family for many generations."

"And who will inherit it now?" Silence followed her question for a moment. Then Jean cleared his throat.

"I am next in line for inheritance. The Saint-Michel always stays in the hands of the eldest son. The rest is part of the family foundation, which the three of us manage equally."

"Well, you've truly earned it. After all, you've been working ... running the hotel for several years now. It must have annoyed you when your brother showed up, was welcomed with open arms and on top of that, you would lose the inheritance that was rightfully yours to Michel."

Jean froze for the length of a deep breath.

"Yes. I loathed him. He took advantage of a nonsensical family tradition that should have been abolished a long time ago. If you're implying I killed him, you're mistaken. Beat Michel up: gladly. Kill him: no. I wouldn't commit murder, even for the Auberge."

"And what happened to your hands? You've recently been in a fight, not a few days ago as you'd like us to believe." The judge's patience was wearing thin, her voice sharpening with every word.

"A bicycle accident." He raised his hands to inspect the scraped knuckles. "It's healing already."

"Enough with your lies. I'm sorry, but we have no choice but to take you in for questioning," Judge Amélie Bonnard said.

Jean Barnais pushed away from the wall and advanced on

her. Renouf immediately stepped between them, causing Jean to halt.

"It's alright, Commandant. I don't believe there will be any issue here. Or am I mistaken, Monsieur Barnais?" The judge wasn't intimidated by Jean's antagonistic demeanour.

This woman is as tough as the rock upon which the Auberge is built. Sandrine re-evaluated her initial impression of the older lady.

"We are mourning our mother, and you are insinuating that my brother had a hand in Michel's death. That's outrageous." Charlotte confronted Madame le Juge Amélie Bonnard.

"Your brother Jean was about to lose the Auberge. You know exactly what that meant to him. His black eye," she cast him a swift glance, "bears witness to the violence between the brothers, and his scraped knuckles match all too well with the injuries on the deceased's face."

"You really believe he could have killed his own brother? That's absurd," Charlotte retorted.

"Didn't he just admit how much he loathed his brother and wished him dead? Pushing him off the wall is just the next logical step. Maybe it was just a tragic accident. It's our job to find out."

"There's nothing for you to uncover. Michel threw himself from the abbey because he was responsible for our mother's death." She stood up and positioned herself beside her brother.

"Leave it, Charlotte. I'll go willingly. Everything will be all right. I had nothing whatsoever to do with his death." He looked at her. "They won't be able to prove otherwise."

Sandrine watched him closely. His last sentence caught her attention. *It's about proof. Is his sister covering for him?* Her gaze shifted to Blanche, who was still crumpling a handkerchief between her fingers. *All the siblings are involved.* The thought hit her as forcefully as Chopard's blow. The three had concocted the plan together and would provide alibis for each other. Blanche avoided her gaze. She was the weakest link, Sandrine was convinced of that. If she could get anyone to confess, it would be her.

What would I have done in her place? Michel was responsible for their mother's death. I probably wouldn't have let him go unpunished either. And yet, she couldn't imagine the twins as murderers. What might have transpired here?

Judge Amélie Bonnard gestured towards the cane that Auguste had left standing next to his chair. The pointed handle matched the wound that had killed Michel. The forensics expert approached.

"Are you allowed to do that?" Charlotte blocked his way.

"Of course we are," Renouf responded in his militaristic tone.

Charlotte stepped aside, and the man sprayed the cane with Luminol. After a moment, he shook his head. Had Michel been bludgeoned with it, there would have been traces of blood on the wood. It wasn't the murder weapon. The technician wiped off the liquid and returned the cane to its place. Amélie Bonnard didn't show her disappointment. It would have been too easy. They would never leave the murder weapon just lying around.

One of the officers led Jean Barnais away. At least he refrained from handcuffing him.

"What will happen to him?" Blanche asked, her voice shaky. "Are you going to lock him up?"

"The injuries will be examined, and his statement taken. I don't see any reason why we'd need to keep him in custody after that."

"Unless they can find traces of his brother's DNA on his hands," Sandrine observed as she watched Charlotte.

"You'd all better go now. We need to take care of our father." Charlotte's steely gaze also landed on Sandrine. "All of you."

The message was clear. She was no longer welcome in the

family home. It was nothing she hadn't encountered in other investigations. She took her leave and exited the house following Commandant Renouf.

"What do you believe?" Judge Bonnard inquired.

"The strained relationship between the brothers, the recent fight, and the freshly scraped knuckles all make him look guilty," she began.

"But?"

"There's no 'but'."

"So, you believe he's the perpetrator?" Commandant Renouf sounded surprised. Had he expected a disagreement?

"I may have a soft spot for the siblings, but it doesn't mean I approach this case with bias. The evidence points to Jean. I would've taken him in for questioning, too."

"So there is a 'but'," Madame le Juge pressed on.

"I fear we might not get much from him. If all three siblings were involved in the act, they would've coordinated their stories and will stick to them. Proving anything against them might be hard, perhaps impossible," Sandrine admitted.

"They had the chance to collaborate then corroborate each other's stories," Judge Bonnard murmured. "But we'll see. Most people end up contradicting themselves. It's all just a matter of time."

Sandrine remained sceptical. The three weren't ordinary criminals, but rather, very intelligent individuals. Siblings who loved and protected one another. Familial ties were often incredibly strong.

"Do you think Jean and his sisters might also be involved in Père Martin's death?" Sandrine inquired.

"That's a complex case," Renouf responded evasively. "I see no motive for either him or his sisters to harm the man."

"That leaves Michel Barnais as a likely perpetrator."

"We'll probably never know for sure, but here's what I suspect: Michel Barnais eliminated a witness."

"That sounds plausible." She glanced at her watch. Adel was waiting at the car. "I need to be on my way."

"What are your plans now?" Renouf asked.

She gently ran her hand over her bruised rib. The pain was almost gone.

"Just as I thought. A good night's sleep was all I needed to get back on my feet." She disregarded the hint of a smile on the man's face, who knew with whom she had spent the night. "The accident in Saint-Malo will be wrapped up by my colleagues. The two deaths in Le Mont-Saint-Michel are outside my jurisdiction, and after today, I'll be officially reassigned by Commissaire Matisse. The only case left on my desk is the human trafficking operation that Michel Barnais set up with Albert Chauvin. That investigation will keep me busy."

"It was a pleasure working with you," Amélie Bonnard said, extending her hand, which Sandrine grasped.

"The feeling is mutual," Sandrine replied.

"Not bad for a Parisienne," Renouf remarked.

"Someday, you'll have to call me a Malouine."

"By then, I'll be long retired." He chuckled and shook her hand as well.

"Keep me posted," Sandrine requested.

"Of course," Madame le Juge Bonnard affirmed with a nod. "You've been a great help in this case. I'll mention your contributions to the Prefect."

She bid the two of them farewell then sent Adel a message to meet her at the large parking lot on the mainland.

Sandrine paused on the bridge, glancing back. The rock stood defiantly in the bay. Two people had died here within a matter of days, but in the history of the Abbey Mount, it would probably only be a brief footnote. Over the centuries, the island had endured many attacks, sieges and lootings. Yet, the fate of the

Barnais family still preoccupied her. Some pieces didn't quite fit together. But that was now Bonnard and Renouf's job.

She boarded the Passeur, the shuttle meant to take her to the parking lot, without looking back.

The shuttle bus pulled into the parking lot station. Sandrine stayed seated, allowing the flurry of tourists, who stood in the aisle or hurriedly gathered their belongings to disembark, to go ahead of her. She exited last, through the back door. A long queue had already formed in front of the bus – more people than the Passeur could accommodate. Even though it was the off-season, thousands would flood the city today. The souvenir shops and restaurants could look forward to a booming business.

After the bus' air-conditioned coolness, the air outside felt suffocating. It was noon, and the sun blazed down mercilessly from a cloudless sky. Today, no sea breeze offered relief from the heat. Adel waited for her in the shade of a tree.

"I'll chauffeur you home," he said, jangling the car keys. "A long, relaxing weekend awaits."

"That sounds tempting."

Unlike her old 2CV, his service car boasted a working air conditioner, which she greatly appreciated on a day like today.

"Let's get going." Adel turned the ignition key and shifted gears.

"We need to run a few errands first," Sandrine interjected. Adel looked at her as if he'd seen right through her, disapproving of her intent.

"After all, we have a case to solve," she said, defensively.

"Which case are you referring to? Dubois took over Camille Barnais' accident, and Michel Barnais' criminal dealings can wait till Monday, given his death. The case is closed."

He pointed in the direction of the abbey.

"Like it or not, you're out of these investigations. Both deaths occurred in Normandy; the victims were from around there. Renouf is competent enough to wrap things up."

"Of course, you're right, as usual," she said. "No need to lecture. We'll take care of a tiny matter, then you'll take me home where I'll spend the weekend lying on the couch or the garden lounger. If I'm lucky, Rosalie might invite me for dinner."

"You want to spend the weekend on the sofa? I'll believe that when I see it with my own eyes," he murmured. "So, where are we headed?"

"A quick visit to our friend Chauvin, then straight to a well-deserved weekend."

"If we must," he conceded with resignation. "I also have a surprise for you." He pulled out several photos from his pocket and handed them to her.

Sandrine smiled. Today was her lucky day.

"I think we'll need a patrol car at the junk yard."

He already had his phone out and called the precinct.

Adel stopped in front of the rusty container office with its barred windows. A crane was loading wrecked cars from a tow truck, stacking them atop one another for later dismantling. Dust hung over the lot. The first clouds appeared in the sky, and Sandrine hoped for a good downpour. Otherwise, she'd be wandering around the garden with a watering can, dousing bushes on Rosalie's orders, the names of which she didn't even know.

The secretary came out and paused next to the door.

"The boss is inside."

She drew a cigarette from the pack and lit it in one fluid motion. *I wouldn't want to see the state of her lungs.*

"It won't take long."

Adel opened the door and allowed Sandrine to enter before

him. He clearly wasn't expecting any danger from Albert Chauvin; otherwise, he would have entered the makeshift office first.

He was right. The burly man looked as if he had been run over by one of his own trucks. His lower lip was split in several places, and his cheeks were scratched. He surely couldn't see out of his left eye. He held a damp cloth to it, which he removed as they entered the office.

"Ah, the police," he snapped at them, grimacing in pain. *That lip must really hurt.*

"What's the matter? Here to harass law-abiding citizens again?" He reached for the phone. "Maybe I should call my lawyer, that'll put you in your place."

"Sure, go ahead." Sandrine pulled up a chair and sat down across from Albert Chauvin. "You've looked better. Not by much, but still."

"Had I known you were going to pester me again, I would have spruced up a bit beforehand."

"Your natural beauty is enough for me."

Chauvin tossed his phone onto a stack of papers. The call to Lianne Roche was nothing more than a bluff. The visit was already proving worthwhile. The source of the scratches on Jean Barnais' hands was now clear. Renouf was mistakenly hoping for DNA traces linking him to his brother's death. Jean must have found out who was behind the accident. *But from where? A police report or from his brother?*

"Spit it out, what do you want this time? I'm busy."

Adel pulled out one of the photos from his jacket pocket and placed it in front of the guy.

"A nice snapshot the English police sent us: the *Émeraude*, Michel Barnais – and the man at the yacht's stern looks a lot like you." Adel's fingertip tapped on the photo.

"That's not me."

"I can clearly see it's you, but we can leave that to the prosecuting judge to decide. I'm sure he'll want to have a chat with you," Adel said. "You might want to call Lianne Roche now after all. Though I suspect she'll have to work some magic to get you out of this mess." He glanced at Sandrine. "She is a witch, after all. Maybe there's still hope for Albert."

"I occasionally go out fishing with Michel, that's not illegal, is it?" Chauvin snapped back.

"Not at all. But smuggling people into the UK certainly is."

"That could have been taken at any time." His gaze shifted from Adel to Sandrine.

"They're from the harbourmaster on Guernsey. He takes photos of his harbour every morning. It's his hobby. The date and time are noted. That will suffice as evidence for the judge."

Sandrine moved closer to the desk. "We've got you on the hook, and we're not letting you off." She tapped on the cellphone. "The brigadier is right, now would be the perfect time to call your lawyer."

"She'll get me out of this, don't worry," he blustered, likely trying to suppress his growing doubts.

"Moreover, we're linking you to the death of Camille Barnais. You commissioned the attack."

"You can't prove that."

"The only question is, who will talk first: Le Bihan or Chopard?" She looked up to Adel, who stood beside her. "What do you think?"

"My bet would be on Le Bihan. He wouldn't admit more than a car theft to protect his boss," Adel replied.

Sandrine turned her attention back to Chauvin.

"I'm curious about one thing. Who did this to you?"

"No idea, the guy was wearing a ski mask. He came from behind and caught me off guard; otherwise, I would've taken him down."

She nodded, despite her doubts about his story. Albert Chauvin was loud and portrayed himself aggressively, but she didn't give him much of a chance against Jean Barnais.

"What did he want from you?"

"None of your business. Probably mistook me for his mother-in-law."

We won't get a word out of him. But she had expected as much; the man was too hardened.

"We're taking you to the station."

Albert Chauvin stood up. He wouldn't resist; he had been arrested too many times before. His best chance of getting off lightly was to stay silent and leave the talking to his lawyer.

What had the man confessed to Jean? That he had acted on his brother's orders? Likely. Albert Chauvin would place all the blame on Michel Barnais. Had that enraged Jean so much that he went back to Le Mont and killed his brother? It was a plausible scenario, but Sandrine didn't believe it. She could see him committing a crime of passion, but premeditated murder? No. She didn't think him capable of that.

Outside the office, the patrol car Adel had called for was parked. The police officers placed Albert Chauvin in the back seat and drove away.

"Will he be back today? I need a few signatures," the secretary remarked, tossing her cigarette butt on the ground and snuffing it out with the tip of her shoe.

"We'll see, but I wouldn't expect him back before Monday." What they could prove wasn't enough for pretrial detention, and there was neither risk of Chauvin tampering with evidence nor of his fleeing. The potential prison sentence was too short for that. Unless they could prove that he was behind the attack on Camille, which would be challenging without a statement from Michel Barnais.

"Well then, I'll get back to work." She squeezed past them and slammed the plastic door shut behind her.

. . .

"I'll handle the interrogation of that guy," Adel declared. "But first, I'll drop you off at home."

The excavator, loading metal scraps into a blue container with its claw arm, caught her attention. It reminded her of something she had missed.

"Damn! How could I have been so stupid?" she exclaimed suddenly.

"What's the matter?"

"I assumed that Michel was already playing the role of the head of the household. But that's nonsense."

"I don't follow," Adel admitted, but he looked at her with a knowing glance which meant there would be no early end to the day.

"Michel complained about the old carpet in front of me and threatened to get rid of it. On my next visit, both were gone – Michel and the carpet. I assumed he'd thrown it in the trash. Mainly to show Jean and the twins who's in charge in the family."

"Renouf's guys checked the trash bins, but they didn't find anything. Not in the Auberge either," said Adel.

"Such a large piece doesn't fit in a regular trash bin. It's not at all straightforward to get bulky items off Le Mont. If I'm not mistaken, I saw it. After his death, Michel still managed to foil his murderer's plan. How ironic."

"Renouf will be thrilled when you send him a message about where he can find that carpet." Adel continued his attempts to convince Sandrine that she wasn't working on the case anymore. Futile.

"I'm still part of the investigation until the evening. Matisse assured me of that."

"De Chezac also said you're off duty today to recuperate."

"A solid lead in a murder case is the best medicine for getting back on your feet. Can you think of anything better?"

"I could think of a few things," he countered. He must have realised that he couldn't dissuade her from going back. "Better if I come with you," he said, resigned to his fate. Their long weekend was off.

In the Abbey

Sandrine waved to the policewoman from the municipal police, and she lifted the barrier. Adel followed one of the Passeurs.
"We can't go any faster," he said.
"I'm not impatient."
"Then why do you keep tapping your feet on the floor?"
"If I'm right, the perpetrator won't be able to escape us."
"Or the women. Don't forget: the twins are the ones who could have most easily brought the body to the abbey. Both had access, and Charlotte even had a key to the freight elevator."
"Or just one of them." With a wheelbarrow from the construction site, even a single woman could have managed to transport the body once she was up there. Now, it depended on what they found.
Adel turned left before the city gate and moved at walking speed through the crowd streaming from one of the shuttle buses toward the city. To the police officers standing in front of their patrol cars, Sandrine flashed her police badge. The firefighter who had taken her to Tombelaine waved back. No one tried to stop them. It felt as though she already belonged to the

Le Mont-Saint-Michel crew. Likely something she would miss soon.

As soon as Adel parked at the end of the street, Sandrine jumped out of the car and ran the last few feet to the blue construction waste container. She pulled herself up by its rusty, dented side to look in.

"*Merde.*" She slapped the side of the container with her open hand, producing a hollow echo.

"What's the matter?"

"It's empty. Gustave must have picked it up today. Damn it. If only I had realised sooner."

"Don't go breaking our stuff," a passing construction worker shouted with a laugh.

"Can you tell me when the container was replaced?"

"Sure. It left about twenty minutes ago."

"Do you know where the construction waste is dumped?"

"There's nothing in it worth keeping." The man looked at Sandrine as if questioning her sanity. She quickly pulled out her police badge and showed it to him.

"The landfill is somewhere near Saint-Malo, but exactly where ... No clue. It's not my job."

"Thanks for your help," said Adel.

"You're welcome." He moved on, leaving the two standing by the container.

Sandrine gave the container's exterior a listless kick. It echoed dully and, most importantly, emptily.

"Easy there. You heard him, don't break anything." Adel chuckled softly and took out his phone. "We'll catch up to it. Twenty minutes isn't much."

"I hope so."

"Hello, Inès. Can you find out who collects the construction waste from Le Mont-Saint-Michel and where it's disposed? Send a patrol car there. The container must not be unloaded under any circumstances. This is extremely important." He listened for a moment, then pocketed the phone.

"It's as good as done."

"Let's go. We know the general direction."

"He probably didn't take the road along the bay. With some luck, our colleagues might catch the truck nearby on the national route."

They got in, and Adel cautiously navigated the tight turns down and back onto the bridge.

"You drive like my grandfather," she muttered, and he burst out laughing.

Before reaching Pontorson, Adel took the national road heading towards Saint-Malo. As they neared Dol-de-Bretagne, they spotted the truck with the blue container parked on the roadside.

"That was quick," she remarked.

"Inès must have put pressure on the gendarmerie," Adel speculated. "She's exceptionally good at that. Just like you."

He parked next to the patrol car. The truck's driver was standing in front of his vehicle, chatting with the policemen.

"What's the issue? I'd like to start my weekend!" he exclaimed as Sandrine stepped out.

"So would we," Adel replied.

"Since when are the police interested in construction waste?"

"Wasn't Gustave supposed to pick up the debris?" Sandrine inquired, addressing the driver whom she had never met before.

"He works in the early morning. But because of the police, he couldn't get the container. Now I had to do it. Throws my entire schedule off. My wife's going to be furious if I come home late."

"How inconsiderate of our corpse," Adel commented dryly.

On the back side of the container, there was a way to climb up. Sandrine grasped one of the horizontal bars and began her ascent.

"Wouldn't it be better if I did it? Your ribs must still hurt," Adel offered. She glanced at his stylish pants and white Ralph-Lauren polo shirt, then shook her head.

"I'm far too curious for that," she lied.

Without further protest, Adel stepped aside, and Sandrine clambered up the container's exterior until she could peer over the edge. A fierce curse threatened to spill from her lips, but she held it back. No trace of the carpet. It was gone. She could have sworn she'd noticed it that morning.

"There's nothing here," she called down to Adel before hopping back to the ground. "Still, get someone from forensics. There must be something they can detect."

"It's Friday afternoon. They won't be thrilled," Adel responded.

"You're right. Better if I call Renouf. Maybe the crime scene team from Cherbourg will be more motivated." She fished her phone out of her pocket. The battery was almost dead. She'd left without her charger yesterday.

"Wait!" Adel exclaimed. "Jean-Claude will have my hide if we bring someone from Normandy into his jurisdiction." He shook his head. "Absolutely not."

"Call him. It's enough if the contents are secured by Monday. Then we can examine everything thoroughly."

Adel climbed into the car and informed Jean-Claude Mazet. Sandrine approached the driver.

"This morning there was an old carpet on the rubble. Any idea where that might have gone?"

"Nope. Why?"

"Are you sure?"

"Yeah. I have to check what's on top before I drive off. Sometimes a net is necessary, for the small stuff that the wind might blow away. But there wasn't any carpet. I would've noticed."

"Do you know where we can find Gustave?" Sandrine wasn't ready to accept that she'd been mistaken. Perhaps the man knew something about the carpet's whereabouts.

"He's off work now. No idea where he lives."

She checked the time. With some luck, they might reach someone at the disposal company's office who could give them the home address.

"Thank you anyway."

"And what about my load now?"

"It stays sealed for the time being. Someone from forensics is on their way."

"What a mess."

Sandrine turned away, heading towards the car when the man called out after her, "Try Gustave's wife. She has an antique shop in Saint-Benoît-des-Ondes."

"Do you know where I can find it?"

"Never been there, but how many antique shops can there be in that tiny town?"

"Thank you." The driver had a point. More than one would surprise her. She was familiar with the small town. It was located on the Route de la Baie, right by the water, and she had driven through it with Léon on Sunday.

Sandrine opened the door and stepped into the cluttered antique store, which barely merited the name. 'Junk shop' would have been more fitting. Behind a 1950's kitchen cabinet, a gaunt woman emerged. She adjusted her glasses on her slender nose bridge and squeezed her way between two chairs, which desperately needed new padding and upholstery.

"How can I assist you?" Her voice was high-pitched and somewhat squeaky. Sandrine had to resist the urge to brush off the dust speck from the woman's shoulder.

"Are you the owner of this antique store?" Adel inquired.

"Of course." She straightened up, seeming to grow several inches taller in an instant.

"We'd like to speak with your husband."

"Gustave?" She deflated slightly, wrinkles deepening on her forehead. Apparently, strangers asking about her husband immediately seemed suspect to her. Sandrine pulled out her police badge and held it up for her to see.

"Has he done something wrong?" she asked apprehensively, her tone suggesting she wouldn't be too surprised if he had.

"Not that we're aware of. We just need some information from him, then we'll be on our way."

She craned her neck, looking past Adel to the dusty window facing the street. "You haven't parked a police car outside, have you?" She clearly believed a police vehicle at the entrance would be bad for business.

"No. We're not from the gendarmerie," Adel reassured her. "Is your husband around?"

"Where else would he be?" She glanced towards the door they had entered from. "I'll go get him. He's probably lounging in front of the TV watching some nonsense again."

"We'll wait here."

"Feel free to look around; perhaps you'll find something nice for your home. Furniture with a history always adds a certain charm." With that, she turned abruptly and disappeared through the door.

Adel lifted a porcelain figurine of a chubby, naked angel.

"If any home is in desperate need of decor, it's yours. Here's something for you."

"I don't have much fondness for such kitschy stuff," Sandrine responded. "But if you need a birthday gift, I can have the department pass the hat around."

"No need," Adel replied. Footsteps approached, and he promptly returned the figurine to its spot.

Gustave entered the room, followed closely by his wife.

"The nice policewoman," he greeted Sandrine. "What a surprise."

"I hope we're not intruding," she replied.

"Not at all. There's a documentary about Edith Piaf on Arte. But it'll be replayed tomorrow."

Adel picked up one of the business cards that lay on a small cabinet next to the door, glancing at it.

"Monsieur Flaubert?" he asked, looking at the man quizzically.

"That's right," the driver confirmed with a nod.

"Gustave Flaubert?" Sandrine probed further.

"Neither related nor connected," he replied with a grin.

"It's a famous name."

"Yes, it tends to surprise most people. My mother was a librarian and held the steadfast belief that someone named Flaubert could only be christened Gustave."

"Understandable," Adel muttered.

"I've always wondered if she married my father just for his surname. She was in love with French classics. She devoured *Madame Bovary* regularly."

"You mentioned this morning that the residents of Le Mont-Saint-Michel often misuse the construction waste container as a dump for their bulky waste." Sandrine steered the conversation back to the reason for their visit.

"That's true. It's a real issue. You wouldn't believe the things we find," Gustave replied.

She looked around the store, slowly getting a sense of the kind of items one might find discarded as bulky waste.

"I noticed a carpet sticking out from the edge of the container. But now it's gone. Do you have any idea what might have happened to it?"

"A carpet, you say?" He seemed to stall, likely needing a moment to think. His wife placed a hand on his back. A warning to keep quiet?

"This is about a murder," Sandrine asserted, looking him squarely in the eyes.

"If someone throws something in the trash, it's not a crime to take it out and fix it up, right?"

"Of course. We throw away far too many things that could still be useful," Adel pitched in, seemingly throwing Gustave a lifeline.

"You can't be blamed for that. However, this involves a police investigation, and that carpet might lead us to the perpetrator. It would be extremely helpful if you could assist us in locating it."

"I might have taken it," Gustave confessed.

His wife jabbed a finger into his back, prompting him to turn towards her.

"Let it be. We need to return it."

"Once the case is concluded, you'll get it back," Adel promised. The woman's eyes sparkled with greed. She seemed to be well-aware that this was a valuable antique rug. Probably worth more than all the junk scattered around the store.

Gustave Flaubert disappeared briefly, then returned with the rolled-up carpet in tow.

"It's quite dirty though. We haven't had a chance to clean it yet," Gustave remarked.

"The lab folks will be delighted to hear that," Sandrine said, unrolling the carpet to examine it.

"Well, what do you know," she commented as her gaze fell upon a dark stain situated almost exactly at the carpet's centre.

Adel knelt down to get a closer look.

"Looks like blood."

"Blood is so hard to get out," Madame Flaubert grumbled.

"Was there perhaps anything else you salvaged from the dump?" Sandrine turned her attention to Gustave. He let out a loud sigh, and his wife's shoulders drooped in resignation.

"Now that you mention it ..."

Gustave began, turning around and tugging at a drawer of an old kitchen table. The drawer opened with a gritty sound.

"This was beneath the carpet. But I didn't break it. It was already like that."

"Bingo," Sandrine remarked.

Adel held out a hand. Gustave Flaubert reluctantly handed him the two parts of a broken walking stick.

* * *

Commander Renouf awaited them at the entrance to the abbey.

"The guard recalls seeing Blanche and Auguste Barnais entering the monastery about an hour ago." He cast a glance over his shoulder toward the steep staircase leading upward. "Remarkable how he managed to climb le Gouffre in his condition!"

"It's a matter of will. He's on an urgent mission. He knows time is slipping away," Sandrine speculated.

"Any idea what it might be?" Renouf inquired. "Should we expect the worst?"

"You're thinking of suicide? That he wishes to follow his son and leap off the abbey walls as well?"

"Do you believe he's capable of it?"

"I don't think so. But we'll find out."

"I'll wait here for Madame le Juge. She should arrive any minute now. Hopefully, I haven't called her in without cause."

"If that's the case, I'll take responsibility."

Sandrine and Adel swiftly ascended the steps. Noon had passed; dozens of tourists filled the grand inner staircase. She remembered the route from early morning, and soon they found themselves on the open square on the west side of the abbey church. There was no sign of the crime scene technicians' earlier work. Visitors stood by the wall, the very spot from which Michel Barnais had been thrown, admiring the landscape stretching out far below them. Likely none suspected the tragedy that had taken place mere hours before.

"He's not here," Adel observed after a quick survey. "I expected him at the spot where his son fell."

"That wouldn't matter to him, because his son didn't die here. And Auguste Barnais knows very well when, where and how Michel passed." Sandrine's gaze shifted to the entrance of the abbey church. "I suspect he's in there."

Cool air greeted them as they stepped inside the church. The imposing walls kept the summer heat at bay; the stained-glass windows in the choir gleamed brightly in the sunlight.

"Over there." Adel pointed out the two of them seated in one of the front rows. They were the only ones sitting on a pew. The rest of the visitors were following the guided tour, walking around the rows of benches. Several wore headphones for the audio guide – information that neither Blanche nor Auguste needed. Few were as intimately connected to the history of this place as these two.

"I'll speak with them. Can you let Renouf and Bonnard know where to find us?"

"On it."

Sandrine walked unhurriedly to the row where Auguste Barnais and his daughter were seated. He was wearing the same dark blue suit he'd worn to their Sunday dinner, a time when Camille, Père Martin, and Michel were still alive. She took a seat next to them on the bench. Blanche flinched in surprise, but Auguste only briefly met her gaze before returning his attention to the altar. His hands rested on the knob of the walking stick he had placed in front of him – likely the one the forensics team had examined for blood traces.

"Do you find it appropriate to enter a house of God armed?" he asked her softly.

She barely noticed the weight of the pistol in its shoulder holster anymore. She had grown accustomed to it, just as she had to the routine of carrying it during her assignments. But to Auguste Barnais, it stood out immediately.

"I'm certain that, in the history of this place, I'm not the only one who's entered the church armed, and many with far more violent intentions than mine."

"You're right. The monastery's history is all too often intertwined with war and death. The world doesn't spare the house of God."

The servants of God who lived here weren't always peaceful individuals either.

Blanche shot her an irritated look. "What do you want from us? My father is ill and is seeking a moment of inner peace here. You can't interrogate him in this place."

"Let it be, Blanche. Things are as they are, and we have to accept them. What choice do we have?" He turned to Sandrine. "My daughter is right. My time is drawing to a close. This will be my last visit to the abbey."

"You've come to say your goodbyes?"

"The doctors give me weeks if I'm lucky." He laughed bitterly. "What do doctors know of luck? Fate has taken too much from me, in too short a time. The love of my life, an old friend, and my firstborn and heir."

Auguste coughed, wiping his mouth with a handkerchief. Sandrine noticed traces of blood on the white fabric. He wasn't exaggerating. He didn't have much time left.

"Why did you take on the strenuous journey here? To confess and seek absolution?"

"You're not a believer." It wasn't a question, but a statement.

"Not really. Can you tell?"

His hands tightened around the knob of the cane, and Auguste Barnais' breathing became laboured. Blanche pulled out a pill bottle from her handbag, but he shook his head. Sandrine suspected it was a painkiller. Why did he refuse? Did he want to experience his last visit to the church with full consciousness?

The older man's breathing steadied. The episode seemed to have passed.

"I have much to confess," said Auguste. "But there is no absolution for me. One only receives when they genuinely regret their actions. I regret little of what I've done."

For a while, she sat silently next to the man, soaking in the peace that radiated from the church – a tranquillity undisturbed even by the chattering tourists. But reality couldn't be held at bay by these walls. It was time to bring this case to a close.

"It took me some time to piece together everything I saw and heard. Far too long." *Perhaps Michel Barnais might still be alive if I had been more vigilant.*

"But here you are now," remarked Auguste.

"I want to prevent Jean from going to prison for a crime he didn't commit."

"You can't prove anything against Jean," hissed Blanche, like a cornered wildcat.

"He's doing his best to appear guilty," Sandrine countered.

"No one wants him to be punished for a deed he did not

commit," Auguste said calmly. "You know as well as I do that he's incapable of taking someone's life."

"It's not up to me. It's up Madame le Juge to decide whether charges are brought."

He stared silently ahead at the altar.

"It wasn't him."

"I believe the same. He didn't harm Michel, but he did give Albert Chauvin quite a beating. Hence the abrasions on his hands."

"Did he?" Auguste looked at her in surprise, seemingly unaware of this.

"He had no hand in the other deaths either. That was you and Michel's doing."

"Can you prove it?"

"By now, yes. Did you think we wouldn't trace it back to you?"

"Do you think I particularly care at this point? I'm as good as dead, and soon I'll be facing the only judge who truly matters." His gaze returned to the altar where three tall candles burned. Sandrine suspected Auguste had brought and lit them. Earthly justice did not intimidate this man. He had nothing left to lose in this world.

"Why did Père Martin have to die? He was your friend. For many years."

"A tragic accident."

"He was poisoned intentionally. The doctor found psilocybin – a high dose. At that point, I should have suspected you, but your friendship misled me. That was my mistake."

"So what, the man ate some mushrooms. Even priests have their vices," Blanche interjected, trying to come to her father's aid, but Auguste ignored her.

"Did the Leriches introduce you to them?" Sandrine asked. "Suzanne mentioned your fondness for mushrooms. At that time, I was thinking of champignons or chanterelles, not magic mushrooms."

"It was a wild time. We were young, free, and careless. I look back at those times with fondness."

"Père Martin was not one to endorse a wild lifestyle or tolerate it in others."

"Absolutely not. But he loved my mushroom ragout. He was a real glutton when it came to mushrooms. The red wine sauce masks the slightly bitter taste of the magic mushrooms."

"Why did you drug the priest?" She had a suspicion, but she wanted to hear it from him.

"Don't play the fool; it doesn't suit you and comes off as insincere. Léon always had a soft spot for sharp-witted women," Auguste retorted, slightly irritated.

"Thank you for the compliment."

"I noticed how you observed Père Martin during the last visit. You too realised he knew something about Camille's death but kept it hidden. I've known the man for decades; how could he betray me?"

"He didn't want to break the Seal of Confessional, not even for the sake of your friendship."

"I couldn't take that into account. I needed to know what he had discovered, what weighed on his conscience. You understand, don't you?"

"A set-up in the chapel?"

"Papa!" his daughter hissed, trying to silence him.

"It's okay, Blanche. What do I have left to fear?"

"You drugged Père Martin and waited for the effects to kick in. Projecting that eerie film onto the wall with a mini projector and a laptop was a diabolical plan. How did you get hold of the footage? Was Blanche involved?"

A gentle smile played on the man's lips as he lovingly gazed at his daughter. Tears filled Blanche's eyes.

"I could never have convinced her to be part of that. So, I

had to copy the film secretly. No one locks their room in our house, and I knew her computer password all too well: Camille's birthday. The rest was easy."

"Until everything spiralled out of control."

The smile vanished, and he nodded thoughtfully.

"I must have misjudged the combined effects of the mushrooms and the little show. They induced hallucinations in Père Martin. He saw devils everywhere, chasing after his soul, and screamed in fear. Before I could restrain him, he leaped up and fled from the chapel. I pursued him, but he was uncontrollable, and in his panic, he ran straight into the bay. Right into Le Mascaret, the tidal bore. He had no chance, if he even understood what was happening to him. It was a tragic accident. I didn't want any harm to come to him." Genuine regret filled his voice, and his head dropped.

"It's not up to me to decide whether it was an accident or not.," Sandrine replied. "But he did reveal something to you before the hallucinations took over, didn't he?"

"From the fragments of words he shouted, I could piece it together. His nephew aids refugees. One of the refugees told him he'd be crossing to Britain on a yacht named *Émeraude*. He spent all his remaining money for that passage. The nephew informed his uncle, and Père Martin followed the man to the boat. There he confronted Michel."

"Then my suspicion was correct. Michel confessed his involvement in human trafficking to Père Martin, trying to bind him to silence."

"He knew the priest's weakness and was sure he would never willingly break the Sacramental Seal."

"That the priest has broken his vows, must have been quite a shock for your son when you confronted him."

"Father, be quiet! The police can't prove any of this, it's all just conjecture," his daughter hissed quietly. A woman with a camera hanging around her neck turned to look at them curiously. Blanche stared her down until she turned away and continued her rounds.

"But we can," Sandrine countered, leaning back against the bench's backrest, forcing Blanche to lean forward to see her.

"It's a peculiar coincidence, but Michel ensured that we could trace his murderer."

"It wasn't murder," Auguste whispered almost inaudibly.

"Had he not parked his car again in front of the container, the entire load would have ended up at the dump without us ever having a glimpse of the contents. Since he couldn't load the container, Gustave had time to look around and stumbled upon the body. Unfortunately, a bit too early."

"Anyone could have dumped their trash in that container."

"You have identical carpets in your home. It won't be hard to determine if the one we found belongs to you."

"So what!" Blanche took over the conversation.

"It's soaked in blood. Michel's blood."

"I have no idea how it got there. Maybe he had a nosebleed and threw the carpet away afterward. He never liked that thing anyway."

"And he hit himself on the nose with your father's cane? Not very smart of him."

"Father has his cane with him. You've examined it and found no traces of blood."

"That's true. It's also a detail I overlooked. Do you remember when your father spilled wine on his jacket during Sunday's meal? I was surprised at how quickly he cleaned it, and Camille explained to me that out of habit, he purchases multiples of his favourite garments. I'm sure we'll discover another cane. Commandant Renouf's team is searching the house as we speak." She pressed Auguste's forearm. "Will they also find a mushroom cultivation box?"

"Léon should never have brought you here." Blanche slapped Sandrine's hand away from her father's arm.

"I'm convinced you didn't intend to seriously hurt or kill him. You confronted him, and it led to a quarrel. Isn't that right?" Sandrine offered the man a way out.

"It's true. After learning from Père Martin why he wanted to prevent Camille from boarding the boat, I confronted him; at least that much of your assumption is accurate. He denied nothing. He seemed almost proud of his criminal endeavours and boasted about the money he was making. Camille would have exposed his operation, so Michel called his friends, who ambushed her in Saint-Malo to involve her in an accident. He never intended for her to get hurt. She was always a woman who knew how to handle herself. Even when things went awry and she ended up in the bay, she could have escaped. She would never have drowned; my wife was an excellent swimmer. Perhaps I could have forgiven all that, considering he was my firstborn."

"The chocolate truffle, right? That was more than you could bear."

"How could he not say a word when his mother consumed it? She must have been under the influence when she was pushed off the road. The drugs combined with the shock of the accident must have left her disoriented and panicking. She didn't stand a chance of freeing herself from the seatbelt." His voice broke off, and a tear streamed down his cheek.

"You struck him." Sandrine pondered whether she would have acted similarly in the same situation. "In the heat of the moment."

Auguste lifted his head and met her gaze. His eyes looked weary.

"I'd like to claim I wasn't in my right mind, but that's not true. I let him get away with so much. I even tolerated the thought of him selling the Auberge, but with Camille's death, he crossed a line. He had to pay for that."

"You weren't on the list of suspects for a long time. How could you have dragged him here? Maybe I underestimated the love your children have for you?"

"I know I did. It's one of my sins that I deeply regret." He grasped Blanche's hand and held it tightly.

"Throwing him from the abbey almost worked. His face was badly battered, and the wound from the cane strike was barely noticeable. It looked like a suicide. However, the forensic examiner looked very closely."

"A competent man."

"Someone with a key dragged the body to the freight elevator and took it up. At the top, he was received and taken to the square in front of the church. Forensics will examine the wheelbarrows and hand trucks used in the renovation work. Throwing him over the wall wasn't particularly challenging after that. I'd guess two or three people could have managed it with ease."

"We ..." Blanche began, but Sandrine interrupted her.

"It's going to be damn hard to prove these people were involved in the act. I fear they'll get away with it. It's my personal assessment, but I can't imagine the prosecuting judge will come to a different conclusion."

"Thank you," said Auguste; he sounded sincere.

"I'm leaving now. Madame le Juge Bonnard will want to speak with you."

Sandrine got up and left the two of them behind. On one of the back benches sat Charles Renouf and Amélie Bonnard.

"Did he do it?" asked Madame le Juge.

"Yes. He confessed to everything. You can take him."

She stood up and walked down the aisle, but Commandant Renouf remained by her side.

"You've done excellent work again," he said. "For a Parisienne."

"Thank you, I'll take that as a compliment." She shook his outstretched hand. "You were also quite good, for a Norman."

"Perhaps I was wrong, and you might just become a true Malouine yet."

A few months ago, such a thought would have seemed completely absurd to her, but by now she was starting to feel at home in Brittany. She had found friends, perhaps even more than that.

"I doubt that."

Renouf looked at her with surprise. "I assumed that would be your wish?"

"You forget, I hail from Cancale, which makes me a Cancalaise."

"A locale famous for its strong women," he said approvingly.

Sandrine remembered Madame Morvan, who had introduced her to the history of the women of Cancale. They were the ones who provided for their families and did the hard work during the long months their husbands spent fishing off Newfoundland. Anyone who wasn't tough couldn't survive in Cancale back then. And it was still evident in them today.

Sandrine exited the church through the grand entrance. Adel was standing by the wall, gazing in the direction of Brittany. The day was clear, and the coastline's silhouette was starkly visible. She turned and looked up at the statue of Saint Michael. At that moment, she remembered he wasn't a peaceful angel, but the vanquisher of the devil, who had taken the form of a dragon. Archangel Michael had defeated him and cast him from heaven to earth, just like Auguste had killed his son and his siblings had thrown him down from the monastery. Here in Le Mont-Saint-Michel, the monastery was revered so highly it was almost akin to heaven. Auguste probably saw his son as a devil in human form and didn't think of confessing his act since he didn't regret it in the slightest. His words now made sense to her.

"I waited for you outside. It's not my case, and I wanted to leave the arrest to our colleagues from Normandy," said Adel, approaching her.

"They'll appreciate that."

"What will happen to the old man?"

Sandrine sat on the wall and looked towards the church.

"What can Amélie Bonnard really do? In his condition, she won't place him in pretrial detention. Why would she, anyway? He's confessed, and the notion that he might flee is ludicrous. Madame le Juge is wise, she won't expect Auguste Barnais to live to see his trial. She'll just wait and let things take their course. His death will make it easier for everyone involved."

"So there will be no punishment for the two deaths?"

"He's dying. He's lost his wife, whom he dearly loved, a long-time friend, and his eldest son, who had just found his way back to the family. I can't think of a much greater punishment."

"When you put it that way, I see your point."

"Let's go. We're not needed here anymore."

"What are you planning to do about de Chezac and the raid?" he asked unexpectedly.

"I'll deal with that next week. Today is my day off, and I plan to enjoy it." She checked her watch. The day had started early, and it was only the afternoon. "Do you have any plans?"

"Not yet."

"On the way, we'll stop at the market, pick up something nice, and inaugurate my new grill. I'm sure Rosalie will bring some tasty treat as well. How does that sound?"

"Only if I get to man the grill."

"You don't trust me?"

He suppressed a reply and smirked.

"Alright then. I'll watch and pamper myself. After all, I'm injured and need some rest."

"Then everything's settled."

Together, they strolled down Grande Rue, passing by Auberge Saint-Michel. The Auberge would be in good hands with Jean. She fondly remembered the night she had spent there. Maybe I should call Léon and invite him too, she thought, and a smile crept onto her lips.

How could I ever miss my old life in Paris?

List of Characters

- Sandrine Perrot: Stubborn Saint Malo Detective
- Adel Azarou: Brigadier with a penchant for fashionable outfits
- Jean Matisse: Head of the Police Department
- Jean-Claude Mazet: At first glance the often underestimated forensic technician
- Inès Boni: Office manager and invaluable source of local information
- Doktor Hervé: Meticulous forensic pathologist from Saint-Malo
- Renard Dubois and Luc Poutin: Police Brigadiers
- Antoine de Chezac: Career-driven Prosecuting judge
- Auguste Barnais: Owner of the Auberge Saint-Michel
- Camille Barnais: Co-owner of the Auberge and Auguste's wife
- Michel Barnais: A man with a criminal past
- Jean Barnais: Runs the Auberge Saint-Michel
- Blanche Barnais: Historian and author

- Charlotte Barnais: Civil Engineer overseeing work at the Abbey
- Père Martin: a priest and friend of Auguste Barnais
- Amélie Bonnard: Prosecuting Judge from Normandy
- Charles Renouf: Commander of the Gendarmerie Avranches
- Doktor Deschamps: Forensic Pathologist from Cherbourg
- Albert Chauvin: Has his fingers in many criminal pies
- Jori Le Bihan und Jacques Chopard: Petty criminals working for Albert Chauvin
- Suzanne Leriche: Psychologist
- Rosalie Simonas: Successful crime novelist and Sandrine's friend
- Deborah Binet: Ambitious journalist always hoping for inside scoops
- Léon Martinau: Club owner who becomes a target of Sandrine's adversaries

Thanks

I am delighted that you joined Sandrine Perrot and Adel Azarou in their investigation in Brittany and Normandy. Feedback from my readers is very important to me. Critique, praise and ideas are always welcome, and I am happy to answer any questions. My email address is: Author@Christophe-Villain.com

Newsletter: To not miss any new publications you can sign up to the newsletter and get the free novella: Death in Paris - The prequel to the Brittany Mystery Series.

Free Novella

Subscribe to the newsletter and receive a free eBook: Death in Paris.
Sandrine Perrot's back story, her last case in Paris.

Sandrine held the warm coffee cup in her hands and looked out through the café window. The gusty wind drove dark clouds across the sky and swirled leaves along the boulevard. Pedestrians zipped up their jackets and scrambled to keep dry before the impending rain. She wasn't particularly excited about the prospect of having to take her motorbike on the road. Sandrine forgot to shop most of the time and hated to cook. Café Central was her salvation so she wouldn't turn up at work with her stomach growling.

"Would you like anything else to drink?" asked the waitress, who regularly saw Sandrine during her morning shift. She bet the young girl was a student who worked here to earn a few euros. Judging by her distinct accent, she was probably from Provence.

"Thank you but I have to get on the road pretty soon."

"Not a nice day." The young woman took a peek outside and picked up the used plate on

which the remains of scrambled eggs and baguette crumbs lay.

"That's why I hold on to my coffee cup for a while and enjoy the warmth in the café before I have to go to work." A bad feeling swept over her that she couldn't pin down to any specific event, but it nagged at her, as if the day could only get worse. The case she was investigating was stuck in her head and she couldn't shake it, which she usually could.

"No hurry," said the waitress, looking around the half-empty café. "It doesn't get crowded again until lunchtime, so until then I don't have much to do."

Sandrine's cell phone, which was lying on the table in front of her, vibrated and she glanced at the display.

"I'm afraid I have to take this call."

The waitress took the hint and took the dirty dishes into the kitchen. "Hello, Martin, what's up?"

She listened to her colleague in silence for a while.

"On the Richard Lenoir Boulevard? I'll be there in fifteen minutes."

Sandrine ended the call and cursed under her breath. Her gut feeling had proved to be right; the day lived up to its promise. She put money on the table, pulled on the waterproof motorcycle jacket and picked up the helmet that was lying on a chair.

She quickly drank the rest of the coffee. The waitress gave her a friendly wave as she left.

Her motorcycle was parked on the wide sidewalk between two trees. She wiped the wet seat with her sleeve before climbing on and pulling on her gloves. She took a deep breath and started the engine. Shortly thereafter, she merged into traffic.

Half a dozen patrol cars and an ambulance were parked by the Saint-Martin Canal. The paramedics were hunkered down in the car and puffs of smoke rose through their slightly ajar windows. They were more comfortable than their police colleagues, who had to go out to cordon off the area. The first onlookers were already gathering on one of the narrow bridges that spanned the watercourse. Sandrine drove through a gap in the metal fence separating the canal from the boulevard and parked the motorcycle on the wide pedestrian promenade. Bollards – stocky

vertical posts – were set at regular intervals, but today no boats were moored here and the lock gate was closed.

"Good morning, Sandrine," a grey-haired man with angular features greeted her. His badge identified him as Major de Police. "Kind of shitty weather to be out on a motorcycle."

"Hello, Martin. It's still a lot quicker than driving a car. Not to mention parking." She stuffed her gloves and scarf into her helmet and stuffed it into one of the panniers. "Is it our guy?"

"The Necktie Killer? Looks like it."

"Is that what they call him now?" She shook her head in disgust. "Far too friendly sounding. He's a sadistic murderer and should be considered and referred to as such."

"I didn't invent it. We owe that to the journalists who needed punchy headlines." He held up his hands defensively.

"I'm sorry. I was thinking of the victims."

"That's all right. Whenever things like that don't get to you anymore, it's time to change careers."

"In there?" she asked, looking toward the entrance to the Saint-Martin Canal, which ran underground for the next few miles. Even on sunny days, this gloomy place seemed ominous to her. "Who from our team is here?"

"Brossault, the medical examiner with the forensic guys and some cops cordoning off the area. The big boys are on their way, it was probably too early in the morning for them."

Sandrine laughed softly. The chief of homicide and the juge d'instruction, the prosecutor in charge of the investigation, would not be long in coming. They were forced to demonstrate that

the police were doing everything they could to take the perpetrator off the street since the series of murders was dominating the front pages of the newspapers. However, they hadn't even come an inch closer to him since they'd found the first victim in the summer. It was now February and two more dead women had joined the list of victims.

"Let's go then," she said, walking towards the scene of the crime.

The rain started, pattering on the dark water of the canal. Major Martin Alary pulled up the collar of his raincoat and walked faster across the slippery pavement. A uniformed cop stepped aside and waved them through the barricade.

"Was it closed?" Sandrine asked, looking at the lock where the water was damming up. The Saint-Martin Canal was just under two-and-a-half-miles long, and connected the Bassin de la Villette in the north with the Seine in the south. It had a total of five locks – enclosures with gates at each end where the water level could be raised or lowered.

"Most people only use the exposed area: a few tourist boats, but mostly paddle boats and small motorboats used for family outings in the Bassin de la Villette. Hardly more than a dozen boats a day traverse the entire length of the canal."

"The less water traffic, the more noticeable things are. Let's hope someone noticed something."

They entered the tunnel through an open metal door guarded by another police officer. Martin Alary wiped raindrops from his shoulders and adjusted his gun holster. A brick path, on which two people could comfortably walk side by side, ran along the length of the canal. The dim light of the rainy day reached only a few feet deep into the tunnel, and the antique-looking lamps that hung at regular intervals on the wall allowed one to see the way, but were useless for forensic

work. The forensics team had already set up blazingly bright spotlights so they wouldn't miss a thing.

A thin man with a pointed beard and a bald head walked towards them.

"Ah. Capitaine Perrot and Major Alary. Already here?" Marcel Carron, the forensics manager, patted Sandrine's companion on the shoulder and gave him a wink before turning to face her. He refrained from giving her a chummy pat on the back.

"How far along are you with securing the crime scene?"

"Almost done. However, there was hardly anything to secure."

"What can you tell me?"

"An employee of the city building department discovered the body during a routine examination. She was floating in the water. He informed us immediately and left the site. Very prudent."

"Is this also the scene of the crime?" the major asked.

"There's no evidence thus far," Carron replied. "We've searched the path for evidence of a struggle, but to no avail. The corpse is unclothed, but we couldn't find clothes anywhere."

"Not surprising."

"I concur."

"Any idea how the body got here?" Alary asked.

"There aren't many options left. There is no current in the canal sufficient enough to move a human body. She would have been spotted within one of the locks."

"Then she was put here," said Sandrine.

"The question is how." The forensic scientist pointed to the metal door at the entrance to the tunnel. "Entry is forbidden and the door is normally locked. However, there's no problem climbing over the door but dragging a corpse of an adult person up and over would be almost impossible without risking being discovered."

"Then there's only one option left," Sandrine said, stepping up to the railing that was too dirty to touch. "The perpetrator threw her off a boat at this point."

"An ideal location," the major agreed. "Nobody would notice since people seldom come in here."

"I'm assuming there's no security camera in the tunnel." Despite saying this, Sandrine looked around.

"Maybe the doctor can tell us more." She wasn't particularly hopeful. So far, the killer had left no usable evidence.

"Good luck."

Sandrine pulled a pair of disposable gloves and shoe covers out of her jacket pocket and put them on. Even though the forensic scientist assumed there wouldn't be anything of interest here, she played it safe.

A few feet away, she found Doctor Brossault standing next to the victim, a blue blanket spread over it.

"Bonjour," she greeted the older man in a dark suit, bow tie and handkerchief in his breast pocket. He turned to face her and used his forefinger to push his rimless glasses up the bridge of his nose. "An ideal place to dump a body, isn't it?"

"Absolutely." He nodded enthusiastically. "The murderer has a soft spot for historical places. You have to give him that."

"The canal dates back from the early 19th century, from what I remember from my history class." "1825 if you want to be exact, but who cares about that anyway?"

Sandrine suppressed a grin. The medical examiner was the type of person who always wanted to be as precise as possible and didn't withhold his knowledge.

"The canal, anyway. The structure built over the canal did not take place until much later: in 1860. At first, it was designed by Haussmann to improve traffic in the city."

"At first?" Sandrine asked. The man loved sharing his knowledge of history and enlightening those around him. It made him happy, so she let him have his fun.

"Naturally. Napoleon III was not exactly a popular head of state. Resistance to his rule simmered particularly in the revolutionary neighbourhoods such as Faubourg-Montmartre and Ménilmontant. So the plan to build over the canal came in handy. A wide swath through the city along which to send cavalry to maintain law and order."

"Interesting," said Major Alary, who Sandrine heard come up behind her. "But it didn't do him any good in the end."

"Fortunately," the doctor agreed.

Sandrine knelt down next to the body and looked inquisitively at the medical examiner. Only when he nodded did she lift the blanket under which the victim lay. A young woman's bloodless face stared at her with lifeless blue eyes. Blonde hair clung damply to pale skin. She wore a silk tie around her neck, where strangulation marks could be seen.

"She was strangled," Sandrine murmured, more to herself than to Doctor Brossault. "Just like the previous two victims," he confirmed.

"What can you tell me?"

"I'd put the woman in her mid-twenties, blonde and attractive like the other victims. She was strangled with the necktie. There are cuts on her wrists. Without wanting to commit myself, I would conclude that plastic restraints were used. The police use those things, too."

"Any other signs that she fought back?"

"I can't imagine that she didn't, but she had no chance of surviving. Not with her hands tied. Of course we are also looking for narcotics."

"Maybe the tie will get us further."

"A silk tie. Quite expensive and downright exclusive. Forensics will confirm that, although I can't imagine Monsieur Carron being an expert on the subject."

She looked up at him probingly.

"Have you ever seen the man properly dressed before?" His brow furrowed as if surprised at her lack of awareness.

"What's so special about these ties?"

"The quality of the silk is impeccable. In terms of design, I would guess mid-century. In addition, our killer is able to tie a perfect Windsor knot, something that is becoming increasingly rare these days. People either forgo a tie completely or fasten it sloppily. I would narrow the circle of perpetrators down to people with style and money."

He finished the sentence and straightened his bow tie.

Sandrine put the blanket back over the woman's face. She would see her again in the medical examiner's office. She'd seen enough for now.

To subscribe to the newsletter, please use the QR code.

Other Books

Emerald Coast Murder

Sandrine Perrot's investigation takes her from the picturesque fishing towns to the rural hinterland of Brittany's Emerald Coast.

Police Lieutenant Sandrine Perrot is on leave from her post in Paris and has settled in Cancale, the oyster capital of Brittany. She is temporarily assigned to the Saint-Malo police station for this case. The body of an unidentified woman is discovered on the Brittany coast path along the bay of Mont- Saint-Michel.

With her new assistant, Adel Azarou, she takes on the investigation, which leads them to a cold case from Paris, but also deep into the tragic history of a venerable hotelier family.

Saint-Malo Murder

Death of an influencer

The tranquillity of the picturesque old town of Saint-Malo is shattered by a gruesome murder. The dead woman is a well-known influencer and radio presenter who has made many enemies in the region with her controversial opinions and themes. The killer has not only professionally staged the body and crime scene, but also meticulously recorded the crime.

Will she find the perpetrator in the dead woman's private surroundings, or will she have to dig deep into the victim's past?

Boolover's Death

A dead book collector

A new case takes Sandrine Perrot to Bécherel, the Cité du Livre of Brittany. A place where life revolves around books. The president of a well-known book club has been found murdered in his private library. Did contempt and rivalry among the book lovers lead to murder or does she have to look elsewhere for the motive?

While Sandrine investigates in the city of books, the prosecutor de Chezac builds a case against her. From the sidelines, she has to watch as the situation in Saint-Malo escalates.

Printed in Great Britain
by Amazon